CIRCLE OF POWER

CIRCLE OF POWER

A Circle Sleuth Mystery

Betty Lucke

Spearmint Books

Circle of Power
A Circle Sleuth Mystery, Book 1

Published by Spearmint Books.

This novel is a work of fiction. Any references to real people, living or dead, business establishments, places, organizations, or events are intended only to give the fiction a sense of reality. These references are used as background in which the fictional characters live, move, and have their being. All other names, places, characters, and incidents portrayed in this book are the product of the author's imagination.

To contact the publisher, please email: spearmintbooks@gmail.com.
Editor – Wendy VanHatten
Cover Design – Tara Baumann

Library of Congress Cataloging-in-Publication Data

Lucke, Betty, Author
Circle of power: a circle sleuth mystery / Betty Lucke
First Edition   Spearmint Books, 2016
Library of Congress Control Number: 2016910487
ISBN 978-0-9884631-3-4

1. McCreath, Cliff (Fictitious Character) – Fiction
2. Mystery—Detective—New Mexico—Santa Fe—Fiction
3. New Mexico—Santa Fe—Fiction
4. Kidnapping—children—Fiction
5. Dogs—Terriers—Airedales—Fiction
        813.6 DD   PS – LCC   1. Title

Printed in The United States of America

Acknowledgements

I wish to thank the following for their expertise and encouragement. The journey with Cliff and his friends in the Circle of Sleuths—exploring the characters, bouncing ideas back and forth, and digging deeply into the world of writing fiction has been truly amazing. This mystery is dedicated to the Town Square Writers and the others who have traveled with me and welcomed Cliff into their lives.

Beta Readers: Cheryl Potts, Dotty Schenk, Dwight Blackstock, Jean Norrbom, Kelly Hess, Kevin Tolley, Margaret Lucke, Meredith Wilson, Page Frechette, PJ Loomer, Susan Rounds, Terry Murray, and the members of the Town Square Writer's Group.

New Mexico Field Trip – Bev Morlock, Sue Young
Bjornson House Design – Dotty Schenk
Consultants: Gary Tatum, Mary Garcia, Greg Carlson, Dale Rich,
J. David Wiseman, Deni Harding, Ray Posey, Syl and Don Bestwick

Editing: Wendy VanHatten

Cover Photos - Betty Lucke and Terry Murray

Cover Design– Tara Baumann

Airedale on the cover – Terrorific Let's Get It Started At Pindale (AKA Fergie)

PROLOGUE

Finally, everything is in place.

I've hated them all for so long.

Then I happened upon Sonja's accident five years ago near Taos just after her tire blew, and my plan was born of an instant.

She was trapped inside that car teetering precariously on the edge of the cliff. I saw her relief when I arrived. She pleaded for help. I knew what needed to be done. Relished her horror when she realized what I meant to do. With her and the rest of that damned family gone, it could all be mine.

So instead of helping her out of that car, I pushed it. Wasn't hard. I heard her screams as it rocked and went over. Heard the rend and screech of metal as the car banged down the ravine to its final fireball end.

Great views from up there.

The power I felt as she went off the edge! It gave me the biggest rush; the best high I have ever experienced.

Now, at last, I'm ready—everything is falling into place. I'll take whom they love. Frighten the hell out of them. Make them suffer, and one by one... watch them die.

My planning is flawless. I've cultivated the right people for the tasks. And when they're no longer useful to me? Well... accidents can happen to them, too.

CHAPTER ONE

On her way home from the summer activities program, Krista bounced with excitement as the small school bus traveling past the dusty landscape of piñon and juniper neared the familiar adobe wall. She tucked her well-used book of dog breeds into her backpack as the bus stopped at her driveway. She was the last student to get off as their ranch lay in the outskirts of Santa Fe, with no near neighbors.

An opening in the stepped adobe arch above their gate held a brass bell—more ornamental than functional. The driveway was far enough away from the house so that even if someone rang the bell, it wouldn't be heard anyway.

As the school bus stopped, she saw a dark-colored SUV parked in the turn-around spot by their gate. The sign on the side advertised Ortega Landscaping. The hatchback was open and a couple containers of lavender sat on the ground nearby. Waving goodbye to the bus driver as he pulled away, she skipped toward the gate past the SUV. The yapping of a puppy stopped her in her tracks. A furry, young golden retriever leaped toward her, straining at the end of a rope held by a dark-haired man.

"Do you know whose dog is dis one?" he asked. "I find him running loose. I afraid he lost."

"No, haven't seen him before. We don't have a dog," she responded, setting her purple backpack down and kneeling to pet the enthusiastic puppy. "Oh, isn't he just the cutest..."

Another man came up from behind, grabbed her, and swung her into the air. He clamped his hand tightly over her mouth. She fought as hard as she could, struggling against his strong arms. She kicked backwards, and he grunted with pain. Krista caught one of his fingers between her teeth and bit down, feeling the skin break and tasting the blood, grinding her teeth until she could feel the bone in his finger.

"*¡Pequeña gata del diablo!*" he screamed, "Ahhh!" ripping his hand from her mouth, leaving behind layers of skin and a bit of flesh that she spat out.

She twisted and fell, but before she could scramble to her feet, he grabbed her again. Krista screamed. The man backhanded her across the face, jerking her head to the side, her long, blond hair flying. She screamed for help again, using her fingernails to scratch his face and arms. He held on tightly.

The first man let go of the puppy, dumped out Krista's backpack, and snatched her cell phone. He put a plastic envelope with a message inside on the ground, wedging it in place with the pots of lavender. Then he slammed down the hatchback. He grabbed a blanket from the back seat, and the two men rolled her into it immobilizing her arms and legs. The younger man who held her hauled her into the back seat, and they forced her mouth open. A bitter-tasting liquid was poured past a scream, causing her to choke. Wide-eyed with fear, she struggled, turning her head back and forth frantically. He slapped her again when she tried to avoid the drink, which they finally tipped into her mouth, holding her nose shut until she had to swallow.

The older man got into the driver's seat and drove quickly away. A mile or so down the road, he punched some numbers into her cell phone. When the phone was answered, he said, "No, but I got her phone. Your daughter is kidnapped. You want her back alive, go to end of your driveway. Find directions in envelope." Then he threw the cell phone out the open window into the brush along the road.

The younger one held her until her struggles quieted; her screams became sobs, then whimpers for her daddy. She tried to move, but the rough blanket and the cruel arms prevented her. Her mouth tasted horrible; she felt like she might throw up. Her eyelids drooped, and she felt woozy. Soon she slept.

CHAPTER TWO

Cliff drove south on Highway 84 through northern New Mexico toward Santa Fe and home. He had been visiting his sister, Erin, and her family up in Pagosa Springs, Colorado. Wide vistas of pines, grasslands, and rocky slopes unfolded past his thoughts as the road followed the Rio Chama Valley. He watched a red-tailed hawk drifting in the hot July sun swoop and dive, coming away with a little mousey lunch.

He glanced in the rearview mirror at his Airedale terrier in the back seat. Gandalf lay stretched out on his back making faint doggie snores. Gandalf loved kids, but Cliff's two little nephews had exhausted him.

It's always fun to see my sister, he reflected, and it was great fun to go rock climbing with my brother-in-law. Wow—in December I'll be Uncle Cliff for the third time. He pushed his sunglasses up on his nose and ran a hand through his red, curly hair. His sister doted on her kids, their endless questions, the giggles, and the squabbling back and forth. She excelled at making peace and diverting energy in positive ways. And, yesterday when she and Cliff had walked into the kitchen to find that her boys had decided to surprise them by making cookies, she'd been very patient. He chuckled at the picture. Jeffie had turned around when he heard them come in and spilled the canister of flour on his little brother's head. Shock, surprise, and guilt. And the little guy peering through the mountain of flour sifting down. His blue eyes blinking through the white, sending more flour over his cheeks, just before he burst into tears, rubbing his eyes and making it worse.

Cliff turned the radio on to a music station. The miles melted away as he thought about his nephews. *I'd like kids of my own—little red-haired toddlers, stubborn tykes with big trusting eyes and grubby hands reaching up to take mine. But it scares the hell out of me. Can't see myself as their dad. Or even as a husband.*

I'd need to find someone who loves me for who I really am, not for who they want me to be. I'm 28 years old, for God's sake, not that bad looking if you like thin, scruffy guys with glasses. Reasonably successful in my career, own my own home. But I can't see it yet—I'm a far cry from finding a mate and having a family.

The music was interrupted by the blare of an emergency signal. "This is an Amber Alert. Be on the lookout for a kidnapped child. A girl, Krista Bjornson, aged ten, was taken by one or more strangers as she returned home from school on Tuesday, July 21 at 3:00 p.m. Krista is about 52 inches tall, weighs 70 pounds, has blue eyes, and long, blond hair. She was last seen in the Tano Road area of Santa Fe, New Mexico. She was wearing a lavender t-shirt, blue jeans, and white tennis shoes. The abductors are believed to be traveling in an older model SUV in a dark color, possibly with a landscaping company sign on the side. If you have any information, please call the Santa Fe Police Department." The announcement was followed by their number.

"Bloody hell," Cliff said. "Not another one. I hate this. Another family torn apart. God, I hope someone finds her." Once again Cliff was the frightened four-year old, seeing his older brother carried away. *What happened to him?* he wondered, looking at the little figure of Koda on his dashboard that reminded him of Johnny. The pain of losing Johnny flooded into his mind with the horror of that long-ago night.

They had been playing at the park next door to their house. Their friends had just gone home to dinner leaving the playground to Johnny and Cliff. It was quiet except for the softball game on the other side of the park, the crack of the bat hitting the ball, and the cheers as a runner made it to a base.

"Just a few more times on the slide, Cliffie," said six-year old Johnny. "Then we gotta go, too."

A car quietly pulled into the lot and backed into a space. The engine continued to run.

"Four slides, Johnny," pleaded Cliff. He had just turned four a few weeks earlier and was proud of his new skill with numbers. He liked to boast he could count all the way to twenty-teen. Johnny watched as his red-headed brother clambered up the steps of the slide. Johnny's hair was just as red, but lacked the wild, curly messiness of Cliff's.

Cliff reached the top and carefully sat down. "Whee!" Cliff yelled as he swooped down. Johnny was already half-way up the steps. "Johnny, do ya s'pose this is like Jussi slidin' down that big icy hole?"

Johnny reached the top and slid down. "Might be. Not as cold on your butt, though." Cliff giggled as he began his climb again. *Koda and the Sami* was their most favorite movie. They often pretended they were Matti and Jussi, the brothers in the movie, whose heroic efforts had rescued the magical snow fox from the evil troll. Cliff had a stuffed snow fox from the movie. Their two-year-old sister, Erin, was too little to care about the movie, but she did drag around the soft cuddly polar bear. Johnny's favorite toy was a stuffed Koda. The wise gnome-like creature had guided the Sami brothers to find and rescue the snow fox. Koda wore a funny red and blue Laplander coat and carried a battery-operated lantern. Johnny often took Koda to bed with him and talked to him. He always told Cliff that Koda listened. Cliff believed it, too.

"I'm gonna go fast this time," Cliff called from the top of the slide. Johnny laughed as his brother came down so fast he couldn't stop, shot off the slide, and landed on his bottom in the dirt. Cliff was slower to join in, but brushed his pants off, and by the time he'd gotten to the steps again he was laughing. His brother was already on his way down.

The softball game sounds rose louder. Someone had knocked the ball out into the weeds. Screams and calls for home runs filled the air.

"Watch me!" Cliff said when he turned around and sat just as Johnny let out a frightened yell.

A big, burly man had come to the slide unseen by them. He grabbed Johnny and threw him over his shoulder. "Put me down! Help!" Johnny shrieked. The man turned and ran toward his car with Johnny bouncing and kicking on his shoulder. "Cliff, run. Get Daddy. Run!"

Cliff sat frozen at the top of the slide for an instant, his eyes big. Then he slid down, stumbled and fell at the bottom, got up, and ran for home, his little legs pumping. He burst through the door crying. His dad picked him up asking, "What's wrong, Son?"

Cliff could hardly talk. He was out of breath, and sobs shook him. "Man took... took Johnny," he blurted out. "Go, Daddy ...get him back. Help."

Andrew McCreath pushed Cliff into his mother's arms. "Call the police, Lynn. I'll go find Johnny."

But Johnny never came home.

◆ ❖ ◆

Gone... Cliff had felt so guilty, so helpless.

Would I have the power to protect my kid if he were in danger? he thought. What if something happened, and I couldn't make it right? Idiot, that's stupid. Johnny's snatching wasn't my fault. I couldn't have done anything. There is no reason that I'm not capable of being a good husband, of having a family, of living up to their expectations...except I was powerless.

The ever-present fear mocked him and wouldn't go away. It was as if he could hear the heartbeat of the monster under the bed. The adult in him knew there was nothing there. But, the child in him was not convinced.

"Enough of this already," he said. "I need coffee. Gandalf, wake up. Time for a break. When we get back on the road again, I'll think about my book's mystery plot. Maybe I can figure out what those thick-skulled villains are supposed to be doing."

The shaggy Airedale stood up on the back seat and stretched. Cliff saw a neon sign flashing "Rosa's" and remembered their good apple empanadas. Sounded like just the thing. The diner sat on the outskirts of Tierra Amarilla, plunked in a vista of sparse piñon and sagebrush right off the highway. He pulled off and parked under a cottonwood tree a few spaces away from a dirty, dark SUV.

CHAPTER THREE

A few minutes earlier Krista had waited, playing possum, listening to the sounds of the two men leaving the SUV in which she lay. Through the veil of her lashes she saw the dome light come on when the door opened. She remained still until she heard both doors shut quietly, and the crunch of footsteps in the gravel die away. Her head ached, her tummy was upset, and she still had the nasty taste in her mouth from the medicine. She had no idea where she was, or even why she had been taken.

She remembered snatches of loud voices during the night. They'd brought her inside a building somewhere and put her in blankets on the floor. They'd argued. "Do it now... Be done with it... Don' want to kill no kid... Trouble... Promised... *Es stupido*... Changed mind... Wanted goddam money... You do it... Lie low here 'til morning... Take her to Utah... Double the money... Can always do it later... Change plates... Why me?... Dose her again... She ain't going nowhere... He find us... You screw up... Kill you... Never find her... He won't know... Trouble."

They had given her the medicine more than once, but she'd tried to hold most of it in her mouth until she could dribble it out into the blanket. Now in the back seat again, coming out of her drug-induced sleep, she'd heard them talking about stopping at a diner.

She sat up cautiously, pushing aside the disgusting blanket and peeked out of the dirty, tinted window. The noonday sun shone from a clear blue sky. She had a good view of the entrance. A big, tan mutt waited by the diner door, standing warily as the two approached. The younger man seemed to her the meaner of the two. He aimed a kick at the mutt who backed off, his tail between his legs, before lying down again. The men went in, and she could see them sit down at a window table. Every so often they glanced out at their SUV.

Another car pulled up, parking in the shade of the cottonwood tree. A red-haired man got out, opened the side door, rummaged around until he got a metal bowl, and filled it from a water bottle. A large shaggy Airedale jumped out and lapped up the water as the man snapped a leash onto his collar. After the dog raised his head, the man put the bowl and the water bottle back into the car, and they set off across the road to where sagebrush dotted the ditch. When the dog had finished his business, he jumped back into the vehicle.

"Watch the car, Gandalf," the man said, patting the furry head through the open window.

The mutt by the door stood up and tentatively wagged his tail. The man greeted him, hand out, palm up to be sniffed, and then he scratched the mutt's neck. The dog swished his tail so hard his whole butt wagged, and he watched with a foolish doggie grin as the man went inside.

I can't stay here, Krista thought. Gotta get away. Maybe this is my chance. She arranged the blanket over some of the junk on the seat, bunching it like she was still under it. Then she reached up carefully and pushed the dome light switch to off. She didn't know if the light would show through the tinted windows when she opened the door, but she didn't want to chance it. With a quick look around, she picked up a few small items and tucked them into the pocket of her jeans. They might be important.

Keeping low in the back, Krista moved toward the far side door, unlocking it. She ducked down again as a large pickup drove in, gravel crunching beneath its wheels, and parked between the SUV and the Airedale man's car. A man got out, slapping a dusty cowboy hat onto his head. He glanced over at the Airedale and went to pass by the car. As he approached, deep growls rose in volume, punctuated with bass barks and a display of strong teeth. The ferocity of the dog's barks increased until the cowboy passed. He ignored the tan mutt greeter by the diner door.

◆ ❖ ◆

"Whose dog is that?" the cowboy asked as he entered, closing the door against the barking now trailing off into occasional woofs. "He shore is noisy and unfriendly."

"Mine. He doesn't like people around my car. You don't want to mess with him."

"Four-footed burglar alarm, eh?" The cowboy eased onto a stool at the counter and picked up a menu smiling at the waitress. "What's good today, Rosa?"

The two swarthy men at the window looked out and then to each other before attacking the burritos and beer in front of them. One of them had a bandaged finger which hampered the use of his fork and fouled his mood.

Krista eased the door open on the far side and slid out, keeping her head down. She depressed the lock again and pushed against the door until she heard it click shut.

The Airedale watched as she ran to his car, crouching low and out of sight behind the pickup. Krista reached up through the window to let him sniff her hand before scratching him behind his ears. He woofed once quietly, sniffed, and licked her arm. *Know I shouldn't get into a strange car,* she thought, *but I gotta. He's nice to his doggie.* She opened the door and crept into the back. "Don't tell anybody, doggie," she whispered.

She grabbed the water bottle, rinsed out her mouth, and spit into the wet area left outside by the dog's earlier drink. Then she gulped more, put the bottle back, and eased the door shut. She burrowed down on the floor behind the driver's seat, pulling part of the dog's blanket over her. The doggie smell beat the stale smoke and medicinal smell of the other blanket. The Airedale watched intently as she checked to make sure she was hidden before she settled in place.

CHAPTER FOUR

Soon Cliff came from the diner. Pulling his cell phone out of his pocket, he opened his car door, and slid into the seat. He punched in a number and listened to the rings, then spoke to an answering machine. "Hi, it's about noon. Hope you get this message. Coverage isn't too good here. We should be in Santa Fe in about two hours. Pretty quiet trip. Looking forward to seeing you."

He tucked the phone away, put his seat belt on, and started the car. The guys from the window table came out. The Airedale stood in the back seat, a quiet growl rumbling in his throat. "Gandalf, stop that. Be quiet. Lie down. Cut the attitude."

Cliff pulled out and turned southeast toward Santa Fe. He slid a CD into the slot and listened as classical guitar music filled the air. Gandalf stood until they were out of sight of the café and then lay down. "You are a fraud, buddy. You put on a good show. You'd lick somebody to death as soon as hurt them."

The road began to climb a little, and grasslands gave way to more pine forests. It was a peaceful country. Good for dreamers, good for thinkers, good for what ailed him.

Cliff thought about the plot for his young protagonists in the mystery he was writing. He realized he'd tied himself in knots and needed more information about how computers might be hacked by the bad guys. He guessed he'd have to pester his buddies at the police station again so he could get it right.

Behind him he heard honking and glanced in the rearview mirror. "So much for peace. Bloody hell!" The dirty SUV from the parking lot was coming up fast behind him, horn blaring. The driver pulled alongside, and the passenger hollered to stop. Cliff kept on going, but pulled his cell phone out of his pocket. He didn't like the look of these guys. Gandalf stood, the hair on the back of his neck bristling.

They were too close—way too close. "Back off, you idiot," yelled Cliff, his heart pounding.

Suddenly they cut in front of him. Cliff jammed on his brakes coming within inches of the SUV on one side and the bridge abutment rail blocking his way on the other. Gandalf slid to the floor with an indignant yelp. Cliff sprang out of the car in anger. "What the hell do you think you're doing?"

The driver jumped out, gesturing wildly with car keys held in his hand. "My kid's in your car. Kid ran away." Gandalf's barks and growls filled the air with a crescendo.

"There's no kid in my car—there's nobody besides me and my dog." He shouted over the barking. "How can you even think of anybody getting in this car without setting off that racket? Get away from my car. What's the matter with you?"

The man lurched closer, grabbed Cliff's cell phone and hurled it onto the road.

"No, you don't." Cliff made a grab for the phone, but the man stomped hard on it with his boot heel, and kicked it, sending it skidding through the guard rails where it disappeared. Cliff watched in disbelief.

Then the man's eyes grew big as Gandalf appeared beside Cliff, all growling rage at the threat to his master. The man turned and ran into the roadside brush, hurling a handful of gravel at the black and tan blur that launched toward him. "Call off your dog!" He reached for a stick and raised it over his head, turning to face teeth and determination. Paws with fifty-five pounds of fury behind them slammed against his chest and he went flying backward into a cholla cactus, rending the air with an unholy scream. Gandalf came to a halt and backed off. The second man bolted out of the SUV and sprinted toward his buddy.

"Gandalf, come!" Gandalf left the chase, came barreling back to the car, and jumped in. "Let's get the hell outta here." Cliff slammed the car into reverse, screeched around the SUV, and took off down the road. Gandalf stood quivering in the passenger seat. "God! Good boy,

Gandalf. That guy's gonna hurt. A million cactus needles. He won't forget you for a while. Lie down, now. Steady." He petted the big head, rubbing the ears as he sped away.

The adrenaline rush faded, and he eased up on the gas. "Stop it," Cliff said to himself, nervously glancing in the rearview mirror once more. "They won't come after us."

He heard a sneeze. Gandalf lay quietly beside him. "Bless you," he told the dog.

Then he heard another sneeze and caught Gandalf's glance. "What? What the hell? That wasn't you! Who's there?"

Now what was going on? He pulled off onto the shoulder and stopped. He hit the unlock button, got out, jerked open the back door and flung the blanket aside. Frightened blue eyes looked at him through long, tousled hair. The child slowly unfolded herself from the floor and eased away from him onto the seat, backing away as far as she could. Gandalf woofed, his tail wagging.

"My God. There *is* a kid." Incredulous, he noted her blond hair and the bruises on her face. "You aren't their kid. Who are you?"

"They took me. Please, don't leave me here. Mister, can you help me?" said a quavering voice.

Cliff sucked in a breath, his jaw dropping. The world stopped spinning on its axis as he looked into her tear-filled eyes. Johnny's blue eyes flashed into his memory and jerked him backward to long ago. He slowly stretched out a hand and with his thumb gently brushed away a tear from the girl's dirty face. "They took you? …The Amber Alert!"

"Yes, I want to go home." The girl took a shuddering breath and cried, "I want my daddy."

"I'll get you home. You're safe now." Gandalf's tongue enthusiastically washed the girl's face. She gave a gurgly cry and turned her face into his fur, hugging him to avoid his tongue.

Time began to move again. Cliff looked back down the road, his thoughts racing. This child *will* get home, so help me God.

He stood, knowing with his whole being that what he needed the most was to make this child safe and get her far away from the villains who had stolen her from home and a family who loved her.

CHAPTER FIVE

"Get in front. We can't stay here. They might still be looking for us." She quickly did as he asked.

"My name's Cliff. That big furry fellow is Gandalf. What's your name? How old are you? Tell me what happened and where you live."

Glancing nervously behind them for the dark shape of the SUV, he got her buckled in, and drove off.

"My name's Krista. I'm ten years old. My daddy is Anton Bjornson, and we live in Santa Fe. This guy had a lost puppy and asked me if I knew where it came from. Then they grabbed me." A sob escaped her.

"When did this happen?"

"Yesterday... after school. They made me drink some yucky stuff. It made me feel fuzzy and... and sleepy. I heard them talking about stopping to eat, and that's when I snuck away and got in your car. I want my daddy," she ended with a wail. Gandalf poked his head between the seats, licking her cheek.

"It's okay. You've been very brave. Gandalf, lie down." The dog lowered his body onto the back seat, his front legs dangling over. He rested his head on the console and watched Krista through the curtain of his shaggy eyebrows.

"Here's what we'll do. They stomped on my cell phone, but we're near the Ghost Ranch Conference Center. I used to work there and still go hiking there a lot. I know them. It'll be safe there. I'll drive in to the conference center and call your daddy and the police. They'll be worried sick about you."

Cliff spotted the Ghost Ranch sign with its triangular long-horned steer skull logo and turned off the highway onto the gravel road. He remembered that his friend, Lou, would be at the Ranch this week attending a conference for artists. Dust billowed behind his car as he drove up the long, wash-boardy drive. He had happy memories of his summers there on staff. What could be better than being around congenial people who were there to create works of art, to solve problems, or just to explore invigorating ideas, all topped off by an inspirational physical setting? They reached the alfalfa field and saw welcoming trees shading the low adobe-type buildings. Brown-eyed Susans bloomed by the walkway.

He parked by the office in the shade. "Stay, Gandalf," he said. He offered Krista his hand as they got out of the car. She hesitated, looked up at his eyes, glanced back at Gandalf as if for reassurance, and then placed her hand in his. He kept his hold loose, trying to offer comfort without being scary. Poor kid, he thought, pretty brave having to trust a stranger, a man, after what those two did. I didn't even think when I put out my hand what her reaction might be. I truly hope Lou is available.

As they entered the office, the gal at the front desk looked up from her computer and smiled. "Cliff, good to see you again. Who's this with you?"

"Hi, Marge. This is Krista Bjornson. She was kidnapped, but she got away. There was an Amber Alert. Can we use your phone to call her family and the police? And can you find out if Lou Schultz is around, please? She's here for the artist's conference this week. We could use her help."

"Wow, we heard the Amber Alert." The secretary handed Cliff the phone and smiled warmly at Krista. "I'll see if I can find Lou. She's probably still at the dining hall. I think they have free time this afternoon."

Cliff rang the Santa Fe Police Department and told them about Krista's getting away from her captors and finding him. They put him through immediately to the task force leader working on the case. He was glad to find out it was Pete Schultz. Pete was Lou's father, and he had been very helpful to Cliff. He'd taught him a lot about how police worked when Cliff first began writing mysteries.

The familiar voice came on. "Cliff, are you in a safe place?"

"Yes, we're at Ghost Ranch." He told him about the confrontation with the two men, and about finding Krista.

"Is she hurt?"

"She's bruised a little, but seems to be okay, except for feeling sick with whatever they used to drug her. She's awfully anxious about her father."

"It's important we see her as soon as possible, get her checked out, and find out from both of you what you know. They shot her dad when he went to where they told him he could pick up Krista."

"No! Is he going to be okay?"

"I think so. He's in St. Vincent's. Might be in surgery about now. You must have been in the right place at the right time, Cliff. Can you give me a description of the kidnappers?"

"Sure. Two Hispanic men - One is about forty, dark hair, about five-foot-ten, mustache, wearing a light blue t-shirt, jeans, and boots. The other one is, I'd say, about twenty-five, about five-foot-eight. He's heavier than the other guy. He also had a mustache. They spoke both English and Spanish."

"How about their vehicle? We'll get out an APB."

"They're driving an old, beat-up SUV. Black with a yellow New Mexico plate. It was dirty, like they'd driven through a lot of mud. Dark-tinted windows on all sides and back."

"Good. That fits with what the school bus driver said. Did you see any signs on the sides?"

"No, no signs."

"Anything else?"

"Saw them first at a diner north of Tierra Amarillo, little hole in the wall called Rosa's. They came after me when I left, driving like idiots, and stopped me. They hollered that I had their kid. I didn't know then that Krista had hidden in my car at the diner. My dog chased the one who destroyed my phone and knocked him into a cholla cactus. We got the hell out of there. I don't know if they'll be after us, or if they'll be busy dealing with the cholla. The cactus really got him."

"Did you get their license number?"

"No, sorry."

Lou had come in while Cliff was talking, and the secretary quietly filled her in. Cliff caught a glance from Lou's gray eyes, nodded to her, and continued listening to Pete.

17

"Did you see any weapons or hear of any weapons?"

"No, didn't see any weapons." He glanced at Krista who was listening avidly by his side. "Krista is shaking her head no. If they had them, they're hidden."

"Did you or Krista find out a name for either of them?"

"Their names?" Cliff looked at Krista. "I didn't hear them. Did you?"

"The guy who grabbed me, the younger one, his name's Alfonso. He's mean."

"Did you hear a last name?" Cliff asked Krista. "She's shaking her head no. Anyway, I'd just passed Echo Amphitheater when I realized I had a stowaway. I figured the Ranch would be the closest safe place to stop and call. Didn't think they'd drive in here. I'll ask Lou to come back with us. She's here now. It will make Krista feel better."

"Good. I'm going to put you on hold for a minute and arrange for an escort to the hospital. Listen, Cliff, don't clean her up or anything. You know the routine. The doctors will be looking for any kind of evidence that will help us capture those guys and put 'em away. Hang on just a minute."

Lou greeted Krista. "Hi, my name is Lou. I'm a friend of Cliff's. Would you like some water? I think we have some snacks here, too. Are you hungry at all?"

Krista drank the water thirstily and selected a couple of chocolate chip cookies from the tray near the coffee maker.

"Let me show you where the bathroom is. Then we'll be ready to go." Lou led her out of the room. As they left, Cliff heard Lou tell Krista not to wash her hands. The police wouldn't want her to clean any evidence away.

Cliff turned to listen as Pete came on the line again. "We've arranged a State Police escort for you to the hospital. They'll be starting out from near Española, coming your way to meet you. What kind of car are you driving?"

"A silver 2014 Honda Fit," he said and gave Pete the license plate number. "That'll be great. Those guys won't bother us with lights flashing. Thanks."

"We'll tell her grandmother Krista's on her way home. You can tell Krista her dad's been hurt, and the doctors are patching him up. Reassure her he will be okay. If Lou is there now, I'd like to talk with her."

While Lou was on the phone, Cliff went back to his car and rearranged his stuff to make room for passengers. Lou and he went way back to when they had begun school at the University of New Mexico. They only lived a few blocks apart in Santa Fe now and had gotten to be good friends as they traveled back and forth by car and by Rail Runner. She'd kept on for her Masters in Fine Arts as he had, though her focus had been more on art than creative writing.

As Lou came down the walk holding Krista's hand, he was glad again for her quiet dependability. She wasn't too hard on the eyes either, seemingly taking the best features from her Japanese mother and her father's German ancestry.

"All set?" he asked. "I've left the back seat for you two. Come on, Gandalf, in the front. We'll soon be in Santa Fe."

CHAPTER SIX

At the end of the Ghost Ranch drive, Cliff stopped and looked carefully in both directions. The highway ahead snaked through a wide open vista with no place to hide a large vehicle. He was pretty sure the kidnappers couldn't have gotten on the road soon enough after the cholla incident to see him turning into the Ranch anyway. He pulled out and turned to the left.

Normally this stretch of highway between the Ranch and Abiquiu vied for the top on his list of favorites. The beauty and the solitude soothed and inspired him. He loved the colors—the purple-blue of the distant, flat-topped Pedernal dominating the mountains to the southeast, Abiquiu Lake, the cream, gold, and red rocks of the sandstone mesas, and the wide, open spaces dotted with green piñon and sage under the bowl of a bright blue sky. But today he felt edgy, on the lookout and yearning for the flashing lights of the promised police escort.

Gandalf was restless, too. Cliff had trained him to lie down while the car was moving, but the big Airedale wouldn't settle now. Cliff wondered if he'd picked up on the tension as they sped toward Santa Fe and safety. Gandalf sat in the front, facing the rear, looking at Krista. Then he stood. Repeated commands didn't make him lie down. Finally, he stood with his front feet perched on the console. Gandalf looked at Krista and then looked at Cliff, who could not see in his rearview mirror at all. With no warning, Gandalf leaped into the back seat, startling Cliff greatly. Krista shrieked and then giggled.

"Gandalf," Cliff yelled. "That wasn't too bright. Sorry, back there."

"I could read his mind and knew it wouldn't be long," Lou said, laughing as Gandalf curled up by Krista and put his head on her lap. Krista began petting him and he let out a big doggie sigh, closing his eyes, finally content.

Now that he could see in the mirror again, Cliff kept checking. Where the terrain allowed he could see quite a way back, and this two-lane road carried only light traffic. In the distance he spotted a dark shape coming closer. A little frown played on his brow. Could it be them? If so, what would they do this time? The dark shape passed a white car. Cliff sped up just a little. It seemed to keep pace, maybe even gaining a tad bit. A delivery truck pulled onto the road behind him, and blocked his view in the mirror. His palms gripping the steering wheel began to sweat before he realized the truck might be good company. Certainly those two jerks wouldn't pull their trick from earlier while people from nearby cars watched. Ah, better. He eased up on the accelerator and kept an even distance ahead of the truck. But after several miles the delivery truck slowed and turned off the road, leaving him vulnerable again.

Ayeee! The black vehicle loomed right behind. It pulled alongside to pass, and Cliff gripped the wheel harder, his heart pounding. He glanced over with dread only to see an SUV full of women chatting and laughing. They passed him and cut into his lane again, their vehicle with its California license plate soon disappearing ahead. Whew! Guess I'm a little too jumpy, he thought looking in the mirror, hoping his alarm hadn't been noticed by his passengers.

They neared Abiquiu. As their road curved in and out of rocky formations, they caught the occasional glint of sun on the Rio Chama. "There's our escort," Cliff said. "I see the lights." He blinked his headlights on and off and put his flashers on. One New Mexico State Police car pulled in behind and the other in front, and with red and blue lights going set the pace. He let out a deep breath. The first part of getting Krista home safely was done.

"How much farther is it?" Krista asked.

"We're just about to Española. Pretty soon you'll see the Rio Grande. That's about half way from the Ranch to Santa Fe." Cliff had relaxed enough to appreciate the reaction of the other drivers on the road to the lights, and began to enjoy the smooth, hassle-free trip with their escort.

"My cousin lives in Española." Krista said. "Lou, what will happen when we get to the hospital? Are you sure Gramma and Daddy are going to be there, too?"

"Yes, I'm sure. You'll get to see them real soon. The doctor might want to check you out first and make sure you're okay."

"Will I have to talk to the police and tell them what happened to me?"

"Yes, what you tell them will help put those guys in jail where they can't take more little girls. My dad is a policeman. I think he'll be there, too."

Cliff could hear the reassuring tones from the back seat as Lou explained to Krista about her daddy and what she might expect. He trusted the doctor would be as understanding and patient as Lou. Krista seemed like a good kid, and he didn't want her to have more trauma on top of what she'd already been through. The black and blue marks on her face and the dark, finger-sized bruises on her arms spoke of brutal handling. He hoped to heaven those guys hadn't hurt her in other ways. He really wanted them put away so they could never take another child. Being powerless was a horrible feeling.

"I live not far from here. There's Camel Rock. Pretty soon we see the Opera," Krista said. "Hey, look. We got more lights in back now."

Lou looked back. A Santa Fe patrol car had now replaced the rear escort, red and blue lights going. She smiled and waved. "It's Sam. He's joined our escort."

Cliff looked in his rearview mirror, seeing his friend and hiking buddy from the police department at the wheel of the patrol car. He relaxed a bit more. Soon they were at the hospital following the police car around to the back. Cliff turned off his flashers as he drove by a group of waiting press people. Wonder what happened, he thought. Then he realized. Well, duh. This is about us! They would have heard of the kidnapping, the Amber Alert, and that it had been canceled. They probably knew Krista had gotten away and that her dad had been shot. It was big news, and they would be all over the place trying to get pictures and sound bites for their TV broadcasts. They pulled up into a sheltered area. Krista looked eagerly out of the window.

A tall, willowy blond woman hurried from the entrance. "Gramma, Gramma!" Krista shouted as she flung open the door and ran to her. The woman threw her arms wide and caught Krista up in a tight hug. Both were crying.

Lou had grabbed Gandalf's collar to stop him from following and snapped on his leash. Tail wagging, he watched his new friend, pulling to go after her. Then distracted, he looked across the parking lot, intrigued by a familiar whistle.

Lou and Cliff heard Sam before they saw him. His whistling was part and parcel of his personality. Some folks found it gave Sam an aura of cheerfulness, while others found it downright annoying. He was very good–Bach or bird songs, cell phone rings or country western tunes—all were part of his repertoire. He came up, breaking off his whistle with a wide smile. He settled his uniform cap on his short, dark hair and took Gandalf's leash. "You two go meet with Pete. Karen will want to meet you. Gandalf can stay with me till one of you comes back."

"Thanks, Sam. Great to see you watch our backs," Cliff told his friend.

Lou's dad, Lieutenant Pete Schultz, came from the hospital entrance with a spring in his step. He greeted Lou with a hug, a smile lighting his face and his demeanor relaxed from its usual all-business stance. His wavy brown hair was flecked with salt and pepper, and the years had made his high forehead march even further back. A welcome shone from his warm, gray eyes, and he clapped Cliff on the shoulder and squeezed. The loose tie at his neck and the beginning of a five o'clock shadow testified to their long wait.

I'm ready to hear the rest of this story, Cliff thought. Wonder how Krista's dad is. Odd that he was shot. How and when could those two creeps do that? Wonder how long it'll take to get them in custody.

CHAPTER SEVEN

As they were already peppered with flashes from local press cameras, Pete shepherded them inside to a small conference room near the hospital emergency entrance. Cliff figured they must have been waiting there in private when the word came Krista had arrived. Pete's laptop sat on the table next to several coffee cups. A tote bag, knocked over in Karen's eager rush to see Krista, spilled some kid's shoes. Though the little room welcomed them, Cliff found that it didn't quite surpass the too-much-gray institutional look. A small couch and upholstered chairs took up one wall. On the other side of a table a counter, sink, tiny refrigerator, and microwave provided the amenities.

Karen hugged her granddaughter again. "Oh, Krista, Honey. Are you okay? You've got bruises."

"I'm okay," said Krista, her face scrunched against her grandmother's tight hold. "I got away. So scared I couldn't find you again, Gramma. Cliff and Lou brought me back. 'N Gandalf."

Cliff swallowed past the lump in his throat. God, to see this reunion, to see the love and closeness between Krista and her grandmother. It was a little—no, a big victory to have her back with her family. It felt damn good to have this ending to a kidnapping, rather than the long nothing of Johnny's.

The grandmother turned to them, brushing her hand over the tears on her cheeks, still holding Krista tightly. "Thank you so very much. I don't have the words…"

He could see the relief, the joy in her blue eyes, that looked a lot like Krista's. "Really glad we could help. Mrs. Bjornson, I'm Cliff McCreath. This is Lou Schultz."

"Call me Karen, please." she reached out to him with a heartfelt hug, scented slightly with lavender, then turned to Lou and embraced her.

"Lou is my daughter," said Pete. "She was at Ghost Ranch at an artist's conference when Cliff stopped there to call 911."

"I'm so glad. An artist's conference—later I'd like to hear about that. But who...where's Gandalf? I should thank him, too."

"He's Cliff's doggie," said Krista. "They probably won't let him in the hospital."

"Maybe later. I'll see what strings I can pull." Pete sat down at his laptop again, pushing his dark-framed glasses up on his nose.

"When can I see Daddy?"

"The doctors are still patching him up," said Karen. "He's going to be okay, but he's not feeling very well right now. We will only be able to stay a few minutes at first. We'll see him again after you have told your story to the police. But before that, Krista, the doctor wants to check you out and make sure you're okay."

"I know. Lou told me in the car, so it wouldn't be a surprise." Krista looked down, and her lips wobbled. "She told me they'd do a blood test, 'n ask me lots of personal stuff, 'n look me over, 'n that it might be embarrassing, but I'd feel better after. Can you come with me, Gramma?"

"They better not try and stop me." Karen squeezed Krista's hand, looking gratefully at Lou.

They heard a knock on the door and a nurse entered. "Mrs. Bjornson, Krista, if you'll follow me, the doctor is ready to see Krista now."

◆ ❖ ◆

"I'll relieve Sam from Gandalf duty," said Lou, "so he can get back to work. My cell phone is on if you need me, Dad."

Cliff looked at Pete. He saw worry mixed with relief on his friend's face as he watched Lou leave. "What is it?"

Pete turned to Cliff. "I need to find out as much as you can tell us about the kidnappers. Help yourself to the coffee—in that big thermos. I could use a little more, too."

Cliff poured the coffee and sat down. Taking a sip, he wrinkled his nose. "When did they brew this? How can you stand this stuff?"

"Starbucks, it ain't, but needs must. Go ahead."

Cliff told the tale of events beginning with his stop at the diner. It seemed like ages ago. "Finally we got to the Ranch to call. And then you said her dad had been shot. How is he?"

"Right now," Pete glanced at his watch, "he's out of surgery and in the recovery room. Anton's very lucky to have survived the attack. The surgeon talked with Karen and me just before you got here. They shot him twice; one shot grazed his head; the other hit his shoulder. It looks like he will recover fully. You can imagine Karen's fright—her granddaughter kidnapped, having her son shot, and Krista wasn't where they said she would be."

"She looks like she's holding up okay. I admire her." Cliff took another sip of coffee and made a face. He went over to the counter and got some more milk for his coffee.

"This whole episode has some strange twists. I'll share more of the details later with you, but for now the highlights. When Krista was snatched, they left a ransom note that said to bring five hundred thousand dollars to the Quick Laundry in Chimayo, put it in the basket on the table in the office at eleven o'clock, and close and lock the office door. They told Anton to call a certain number after he left the money to get directions for getting Krista back. We had an undercover officer there at that strip mall from nine on, doing loads of laundry. She said no one went near or opened that office door. Other officers covered both the front and back parking lots. The office has no outside door. After Anton was shot, we contacted the laundromat owner and had him open up the office. The money had vanished." Pete sat back and watched Cliff.

"You trust your officers?"

"Absolutely."

"No diversion that may've distracted them? Nothing exciting happening? Did anyone engage them in conversation?"

"Nothing. No fender benders in the parking lot, no phone calls, no arguments or fights. Only a few words of casual conversation the whole morning. Not even a TV in the laundromat to pass the time."

"Did they get a list of who used the laundromat throughout the morning?"

"Yes, the policewoman was pretending to write letters. Actually she took very detailed notes of all she saw. No one acted in a way she thought suspicious."

"No one gave them any funny coffee to drink? They didn't leave to go to the bathroom?"

"No." Pete smiled.

"You have a good idea, don't you? This is a test, isn't it?" Cliff stopped to think, pushing his glasses up on his nose. "A strip mall, you say. Stores built in a line, all connected spaces. There were no outside doors on the office? Any windows? Any connecting doors or panels?"

Pete sat there shaking his head.

"If you don't get into a room through a door or a window, you could tunnel under and come up through a trap door." Cliff watched Pete still shaking his head. "Or you could come down through the ceiling. I bet all of the units had grids with acoustic tiles."

"Damn, you're good, Cliff. Bingo! That's why your mystery writing works." Pete grabbed pencil and paper and drew a quick diagram of the strip mall. "There's a restaurant, a tax place, a real estate place, here's the laundry, and then a beauty salon. We discovered in early afternoon that all the units have access to a crawl-space catwalk in the ceiling going the length of the mall. Anywhere along it, you could access the catwalk by lifting out a ceiling tile. The forensic team has been working there all afternoon. They should find something. We don't yet know which of the businesses the ransom grabber used to gain access."

"Clever." Cliff considered the diagram. "Wait a minute. Did you say Chimayo?" Cliff leaned forward in his chair. "And where was Anton shot?"

"Truchas—about twenty-minutes' drive to the east."

"Chimayo. Truchas. What times were they?"

"The ransom was to be left at eleven a.m. Anton did it right on the dot. Then he went immediately to the Truchas spot where they said he could pick up Krista. Supposedly she'd been left tied up and gagged in some old building along the highway. We had undercover folks in Truchas as fast as we could. One had passed the building and parked out of sight. The other followed right on Anton's tail. A sniper ambushed Anton when he got out of his car. When he was shot, our guys were busy giving him first aid and didn't see much else. Of course they checked for Krista right away, but there was no sign that she or anyone had been there. From the dust and cobwebs it looked like the place had been undisturbed for months. It was a set up."

"A set up? You mean they lured Anton there to shoot him?"

"It appears so."

"About eleven-thirty is when I got to Rosa's Diner. The two kidnappers were already there and had just started eating their lunch. They couldn't have gotten the ransom or shot Anton. It's a good hour and a half from Truchas, even if you paid no attention to speed limits." Cliff thought for a bit and swallowed a sip of coffee with a grimace. "I see what you mean about strange twists. So the two creeps who took Krista weren't alone. Who got the ransom money? And how? Who shot Anton?"

"Exactly. How many people are we looking for?"

"Bloody hell, Pete. Doesn't sound like they even planned to bring Krista back. What would have happened to her if she hadn't gotten away?"

"It doesn't even bear thinking about. I'd like your help tomorrow, Cliff. I'd like to talk to the folks at Rosa's Diner, and maybe we can check out the place where you confronted the kidnappers. We'll drop Lou back at her conference on the way."

"Glad to. Maybe we can stop in Chimayo, too? You've made me curious now to see that site."

"Sure. I think I'll have Lou and Gandalf come and join us now. I think you might help when Krista tells her story. Make her more comfortable. You might hear something I miss. Gandalf's being here will ease her, too."

"They'll let him in?"

Pete shrugged and grinned. "He's on police business."

CHAPTER EIGHT

Lou sat on a bench near the front hospital entrance with Gandalf by her feet. She would not be bored as long as there were people to watch. The artist in her saw interesting light, shadow, and color on the faces that passed by. The range of emotions reflected concern, relief, apprehension, and pain of patients, relatives, and friends, as well as the everyday-ness of folks just going to and from work and routine, some tired, some animated. Lou passed the time enjoyably, making up stories of what might be happening in their lives.

One of her upcoming projects was illustrating a children's book about a little boy who had been badly injured and had to stay in the hospital for weeks at a time with many more follow-up visits. This was an ideal opportunity to do some of that research. She took out her cell phone and snapped pictures, not of any particular subject, but getting a feel for the ambience of the hospital setting. When she saw a particularly interesting face, she took several shots as they approached and passed by. A tall, elegant woman moving purposefully toward the entrance, looking around as if she expected to see someone, caught Lou's eye as a good character study.

Fortunately, cell phones don't draw attention to themselves, she thought. No one seems to realize I'm taking their pictures. Good thing. That'd be creepy.

The only ones that did seem to notice her were the dog lovers who spotted Gandalf. Some of those stopped to chat. Gandalf, ever ready to meet his adoring public, obliged with sniffs to determine if they had dogs and cats at home and with licks to their extended hands. Lou snapped pictures of those encounters to add to her collection, too.

Taking out the sketchbook that almost always accompanied her, she sketched some of the folks: an old man, his years showing in wrinkles, shuffling by with his walker, the tall elegant woman, and a skinny child with his leg in a cast, hobbling by holding on to his mother's hand. Then Lou sketched Krista from memory, capturing the myriad of emotions which had affected the little girl during the afternoon. I wonder how she's doing, she thought. I hope her adventure doesn't leave lasting scars. What an awful thing to go through. I was so glad to be there when Cliff needed me. I wish sometimes he saw me as more than just a friend. I wish....

Karen and Krista followed the nurse down the hall into a little bathroom where they had Krista pee, and then into an examining room where a policewoman joined them. Krista looked around at the cupboards, sink, computer screen, and the instruments on the wall. They'd made an effort to make the room appealing and cozy, though it still smelled like antiseptic. A mural of cute animals dominated one wall. A soft teddy bear perched on one of the chairs looked at her with his black button eyes. She eyed the paper-covered table apprehensively. "Just like Lou said."

"First of all, we are going to get your clothes off," the nurse said. "What is this on your shirt, Krista?"

She looked down. "Yuck. It's blood."

"Where are you hurt?"

"Not my blood, the guy who had his hand over my mouth. I bit him really hard. I scratched him, too. Then he hit me. Then he hit me harder and rolled me into a blanket. I couldn't get out."

"Do you know if your bite left a mark?"

"Yeah, his finger was bleeding all over—that's when it got on my shirt."

The nurse helped her undress and gave her a little gown to put on. She handed her clothes to the policewoman who put them one by one into bags and made notes.

"How long do I have to wear this? It doesn't cover me good with these weird ties."

Karen said, "Only a little while until the doctor is through. Maria brought you some clothes to change into before you go see Daddy. I wonder if the doctors might have given your daddy a gown like this, too?"

"Gramma, that'd be silly. Really? With little pink bunnies on it?"

Krista looked up at the nurse who was drawing blood from her arm. "Will they make him wear a gown?"

"Maybe, but they have plain ones for big people. They don't get the special ones with pink bunnies." She smiled. "There, that's all the blood we need. That part's all over."

"How come they need my blood?"

"They can test it and maybe find out what those guys made you drink. Blood tells us all kind of things. They can, like say, test the blood on your shirt. That blood might let us prove who took you."

"Oh, I almost forgot." Krista saw the policewoman putting her jeans into a bag. "I thought when I got away the police might need some clues so they could catch 'em. I stole a candy package from one of 'em. It might have my fingerprints on it, too, but I tried not to touch it 'cept with the piece of paper I wrapped it in. It's in my pocket."

Surprised, the policewoman looked at her. "That was very smart of you. How did you think to do that?"

"I like to read mysteries. Fingerprints are important in catching bad guys. Are you going to fingerprint me so's you won't mix my prints up with the bad guys?"

"I think that's a good idea. When you go back downstairs and tell Lieutenant Schultz your story—tell him he's supposed to get your prints, and what you did with the candy container. I'll make some special notes for him. I think it will be very important. What's your favorite mystery, Krista?"

"I like Trixie Belden and Nancy Drew. I like the ones with the dog, too. Each one of those has a special part that tells something important about how to solve mysteries."

As they talked about their favorites, the police woman cleaned under her fingernails, putting what she found into a little bag, and making more notes.

The door opened, and the doctor came in. Krista looked at her. "This isn't going to hurt, is it?"

"I'm just going to check you over. We'll take your blood pressure, see how fast your heart is beating, and look down your throat and make you say 'ahh.' Then we'll look at your skin all over to make sure they didn't hurt you. We'll also take some pictures of your bruises for the police."

"Okay."

"Do your bruises hurt?" The doctor gently touched Krista's face and looked at the bruises on her arm.

"Just hurts a little."

"Did those men touch you where they shouldn't?"

"I don't think so. They pretty much left me alone after I got sleepy. Sometime in the night they carried me into a house somewhere." As the doctor methodically examined her, Krista told her how she'd avoided taking more medicine and gotten away.

"There, I think we're all done. You tell your grandmother if you remember any more hurts, okay? You did just fine."

Karen said, "I think we'd better get you dressed, and cleaned up before you see Daddy. You can ask him about the pink bunny gown."

Karen led her granddaughter to the elevator to go to Anton's room. "You're going to see bandages on his head and arm, Krista, but he's going to be all right. He will probably be hooked up to some monitors. Sometimes they make funny beeps. All those machines just tell the nurses how he's doing."

When they entered the room he was lying quietly, an IV in his arm. Krista saw a little clip on one of his fingers, too, with a tube that went off somewhere to a machine. A couple of monitors glowed, but she didn't hear any beeping. His head was swathed in lop-sided gauze bandages. Under a loose gown, his shoulder sported another bandage.

He opened his eyes and his face lit up. "Krista!"

"Daddy," Krista climbed on the bed, cuddled down by his side, and laid her head on his chest, putting her arms around him as far as she could.

"Careful," Karen said watching all the tubes and wires.

"It's okay, Honey." Anton moved his good arm to pat her back awkwardly. "This is the best medicine—absolutely nothing could make me feel better than this hug."

"I got away, Daddy. I was scared."

"So was I, Honey, just terrified. Good to hold you again."

"Just a plain gown, Gramma," she said raising her head. "No pink bunnies."

"What?"

Karen laughed, as she wiped away a tear. "No pink bunnies. Anton, they had her wear a gown with bunnies while she was being checked out. We were teasing her about your having one like hers. She's okay. They didn't do anything really bad to her, just scared her. And she got away."

Anton pulled her close again with a big sigh. "Thank the good Lord. I love you so much, Honey. I'm so glad you're safe." He closed his eyes again. "And I'm not the pink bunny type. They wouldn't dare."

"We'll come back in a little while, Son. Rest. Love you."

CHAPTER NINE

"Gramma, can we eat after I tell my story?" Krista asked as they came back into the little conference room. "Oh, good. They let Gandalf in." Karen and Krista settled on the couch. It wasn't that big, but Gandalf jumped up with them and plopped himself down, half on top of Krista, pushing Karen to make space for himself.

"I got to see my daddy," Krista announced. "He said my hugs were the best medicine. He's going to take a nap now, but we get to see him later. Maybe he can come home tomorrow."

Lou and Pete sat at the table. Cliff poured more coffee and gave Krista a bottle of water. They heard the squeak of someone's shoes on the polished hall floor approach and recede. A child's plaintive cry rose and was shushed by a voice of comfort.

"Now, Krista," said Pete, "you can tell us about your adventure. We want to hear everything, even if you don't think it's important. Start when you were getting off the bus."

"Well, there was this big SUV with a sign that said Ortega Landscaping on the side. I thought it was weird. The sign was very clean, but the rest of the outside was all muddy and dirty."

"How many people were in it?"

"Just two. The one guy was outside the SUV when the bus dropped me off. He had a really cute puppy and did I know who it belonged to. When I went over to look at it, the other man came from behind and grabbed me. They left the puppy. From my dog book I think it was a golden retriever. I like doggies. I hope it didn't get lost or hit by a car."

"We found the puppy. He's okay. Go on."

She told them about the medicine, what she remembered about the call on her cell phone, and all that she remembered about the night.

"Can you tell us what the two guys looked like?"

She told them and then added, "The young one had real short hair and he had a stupid, skinny beard. It was like he had a big upside-down U under his nose. It went all the way to his chin." She demonstrated on her own face. "Then he had a line of beard from his lower lip to his chin. The other guy just had a mustache. Oh, 'n the stupid-beard guy had ears that stuck out a lot. I could see them from where they had me in the blanket."

"You said they spoke Spanish—all the time, except when they were talking to you?"

"Pretty much all the time. I take Spanish in school. They used a lot of bad words. Maria—she's our housekeeper—she would have yelled at them and washed their mouths out with soap." She paused to take a sip of water.

"Do you know their names?"

"Only Alfonso, the mean one—the one who grabbed me and hit me. Don't know the other guy's name."

"Do you remember what they talked about?"

"They were going to pull one by takin' me to Utah. Daddy and I went to Utah once. We saw some really neat rock formations—pretty arches and stuff. The wind and water made them."

"Did they say anything else you can remember?"

Krista told them about the snatches of conversation in the night and then added, "They said he was goin' to be real mad."

"Do you know who he is?"

"No, just that he's trouble." Krista paused to stretch out one of Gandalf's ears and run her fingers along the softness. "Oh, and somethin' about Los Ojos, and they hoped they never need to go back there."

"Did they name any other places?"

"I don't remember. When they were talking 'bout being hungry in the car, I pretended to be asleep. They left, and I peeked out the windows and saw them inside the diner. That's when Cliff came." She took another sip of water. "Then the cowboy drove in. I stuffed some stuff under the blanket on the seat, and tried to make it look like I was still there."

"What kind of stuff did they have in the car?"

"More blankets, clothes, and tools and stuff. Some beer. They had a collection of license plates, too. I thought they might be trying to get all the states. They had Colorado, Utah, a couple of different New Mexico ones, and some others. Oh, and Texas, too."

"Tell us more how you got away."

"Well, I saw the candy package and I stole it, and wrapped it up so's I wouldn't get my fingerprints on it. The police lady told me to tell you that you were supposed to take my prints."

Pete smiled. "We will surely do that. You got something even better than the breath mint package. She told me the paper you used to wrap it in was a note with directions to your place and the time when you would be getting home. It has a phone number on it, too. We're checking that out now. You were excellent."

Krista beamed. "Then I snuck out real quiet. When I did that, I saw they didn't have the landscaping sign on the side anymore. It was gone. I got into Cliff's car and hid under Gandalf's blanket. He didn't bark at me at all like he did at the cowboy." She put her face in Gandalf's fur. "He's my friend."

"If you remember anything else, Krista, have your grandmother call me. I'll stop by sometime soon to talk to Maria and Diego. You were a big help."

Cliff looked up as the door opened. A tall, blond man wearing a Rio Arriba Sheriff's Department uniform stepped into the room, head high, shoulders back. Smiling, Karen rose from her spot on the couch and moved forward to receive his hug. "Vidar."

"Aunt Karen, I came as soon as I could get away."

Karen introduced her nephew to them. Cliff reached forward to shake Vidar's hand. This is a guy I wouldn't want to cross, he thought. This family has good connections with the police. Bad guys, look out.

"Lou… McCreath…" Vidar acknowledged them. "I did hear they'd canceled the Amber Alert. So, she's back."

"Hi, Vidar," Krista said from the couch, still cuddled up next to Gandalf. "I got away."

"You're a lucky one. Good job, kid." Vidar turned back to his aunt. "How is Anton?"

"Doing pretty well. They'll keep him overnight. We'll see him again before we go home. We're just waiting for some test results, and to finish our questions here."

"You going to be okay at home tonight, Aunt Karen?"

"Yes, thanks, Vidar. Pete has an officer on duty at our house, at least through the night, and maybe until Anton is home. Maria is there now, and Diego should be there tonight, too. Cliff and Lou are going to give us a ride home when we're ready."

Vidar nodded, poured himself a cup of coffee, and sat down at the table. "Lieutenant, I spoke with the Sheriff before I came over. I requested an assignment to your task force. Anton, Karen, and Krista are the only family I have."

"I don't know, Vidar. Normally our policy is to keep individuals from working on cases in which their families are involved."

"I'm aware of that. I talked the Sheriff into making an exception this time. I'd like very much to help. I know the area and the folks who live there. He'll call you tomorrow. If there's anything I can do, let me know."

"Certainly, Vidar. We appreciate it. I'll look forward to his call. What is the latest from the Truchas site? I understand you were there shortly after Anton was shot."

"Yes, I'd been responding to a burglary call in Truchas. Whoever shot Anton sure made a slick getaway. There was no sign of him. We had reports of a white truck that went racing up Highway 76 after the shots were heard, but they don't have any person of interest yet. The description of that truck could fit at least a dozen vehicles in the area. Pretty common."

"Gramma, I'm hungry." Krista had left Gandalf and was leaning on Karen.

"I think we all are. Let's see what the cafeteria has to offer."

Pete said, "Hold on a minute. I'll get Sam to go with you. And, it'd be a good idea to bring your food back here—avoid the press and the gawkers. If I'm not here, it's because of the news conference that'll be happening shortly. I'm just going to finish my report. I called Akiko, she's my wife, and told her I'll be home late tonight. The Chief will handle the news conference, but I should be there, too." Pete went back to his laptop.

"I have a lot left to do tonight, so I'll be shoving off." Vidar stood, finishing the last of his coffee. He looked at Cliff and Pete. "You two seem to know each other. Are you in the department, too, Cliff?"

"No, but I've known Pete for a long time. I'm a writer. He's one of my main consultants for getting the facts right."

"Don't underestimate Cliff." Pete said. "He has a crazy way of looking at puzzles the rest of us can't fathom, and then he throws in an off-the-wall idea that sets us down a new path—and often it works."

"Ah, …a writer, and do you have an off-the-wall idea for this?" asked Vidar.

"Nope, not yet. Not enough information. Nice to meet you, Vidar. I'm sure I'll see you again." Cliff felt a little amused by Vidar's dismissive tone.

Sam appeared at the door. "Ready for the cafeteria?"

With Krista tugging on Karen's hand, Cliff and Lou followed them out the door.

CHAPTER TEN

Later, after they'd finished, Karen gave Cliff directions, and they left the hospital behind them at sunset time. Built on higher ground, the hospital offered wide views of the Sangre de Cristos and the Jemez Mountains. The golds and reds of the setting sun slowly gave up and faded into purple and blue off to their left. A few high clouds glowed pink before disappearing into the night. In the back seat Gandalf laid his head on Krista's lap, and she stroked him softly, finding velvety spots on his ears and the contrasting wiry fur on his head. Soon her eyes closed, and her head nodded down. Lou sat quietly in back beside them. Karen reached out and touched the tiny figure on the dashboard catching the last light.

"Koda?" she asked.

"Sure is. Hard to believe that kids' movie would have spawned a multi-billion-dollar industry of books, sequels, and all that licensed stuff, isn't it?"

"Maybe the appeal is that it is layered. The kids enjoy it for the story, but the adults appreciate the deeper meaning within."

"You may be right."

"I heard there was still another movie in the series of the Sami legends coming out. Anton will want to take Krista. I remember when Anton was little, he had a toy Koda. Wise little mentor-type of character."

"Yeah, he was my brother's favorite."

Cliff was lost in thought for a while and then began to speak. "My brother was kidnapped when I was only four. Johnny had just turned six—my big brother. Today brought it all back. I feel—felt so guilty. It hurt so bad.

"I'll never forget that day. And it got worse. My parents were crying. There were police and guys from the press all over. I was sure that somehow they would find him and bring him home. But it just stretched—day after day, week after week. It became an ache that wouldn't go away. We never saw him again. We don't even know what happened. They never caught anybody, never found anything. He's just… gone…. Sorry, today's been… I never talk like this, especially to people I've just met." He glanced at her apologetically.

"It's okay. Maybe I need to hear it; maybe you need to say it."

He blinked a few times, and was quiet for a while. Then he spoke again, remembering, "I couldn't make it right again. I couldn't be Johnny for my parents. I remember when my folks, a long time later, months and months later, finally moved his stuff out of our room. They packed it up and put it into storage. I screamed and threw a tantrum and latched onto Koda, Johnny's toy. I wouldn't let go. Johnny always said he talked to it, and it listened.

"My dad told me I could keep Koda for Johnny. I did. I still have it. I talked to it. Told him all the things I wanted to tell Johnny."

"You still talk to it," Karen guessed.

"You're right. Still do—even as a grown man. Koda listens." He slowed to make a turn. "It was hard on my parents. I tried to make it up for losing Johnny by being a good kid. I can't imagine losing your first-born child; never knowing, never having closure."

The wise little figure on the dashboard seemed to look at him. "We still wait for Johnny to come home. The hurt isn't as sharp anymore, but it's still there. It's an emptiness… no bottom, no end, just a void."

"Oh, Cliff, I'm so sorry. How very awful it must have been." Karen touched his arm.

"My little sister and I were very clingy after that, and my parents didn't want to let us out of their sight. Then later they had to push me into life again. They insisted I play with my friends, learn to ride a bike, play softball.

"My folks tried to keep things normal for us—birthdays, Christmas, holidays. But there was always a Johnny-sized hole—at least I felt it. I'm sure my folks do, too. My parents had always been happy, laughing, and fun. They still are, but there's a damper—they'll see a red-headed kid, or a guy who's the same age Johnny would be now, and they get quiet. I know they're thinking about him. Actually, I understand that. More than once I've gone up to a red-haired, blue-eyed guy who's about my age, and asked him if his name was John McCreath. Sometimes I tell them the story. Sometimes not. I keep hoping. Probably stupid.

"Anyhow, late one night, I guess I was a teenager, I got up to get something. It must have been Johnny's birthday or at least some special day. Mom and Dad were sitting on the couch. He had his arms around her, she was crying, and I saw tears running down his face, too. They didn't know I was there; I went back to bed. I felt so guilty—so powerless."

She waited in silence for him to speak as he took the turn off to Tano Road, and then he resumed. "I have a natural ornery, stubborn streak. Sometimes, when people tell me I can't do something, I dig in and *damn* well do it. They say people choose a dog breed for a reason. I have a stubborn, feisty terrier." He smiled and looked in the mirror at Gandalf with his head in Krista's lap, both of them asleep. Lou reached forward and grasped his shoulder briefly. As he caught her eyes in the mirror, he saw from oncoming headlights that her cheeks were wet.

"When I saw Krista in my car all I could think about was getting her home, of not having another family go through that."

"You did stop the bad guys today, Cliff. I realize even more now, the miracle of you being there for Krista. You saved not only her, but Anton and me, too. Krista's mom died in a car accident when she was four. Just before that I lost my husband. So much pain, so much loss—but we had some comfort, I realize, in having funerals, family, and friends... an ending. And, then you pick up and go on. I can't imagine not knowing.... Cliff, I'm so thankful Krista found you."

"I'd walk through fire to stop that happening to another family. I think about those two guys, too. I wonder why they took her, if she was the only one. I write mysteries for a living. This is one mystery I could focus on and solve. If there's anything I can do to help, Karen, please let me know."

"Maybe you can. Maybe you were put in Krista's life for a reason. I want you to come over, you and Lou, when Anton gets home. I want us to get to know you better. I think we need you."

They both drifted off into memories and silence driving through the darkened roads until she pointed out their driveway.

He turned onto a drive that dipped down and then climbed up past a corral, some ranch buildings, and up to a sprawling adobe-style home. The front door opened and light shone past a matronly woman who hurried toward them. Krista sat up in the back seat and got out of the car, rubbing her eyes. The woman enveloped her in a hug.

◆ ❖ ◆

I know him so well, but I've never heard that, Lou thought as Cliff drove out of the Bjornsons' drive and headed toward their homes. He truly continues to surprise me. My heart aches for the pain he's feeling.

As they descended toward the valley, the lights of Santa Fe stretched before them, twinkling in the darkness. Cliff spoke. "I'm glad you were with me today, Lou. It meant a lot, having you there to help with Krista and to take care of Gandalf."

"Thanks. I was happy you asked. You were right in Krista's needing a woman on the trip back. You were safety and strength to her, but she needed someone who could hug and cuddle her, too. She was so clever in getting away." Lou tucked a strand of hair behind her ear, her eyes on the little Koda. "I never knew all that about your brother. I mean, I knew he'd been kidnapped, but I never heard you say what you felt about it all. You never told me why Koda was so important—I guess I thought it was because you liked the movies so well. I'm glad I heard you tonight."

"Yeah, well. Didn't mean to turn the evening into a tear jerker. It's been a bizarre day."

"I really like Karen—she's a very strong woman. She's done a great job with Krista."

"She's sharp. I'm looking forward to meeting Anton."

He turned on the CD player, turned down the volume and let the muted sound of Uilleann pipes surround them.

"How's Ashleigh?" asked Lou. Something within her pushed the question, though she wished the blonde would just disappear.

"Oh, bloody hell. Ashleigh!" Cliff cried, hitting his palm on the steering wheel. "I totally forgot. We had a date for a movie tonight. She'll be royally pissed."

"She should understand when she knows what happened. She probably heard all about the kidnapping and Krista coming home on the news. She might even have seen you on TV. There were enough photographers at the hospital."

"I hope so." They drove in silence for a bit. "I wouldn't count on it, though. She'll probably think I did it on purpose. It wasn't my kind of movie, and she knew it."

"So tell her your cell phone was trashed. You couldn't call her."

"Like I couldn't borrow a phone. No, I'm in trouble." He paused for a red light. "Once when we were sitting out on the patio—No, don't say it, Lou. I know it's the only place to sit at my house without moving a bunch of stuff."

Lou responded with a laugh. "You're right about that."

"Anyway, I was barefoot, and Gandalf started to wash my feet with his tongue. You know how he does, it's like a wonderful, relaxing foot massage. She got all grossed out and said she didn't understand why anyone would let an animal lick them and how unsanitary it was."

"Now she's treading on thin ice." Lou smiled. "Don't mess with your dog."

"Did I tell you what she got for me for my birthday?"

"No, what?"

"A vacuum cleaning gadget with every attachment known to man, even one to use on the dog. Airedales don't even shed, for God's sake. It was totally ridiculous and obscenely expensive. She knew right off I didn't like it. She was hurt, said she thought I'd love it, and that I really needed it. She got all huffy and said she'd take it back."

"You're kidding. You—famous at the University, known as Messy McCreath?

Cliff glanced over at Lou. She tried to keep a straight face, but couldn't stop a little snort from escaping. He grinned and joined her in laughter.

"I'm sorry, but she really doesn't know you very well."

"I think she doesn't want to know me. She wants to change me into somebody I'm not. It's not going anywhere again, Lou. I just can't seem to find someone who sees who I am and likes me—*me*, not some image they have of me."

Lou sobered and remained quiet for a while, thinking, *you could open your eyes, blind guy. I suppose there'll be another soon in the succession of blond bimbos. And he always tells me about them. Oh well, one of these days one's going to trap him into a relationship that* both of them will end up regretting. It's a good thing my career's taking off. I'm enjoying it a lot now and even getting paid well. Maybe I don't need a man to have a happy life. She sighed. Hmm, too quiet in here. Think I'll change the subject.

"Do you think Krista will be able to get back to sleep," she said, "or will she have nightmares? She was sure scared, and just hanging on, but I saw a lot of resilience as she told what happened. That kidnapping is strange, Cliff. It's like somebody has it in for that family."

"I think so, too. Those two guys aren't the only ones involved. I realized that when I heard the two locations where they were supposed to leave the ransom and then pick up Krista. Those spots weren't anywhere near where Krista and the two jerks were. It's really fishy. I would love to solve that mystery."

"Well, why not? Talk with Karen and Anton. You're good at figuring out plots, and ferreting out villains. Sometimes somebody from the outside can see things family can't. Talk to my dad, to Sam, use your connections. Go for it."

"We'll see. Maybe when we're over for that dinner she mentioned."

Lou nodded as they pulled up to where she lived with her family. "Or before. Maybe you shouldn't wait 'til Anton is better. You'll have a lot of time to talk with Dad tomorrow. Think about it. See you in the morning."

CHAPTER ELEVEN

Cliff woke early the next morning with questions buzzing through his mind. Mentally planning his day and carrying his coffee and breakfast, he went into his study, now bright with the rising sun. He opened the French doors for Gandalf who paused first, looked around carefully, then ambled out. Cliff thought Gandalf was always in hope that he might catch the resident squirrels off guard. It didn't seem to occur to Gandalf that the snap of the door lock and the sound of the door opening would give away his presence to the squirrels.

One of the benefits of being an early riser was the morning chorus of bird songs. This summer they'd been lucky to have a nesting pair of blue grosbeaks in the neighborhood, and Cliff heard them now. A few times he'd even seen the flashy, brilliant blue male and his cinnamon-colored mate.

Lined with bookshelves, Cliff's study took up one of the largest rooms in his house. Johnny's large, toy stuffed Koda that he'd kept had pride of place on a center shelf. A bedraggled furry fox lay tucked behind it. The next shelf over displayed his five published books face out, along with the award he had received for his third book. Several hiking guides, to which he'd contributed articles, stood next to his mysteries.

Cliff reached for his cell phone to check messages before he remembered it was gone. "Damn," he swore. "Those bastards! Gotta take care of that today." Stacks of papers and books lined Cliff's Lshaped desk along with the clutter of pencils, paper clips, and other supplies. He rummaged carefully in a geologically-layered pile of paid bills and other "important papers," found his last cell phone bill, pulled it out, and stuck it with his car keys so he wouldn't forget it. "Guess it's about time to do some filing, too. Someday soon. And, there's another ugly task I should do today. Go see Ashleigh. Think I'll break it off with her. Not looking forward to that scene."

How can I convince them to let me work on solving this case? he wondered. Karen is already open to it, and Pete did ask for my help today. Maybe there's something I can offer. I *hate* being powerless. Couldn't do anything about the guy who took Johnny, but I've already dealt with these two creeps.

Now, let me see…what is the best way to organize this sleuthing bit? Huh, you're a mystery writer. Put what you know to work. Try some of the hoops you make your story-book detectives jump through. Motive, means, and opportunity. Well, bit early for the means and opportunity stages yet. But motives—why would someone want to hurt the Bjornsons? Who're the players and suspects in this caper?

He sat down in his office chair and looked over his desk at two dry erase / bulletin board holders. The boards currently displayed a plot-point outline for his next mystery and a diagram of the setting of the immediate scene he was writing. He leaned those boards against a bookshelf and pulled out a couple of blank boards. Flipping one to the bulletin board side he tacked up a map of Northern New Mexico. He used push pins to locate Rosa's Diner, the bridge over the dry wash where the two had confronted him, the location of the ransom drop, and the Krista-pick-up spot where Anton had been shot.

He divided the dry erase board into two columns and labeled them Suspects and Motives. Now who do we have so far? Alfonso and his buddy, the second kidnapper. He listed them. Then he added Shooter and Ransom Grabber. While he ate his breakfast he pondered how to proceed.

Rolling back to his computer, he began a document and started a list of questions and thoughts. Are the shooter and the ransom-grabber the same person? Or doesn't that work time-wise? Five hundred thousand dollars isn't a huge ransom demand. Might the money only be a bonus tacked on to the bigger goal of luring Anton to his death? There is a lot more going on here than that five hundred grand.

Back at the board he listed general ideas and questions for motives in the second column. Who is the enemy? Who stands to profit by the kidnapping or by Anton's death? Who has a grudge or is greedy enough to hatch the plot? Who has a secret to hide that makes them vulnerable? Had anyone recently threatened Anton? Who are his business rivals? For that matter, what is his business?

He did an internet search with Anton's name, finding out he owned Drone Tech, a company involved in the development and manufacture of drones. He also discovered that Karen and Anton had the Carter Foundation, a philanthropic organization which gave grants to various groups and individuals.

Okay, is there anyone who is trying to purchase or acquire Drone Tech? Is there anyone with any reason or some nefarious purpose who would like to stop Anton from pursuing some kind of current technological improvements?

Then he began a new computer folder with a document for each of the players. He decided to look at the family first: Anton and Karen. Then he did another group with employees and business contacts for the Carter Foundation and for Drone Tech. Later he would start an internet search for their names, checking Facebook and other social media, the newspapers, and all other leads he could think of. At this point he was organizing. Later, he'd get to copying and pasting information and links that might be relevant into his documents. Then he would study them. Now he just needed names and threads of information to follow about who might benefit from harming the Bjornsons.

As he worked he periodically switched to his questions document to add more ideas. Coming across Vidar's name in one of the articles, he gave him a page in the family folder as well. Reliving the trip to the Bjornsons' last night he thought of the warm hug for Krista from the woman. Must be their housekeeper. What did Krista say her name was? Ah, Maria. He remembered hearing about Diego, their handyman, briefly at the hospital. He added those two to the employee folder and made documents for their names, too.

Noticing it was almost 7:30 a.m. he finished the last of his cold coffee, shut down the computer, and reached for his cell phone to tell

Pete and Lou he was on his way. "Bloody hell. What a pain. Well, they'll know I'm coming when they see me." He closed the outside doors and made sure Gandalf had plenty of kibble and water.

He wondered what he and Pete might learn from Rosa. Might she know the two guys? Would she be cooperative? And what would they find in Chimayo? Would they find the answer to where the ransom money went after it disappeared from a locked room?

CHAPTER TWELVE

Pete and Cliff entered Rosa's Diner, stepping past the tan dog who thumped his tail. They sat at the counter. Rosa came over to take their order.

"I've heard good things about your apple empanadas. We'll have those and coffee," Pete said.

Rosa gave the order to the cook and brought the coffee.

"Are you the owner?" Pete asked.

"*Sí*, I am Rosa."

"Rosa, my name is Pete Schultz, and I'm from the Santa Fe Police Department. This is Cliff. He was in here yesterday. There were also two men who sat over there by the window, and a man described as a cowboy who sat at the counter. Are any of them regulars? Do you know any of them?"

Rosa's face shuttered as soon as she heard where they were from. She backed away. "We don't want trouble. We don't know anything."

"You're not in any kind of trouble. All we want to do is get in touch with them."

"I don't know them. Why? What'd they do?"

"The cowboy didn't do anything. He just might have seen something that would help solve a crime."

"That cowboy… eh, he comes in here every week. Makes a trip for supplies down to Española. Stops here to eat. His name's Shorty. He's a good tipper, and he don't give me no sass. He works at Cooper Ranch out by Lumberton."

"How about the other two?"

"Don't know them."

"Those two men kidnapped a little girl," Cliff said.

"Kidnapped! *¡Madre de Dios!*" She threw her hands into the air and became more animated. "That's why. She must'a got away. Those two hombres, I seen them before, but not many times. Maybe got family around. Don't know where. They got really loco yesterday! After you go," she nodded to Cliff, "they go, and then they come stomping back in here. Said their kid ran away. No kid here, I tell them. They real upset."

Rosa's hands in the air accompanied the musical cadence of her voice. "No asking, just telling me they gonna search my place, slamming doors, looking behind things—then they go tearing off. *Gracias de Dios* Shorty was here. They looking to beat somebody."

"Did they call each other by name? Can you tell me anything else that might help us find them?"

"Well, they was yellin' in Spanish. Say something about he gonna kill 'em. Then they decided the red-hair gringo stole her and vamoosed." She took a deep breath and calmed down a bit, then turned to pick up the coffee pot, and refilled their mugs. "Never heard any names."

"When they were searching, did they touch anything that might have left fingerprints which could still be there? Did they pick up or move anything? Do you mind if we look for prints?"

Rosa thought and pointed out a few places. "Sure, look for prints if you can find 'em. My prints are all over and my cook's, too."

"If it is okay, we will take your fingerprints and your cook's."

"Okay. Cook, he'll grumble, but those two shouldn't be stealing little *niñas*. They need catching. Did the little girl get away? She is okay?"

"Yes, she escaped," said Cliff. "She's home now. Scared and upset, but safe."

Pete finished the last flaky bite of his warm apple empanada and savored the cinnamon-flavored sweetness. "These are delicious, Rosa."

"*Muy gracias*. Well, glad she's okay. How old is she? I know those two *diablos es muy mal*."

Caught up in the story of the girl who'd escaped, Rosa had become very chatty. She told them about her granddaughters as Pete put on gloves and worked. He checked several areas she pointed out for prints and lifted several. Then he got Rosa's prints and the cook's. Cliff got more hands-on experience at lifting and documenting fingerprints.

"If you hear anything else about them, or remember anything more, here is my card. Just give me a call. Thanks for your help. I'll remember those empanadas and be back." Pete paid the bill and left a generous tip.

◆ ❖ ◆

"Okay, now we'll try to find the place where they cut you off. Do you think you'll recognize it?"

"I'm pretty sure I can find it, especially coming from the same direction I was traveling then. I know I hadn't gotten to Echo Amphitheater yet, but I was almost there. There were guard rails over an arroyo. There was a cholla cactus off to the left side of the road. Just before Gandalf jumped on the guy, he'd grabbed a big stick. It should be off to the side of the cholla. Would it have prints on it?"

"Depends on the surface of it. Rough bark would be hard to get anything good. Weathered and smooth might yield fine prints."

"Slow down. It's pretty soon now.... Here—I think this is where it happened."

Pete parked beyond the rails. They walked back.

"Watch where you step. We don't want to disturb any footprints or possible evidence. We may even come around from behind rather than go the way they did."

Pete got out his camera and took pictures as Cliff recounted the action. "I stopped here. Laid a little patch of rubber, I see. So did they. The driver came around the side of his car and grabbed my cell phone. Here is where he stomped it. You can see little bits. Then he kicked it through the rails, over here." They looked over the edge to the rocks and silt below. It hadn't rained for the past couple of days. "There, see the reflection? It's there."

Giving the cholla cactus area a wide berth, they walked down into the arroyo. Pete put on his gloves again, picked up the pieces of the abused cell phone with tweezers and put them into an evidence bag. He labeled the bag, noting the nearest mile marker and the date and time.

A little lizard darted away and watched from a nearby rock.

Then they walked to the site of the cactus encounter and Pete photographed it. "You don't usually see cholla this high up. We're still in the pines. You really lucked out there."

"I know. Thank God. The guy ran from up there, picked up the stick—I think that's it over there. Gandalf jumped here. He landed

51

there." Cliff pointed out what had happened. "Look at the cactus. It must have been nearly four feet tall. Now it's just scattered pieces. Damn, just hurts thinking about it."

"Look there, he left his shirt," Pete said. "Probably cut it off with a knife. And see those two flattish rocks? I think they may have used those to lift the cactus segments away from his skin. They're smooth enough to get good prints, I think. Look—there are little brownish stains on one edge of each. That is probably blood on those and certainly on the shirt. That's how cholla operates. Whole sections come off when you touch a spine. If you try to shake them loose, they only stick you in other places."

"I don't see anything that looks like decent footprints," said Cliff. "Do you?"

"Not really." The sandy soil showed scuffed marks, messed up with movement of the two. Pete took some more photos, and put the shirt, some of the cactus segments, the stained rocks, and the stick into evidence bags.

"We'll see what the forensics lab can get from these," Pete said. "We should have some that match the breath mint package Krista took. We'll run the fingerprints. Checking DNA will take longer, but we might have enough to nail them. With any luck we'll know both of their names soon. We've already got Alfonso's blood on Krista's shirt. Getting these two should help in finding whoever did the shooting and grabbed the money."

As they were getting back in the car, Cliff decided to broach the subject on his mind. "Pete, if there's any way you see to involve my help in this, I'd really appreciate it. I know you have all the protocol to follow, but I feel like I *need* to *do* something."

Pete pulled onto the highway, not saying anything at first. "I could use your sincerity and ideas, and I do see how important it is to you, but all those rules are in place for very good reasons. I'll have to think on that. I'm not the only one who should be making decisions involving civilians in this particular case. Maybe there is a precedent… maybe. I'll see."

"Thanks. I appreciate it." Well, he thought, at least he didn't say no outright and didn't tell me to back off.

♦ ❖ ♦

Pete and Cliff took a detour through Chimayo and stopped at the strip mall on their way back to Santa Fe. The long building looked fairly new and seemed to be well maintained. A slanted tile roof overhang ran along the front supported by posts with wooden corbels. The overhang butted up to a low façade which boasted rounded crenellations as if the builder had tried to give it a southwest flair. The restaurant had hung chile *ristras* on its posts and had placed a few outdoor tables and chairs in the shade of the overhang. Someone had spaced big pots with pungent marigolds along the edge of the walkway next to the posts. A bench sat next to the flower pots in front of the salon.

The restaurant end showed it must be doing a good lunch business. Pete parked at the salon end and they walked down toward the restaurant. They went into the laundry just so Cliff could get the layout in his mind.

As they headed past the real estate place Cliff remembered Vidar's comment to Pete. "I see what Vidar meant about the white pickups being pretty common. Look at 'em all—ten vehicles in the lot and five are white pickups. Quite a variety though." There was an old, beat up one parked in front of the beauty salon. There was a luxury one, an Escalade, parked in front of the real estate office, and three in front of the restaurant: a big behemoth perched on high wheels, an old Dodge RAM, and a mid-size one Cliff didn't immediately recognize.

Since it was now about lunch time, they went into the restaurant and ordered sandwiches. Cliff went into the tiny bathroom. He stood carefully on the toilet and pushed aside a ceiling tile to look at the catwalk platform. He saw the rope ladder which could be pulled down. Have to be pretty agile to get up there, he thought. Not just anybody could do that.

They finished their lunch and walked back. Cliff looked at the windows, noticing a decal with a red V and a black hawk silhouette on each window as well as posters for local events. He knew of Chimayo's famed church drawing many pilgrims. He also knew tourists came to visit the weaving shops. Other than those draws, Chimayo was mostly a small unhurried community on the high road to Taos.

◆ ❖ ◆

After Cliff got home from his trip with Pete, he stopped to purchase a new cell phone and get it set up. Then he took Gandalf out for exercise. As he walked along he called Sam. "Would it be okay for me to do a ride-along with you tomorrow and bat around more research stuff for my book?"

"I'll check. Shouldn't be a problem. I'm going to Chimayo to interview the two ladies from the beauty salon who may have seen something."

"Great, see you in the morning." Cliff wasn't unhappy with having another chance to find out more about the kidnapping investigation. Chimayo again. Could be very informative, he thought.

Chapter Thirteen

It had been two days since Krista had escaped her captors and returned home. Her dad had come home yesterday from the hospital. As Pete drove toward the Bjornsons' ranch, he hoped that Anton would have given some thought as to who might have shot him and kidnapped Krista.

When Pete arrived at the Bjornson home, Karen brought him out onto the patio off the family room where the morning sun invited one to bask in the warmth and fresh air before getting caught up in the cares of the day. Anton was settled back in a cushioned chair, his feet propped up on a stool in front of him, and holding a cup of coffee in his right hand. A sling held his left arm close against him, and a dressing covered the wound on his head. When he saw Pete, he moved to get up.

"No, stay put," Pete said, making a sit-still motion with his hand. "I won't trouble you for long, but I really wanted to talk with both of you about who might have reason to harm you and be responsible for these crimes. But first, I want to ask how Krista is doing?" He sat next to Anton and accepted the coffee Karen offered before she sat down with them.

"She went back to her summer activities program at school this morning," Anton said. "Mom waited with her for the bus to come, and told her she would pick her up after school. Krista was of two minds, I think, wanting to get back, especially to the art classes, but being apprehensive about leaving. Actually, I was torn myself. It'll take all of us a while to feel comfortable with her doing things on her own. I talked with her teacher and decided it'd be good for her to go back. It's Friday, so that eases her in. Then, Monday won't be such a big deal."

"Any ideas about who would snatch her? Or shoot you?"

"We'd just been talking about that, and why on earth they would want to," said Karen.

"Can you think of any enemies? Or folks who bear a grudge? Not only from your personal life, but perhaps your business or the Foundation?" asked Pete.

"We can't think of anyone associated with the Foundation or anything it's done. Not even a smidge of idea for that," said Karen. Her brow furrowed in concentration.

"I've been thinking about the business end. Of Drone Tech," said Anton. "I've a couple of ideas. There is Jerome Fisher, from CFW Films out of Albuquerque. Drones have a big future in filming, and he wants to position himself to be in that forefront. He can be pretty aggressive. Comes on like a steamroller. Can't see how this would help him, though."

"Are there more possibilities?" Pete asked.

"Well, recently we fended off a takeover by a company owned by a fellow who used to work for us. Brian Cleason was one of our vice presidents. He'd been with us almost from the beginning of our company. He's very astute—mostly in business management, branding, and marketing. He didn't like the direction we were going, and left rather abruptly about four or five years ago. I was pleased, even though he was talented. We butted heads too many times."

"May I ask what your differences were?"

"Mostly about how we do business. My company manufactures here in the states; we seek out young talent locally. We have a reputation for quality. We might not be the cheapest, but our products last. Brian prefers to outsource, cut corners while pushing the limits of the legal boundaries, and make more money, at least in the short haul. Now he's gotten the funding from somewhere to start up his own company. We both bid recently for a development grant, and Drone Tech won it. He vowed that next time would be different."

"Did he threaten you?" Pete asked.

"Not in so many words," Anton replied. "It's not like him to show aggression up front. He's more the grumble-behind-your-back type.

Likes to stir up resentment and let somebody else do his dirty work. I can't see him doing this by himself, but maybe he'd hire somebody? I wonder."

"How about any personal enemies?" asked Pete.

"Sorry. I've drawn a blank there." said Anton. "Why would anyone go to such drastic lengths? That stymies me. I haven't even done much dating since Sonja died, no jealous husbands or boyfriends, no hot-button politics, no grudges that I'm aware of." He paused to take the last sip of his coffee, grimacing as he reached to set the cup down. "Mostly I've thrown myself into my work over the last five years. I'd think any drama in my life would be coming from there. The drone industry's rapidly changing. Lots of jockeying for position and market share, that's for certain."

"I appreciate your candor, Anton. We'll check out these two fellows. Give me their particulars before I leave," Pete said. "It'll be interesting to find out where they were on the day you were shot. Also, I'd like to get your prints, and Maria's and Diego's today."

"Sure," said Karen. "You can do it now if you'd like. Maria is in the kitchen. I'll call Diego." She pulled out her cell phone. When she finished, she turned to Pete again. "There's something else I'd like to talk to you about. Cliff told me about his brother's kidnapping."

"He did?" asked Pete. "I'm surprised. He's not one to say much about it."

"I rather think it was because Krista's kidnapping made it fresh again. He still feels the pain. Could he be of any help to us? I think it would be good for us and for him. You know him well, what do you think?"

"I think your insight is good. It's also interesting, because he has already expressed a desire to be involved. Anton, your thoughts on the matter?"

"I haven't met him yet, but I'm looking forward to it," Anton said. "Mom told me his story. Krista is full of good words about him and your daughter." He chuckled. "Though I must admit, both of them took a backseat to Gandalf. I believe they all three helped considerably in easing her back from what could've been even more traumatic. If you want to involve them, you have my blessing."

"I'll see what I can do."

Diego walked in then, and Pete busied himself with taking everyone's prints. As he packed up his things, he said to all four, "I don't want to alarm you, but if I were you, I'd be careful and be aware of what's going on around you until whoever did this is in custody. They might try something else. Let me know if anything out of the ordinary happens, or if you have misgivings about how someone is acting."

CHAPTER FOURTEEN

Cliff's ride-along day brought sunny, bright skies. Sam told him the forensics team had found long dark hairs, red fibers, and silver sequins on the catwalk in the strip mall. The undercover officers had noticed three women with long dark hair and red jackets while staking out the place the day of the ransom drop. Two were salon customers and interviewing them was Sam's task. Cliff also got a chance to talk with Sam about his mystery plot, the "what-ifs," and questions about fictional villains and juvenile detectives. Then he told him about breaking up with Ashleigh.

Sam only shrugged and said, "No loss. I never did think you were suited to each other. Say, I'm going out to my folk's ranch on my day off. Would you be up for that? Thought we could take a couple of horses up into the Pecos and maybe get in some fishing. Gandalf can come, too."

"Great idea, Sam. Love to. By the way, has your mom ever reconciled herself to your being a cop?"

"Not yet. How many years has it been? She's still hoping I'll see the light and do something more fitting to my status, as she puts it. Needles me every chance she gets. Says it's demeaning for someone from a family who has been important in these parts for centuries. Hasn't stopped her from trying to set me up with a girl with the appropriate Spanish bloodlines. Probably hopes some haughty senorita will talk some sense into me."

"What does your dad say?"

"Listen to your mother, Son. It's easier in the end."

Cliff laughed.

"With any luck we won't run into her. Mom will be at our Santa Fe house when we go to the ranch. It's her regular women's society day." Sam grinned at Cliff. "Why do you think I've maneuvered to get Mondays off when I can?"

During lulls in the conversation, Sam tried out his new skill of whistling two notes in harmony to Cliff's amazement. Soon they were pulling up at a double-wide trailer in Chimayo. A girl in her early twenties, her long black hair pulled back in a ponytail, answered the door. She held a cell phone to her ear. They explained who they were and why they were there.

"Hey, I'll have to call you back. Got company, bye," she said to the phone.

"We're following up on an incident that happened on Wednesday when you were at the beauty salon," Sam said. "You might have seen something that would help us find the folks responsible for kidnapping a little girl."

The phone in her hand vibrated. "Just a minute." She read and responded to a text message. "What did you want?"

"Please tell us if you noticed anything out of the ordinary happening that morning."

"I really wasn't paying much attention," she began, only to be interrupted by the phone ringing. "Sally, I'll call you back in five.... Yeah, Bill's picking me up. Give me five."

Five minutes later Sam and Cliff were on their way back to the car, with no useful information learned, but having watched several messages tweeted, photos shared, and texts received.

"She spoke the truth," said Sam. "She wouldn't notice anything until somebody took her phone away."

"Any number of clowns, weirdos, giraffes, and wandering minstrels could have paraded by, unseen by her," agreed Cliff. Then he began to chuckle as Sam started to whistle "Send in the Clowns."

The other dark-haired, red-jacketed contact lived in an older section of Chimayo. They walked up to a well-kept, modest home with a front yard of blooming drought-resistant plants. They saw a curtain twitch at the window. Sam rang the bell.

"Who is it?" The voice spoke from behind the door.

"Police. We just need your help with a few questions." The door opened, and a lady who appeared to be on the far side of fifty appeared. Sam showed his identification and explained why they were there; they were following up on an incident that had happened while she was at the beauty salon. She invited them to sit down on her porch.

"I would invite you in, but my reputation.... Can't be too careful. I'm sure you understand."

"What do you remember about that morning?" Sam asked.

"Well, I had an appointment to get my hair done. I have Gloria put in this rinse, not a dye, you understand. It makes the lovely dark color of my hair catch the light and gives it body. When I'm fifty, heh, heh, that will be soon enough to start thinking about dying my hair. What did you ask about again?"

"What you did that morning," Cliff murmured.

"Oh, what I did.... Got my hair done and then went by the thrift shop where I volunteer. Those women there wouldn't know how to keep it running if it weren't for me. I have a lot of expertise in antiques, you know. I know what prices they should charge. Why, the other day they got in a set of dishes. 'Just old green glass dishes,' the young gal said, 'And not very pretty even.' Well, don't you know it was a set of depression glass, and they were going to sell it for a song—for a song, I tell you. Well, I soon set them right."

"Did you see anything unusual going on while you were at the salon or as you were leaving?" Sam asked.

"You mean did I see the suspects? How delicious. What did they do? Nip into the laundry and pick up a packet of money? That laundry—I wouldn't take my clothes there at all. You never know who has been using those machines and what they wash in there. Germs, fleas, and worse. What you might pick up there! Absolutely unthinkable." She shuddered dramatically.

"Mrs. Bruton..."

"Oh, it's Miss Bruton. Never married. Though not because I wasn't asked. I had to take care of my sainted mother. My duty, you know. All of my sisters flew the coop and left me to do it all. My beau, Simon, begged me, but I said not while I'm her caregiver. Then, he up and married Eloise Farmer. Didn't wait more than five years for me. No commitment. Well, I can tell you I was fortunate to find that out when I did."

"You are an observant woman, Miss Bruton. Have you been going to this same salon long?"

"Oh, yes. Ever since Gloria branched out and opened her own place. About fifteen years I think."

"What can you tell us about the business owners there? The restaurant and the others?"

"The owner of the restaurant, Lucy. She's owned it for maybe ten years. Her two waitresses—they make the place. They've been there longer than that. Always so friendly and happy. The food's just ordinary, but those two gals keep folks coming back."

"How about the laundry?" Cliff asked.

"I don't know them. I heard they have several laundries in the county. I never see them."

"And the real estate office and tax place?" prompted Sam.

"The real estate place—she's only been there about three years. Moved up from Albuquerque after her husband died. She was a realtor down there for years. She's not here very often, but I've run into her several times at the restaurant. I believe her main office is in Santa Fe. I admire the way she carries herself—very elegant and well put together. I think her husband had money. She drives that nice Cadillac. Course you want to impress your clients whom you take around. I'm appalled at the price of real estate these days. I don't know how a young couple can afford a home. Are you married, young man?"

Cliff looked at Sam who was increasingly exasperated but unfailingly polite.

"No, ma'am. The tax place?"

"Oh, them. They're only here during tax season. Don't know why they rent that spot full time. Guess it might be so people know where to find them."

"Thank you. Now if you can think back to that day you got your hair done. Do you remember anyone carrying a large handbag or tote bag?"

"There's a lot of bags, let me see. Marcia always brings her knitting in a bag. Could have been her. She has a bag with cats on it. Did you ask Gloria? Hairdressers see and hear a lot you know. Why just last month she told me that the waitress at the restaurant, you know the one that sells all those different kinds of pancakes, anyhow she was having an affair with her son's…"

"I'm sorry, Miss Bruton. If you can't tell us about seeing anyone with a bag, or any other woman with long dark hair, or who wore a red top, we really must…"

"Oh, I'm sure I'll remember. A red top...yes, yes, there was a woman. Tall, big-boned lady. She shouldn't be wearing strong colors like that. She'd look much more feminine if she had pretty pastels, or maybe a floral design. Parked right next to me, she did. Dark hair, she had a red jacket."

"Did she have a handbag?"

"Every well-dressed lady carries one. I wouldn't leave my house without one. What if I needed something, like a cough drop or a rain hat and I didn't have my purse?"

"Do you remember her bag?"

"No, but she had gotten to her car before I got to mine. Don't know where she had been. Not the salon. She had just closed the trunk as I came out. I don't know why she would put anything in the trunk. There's no place to shop there. I hate the cars where you can see in the back rather than having a trunk that hides things. So much safer, don't you think? My friend, she didn't have a trunk, mind you, and she put all her shopping in the back, and they went to eat, and they came out to find the window broken and all her bags gone. Now if she'd…"

"What kind of a car did she have?"

"Who? My friend who had her things stolen?"

"The lady in the red jacket who parked next to you."

"I'm sure I don't know. White, or cream…or silver—something light anyway. Or was it red, no, that was the car on the other side of mine. Is it true that red cars get stopped more often for speeding?"

"Miss Bruton, the car next to yours. Do you know what kind it was?"

"Fairly new, I think. I don't know one car from another. It was biggish."

"Can you tell us anything else about the car or the lady? What time did she leave?"

"Oh, that is so hard, Gloria was pretty busy, and she didn't get to me right on time. I didn't get out of there until about 11:30. I had to hurry to get to the thrift shop. Oh, I did notice one thing. As she drove out of the parking lot she was on her phone. That is so dangerous. Why, I remember my cousin Milly's daughter had an accident, just because she was busy trying to phone her boyfriend and wasn't watching the road."

"You say she was tall. Did you notice if she wore high heels?"

"I specifically remember looking. She had on tennies. Poor girl, how is she going to find a man who is taller than she is? It's such a shame when girls grow so tall. Really puts them at a disadvantage."

"Can you tell us more about the lady? Would you be able to identify her? Did you notice the shape of her face, eye color? Age?"

"Probably in her early 30s—not dainty at all. Beautiful long hair. High cheek bones, dark eyes. Nice makeup. Real cupid's bow mouth. I liked the shade of lipstick she used. In a way this woman was very handsome—if that's a word that can be used for a woman. I mean, that word is normally used for a man."

"Would you be able to pick her out of a line-up?"

"Oh, yes, when will that be?"

"If we need you to identify her, we'll be in touch with you." said Sam. "Thank you, Miss Bruton. You've been very helpful."

"Oh, are we done already? Aren't you going to ask me what else I saw? To think I might have seen the kidnapper—too delicious and scary."

Cliff chuckled on their way back to the patrol car. "Sam, do you get many like that?"

"Every so often. She's a very lonely lady."

"I can't see her as our suspect. Can you imagine her swinging around on a rope ladder and getting up to the catwalk? I saw that access yesterday in the restaurant bathroom."

"What? You don't think she has hidden athletic talents?" Sam laughed.

"I'd be real surprised. So, did we learn anything? Other than Miss Bruton's life story?"

"Well, I think she did see the lady from the restaurant who had dark hair and a red jacket."

"And she put something in her trunk. A tall, big-boned lady," said Cliff.

"Who shouldn't wear red, because it made her look unfeminine."

"Are you thinking what I'm thinking? That she may have been a man?"

"Could be. I think probably. We had to work for it, but I think she or he might be the one we're looking for, eh?"

CHAPTER FIFTEEN

Cliff sat in the bookstore coffee shop waiting for his editor. She'd finally finished going over his draft and was ready to meet with him to make her suggestions. It's a little like facing a big exam, he thought, torn between the excitement of feedback to improve his manuscript and the certainty of having his ideas attacked. He was early.

Not far from where he sat, a big black box marked with colored letters saying "Gloom Box" dominated a table display with a poster for the annual Zozobra celebration. Every so often he saw someone stuff some papers or pictures into the slot on the top of the box. Zozobra was a uniquely Santa Fe way of kicking off the Fiesta which took place over Labor Day weekend. Papers representing all the troubles from the year were collected to be burned in a huge puppet, Old Man Gloom, at the festival. Old love letters, paid-off mortgage papers, and shredded police reports went up in flames, wiping the slate clean, and giving people fresh starts. This year, he thought wryly, his picture might even end up in the fire, added to the Gloom Boxes by Ashleigh. Oh, well.

Cliff sat with a notebook in front of him, enjoying the coffee and idly listening to the bookstore noises of baristas and customers. As he often did, he made up back stories and plots for the strangers as they talked and browsed around him.

A couple of teenage boys were looking for books on drones. He heard them talk wistfully, wondering how they could convince their parents to get them drones for Christmas. They had visions of flying them over the city and spying on their friends. They were trying to figure out how they could deliver small packages to each other. They needed a book. Much of what they wanted he figured was impractical, and surely some of it was illegal. Interesting though. It gave him some ideas for his teenage protagonists. He knew Anton Bjornson was in the drone business and wondered if he might be a good resource person. He jotted down some notes from the boys' conversation.

The teenagers moved on, and three folks sat down at the table next to his with their coffee. He listened, seemingly off in another world working, but actually noting anything he heard that could be used in a future plot. From what he learned, they were a realtor and a young couple who were her clients. They had been out looking at houses and were trying to assimilate what they'd seen. Moving to an area that had so much potential for artists thrilled the couple. The wife emphasized the importance of their new home being large enough to accommodate a studio for her painting. The realtor, a tall blonde, had her laptop in front of her. She brought up the different homes as they discussed them. As Cliff listened, he began to admire her skill. It was obvious to him which of the properties she preferred for the couple, and she excelled at pushing them in that direction. She appeared to listen well, and seemed to anticipate their objections and counter them. She flirted with the man, while praising him for his attention to his wife's wishes. This lady realtor knew her stuff. Probably been doing this a long time, he thought. In his mind the trio took on new life, and an imaginary story began to weave itself around the search for a new house, the life they left behind, and what might be in their future. He could even imagine the seeds of conflict planted in the home-buying process that would spring up in the plot later.

His attention shifted to the table on the other side of his. A couple of older women were making short work of cheesecake slices covered in strawberries while lamenting their problems with computers. One had asked her granddaughter to help her print her emails, but she was so busy it never got done. All the woman wanted to do was to print the minutes of the last board meeting she'd been sent. The other lady had just been told by her friends that her email must have been hacked. They'd gotten strange emails with links they didn't dare click on. Amid complaints about passwords, the difficulty of remembering them and keeping them safe, the ladies finished their desserts and moved on.

Their places were taken by a college-age couple who sat down with a pile of travel books on Scotland. They were planning a trip and seeking the best guide for their budget and interests. That piqued Cliff's interest. After he'd received his master's degree, he'd traveled to Scotland and Ireland, thanks to a graduation present from his parents. That trip was also a cutting-the-apron-strings event to a degree—traveling on his own abroad. Cliff played the bagpipes. He'd sought out music to add to his repertoire, met, and played with other pipers. His talent had been well received. Falling in love with the Highlands, he'd explored his family's ancestral roots, meeting some distant cousins. During his stay with them he'd picked up the 'bloody hell' expression. He liked to think his visit refreshed genetic memories, sights, sounds, and stories. He stayed the longest at Eilean Donan Castle, soaking up the atmosphere, writing, piping for tips, and doing research for his books.

Cliff wondered how he could tie the story of the young couple with their new home, the realtor, Scotland, and the computer hackers into one plot. Maybe the teenaged-drone enthusiasts were actually bright enough to hack into the realtor's computer....

"Hi, Cliff. Sorry I'm so late. Tourists everywhere. The traffic is just a nightmare today, and the parking is even worse." His editor plunked down her papers on his table, bringing him back to reality.

CHAPTER SIXTEEN

Cliff was eager to meet Anton and see Karen and Krista again. The promised dinner invitation had arrived. Anton had been home and recuperating from his injuries for about a week now and said he felt much better. Krista had drawn a special picture of Gandalf to include with the invitation, saying he was invited, too.

Cliff and Lou drove through the gate in the high adobe wall near the spot where Krista had been kidnapped, seeing it in daylight for the first time. Just a short distance from the gate, the driveway dipped into a low wash before it began rising through piñon and cedar. The road climbed and passed a corral where several horses stood, looking up from their alfalfa bale. Just past the horses, Cliff noticed the type of fencing changed from wood rails to rectangular wire grids. Half a dozen white, furry critters with long necks crowded the fence and watched as they drove by.

"What are those? Alpacas?" asked Lou.

"I think you're right. They're too small to be llamas." Cliff said as he drove past more wire enclosures with the curious creatures. Most of them were white, but they saw other colors as well. Babies crowded their mothers. Gandalf stood up in the back seat, looking interested, but not quite certain as to what to think of these animals.

Cliff continued up past some outbuildings and a small duplex. He parked by the sprawling house which was built in contemporary Southwest style, partly in two story. A low-stepped adobe wall surrounded an area of turf grass and a riot of lavender and purple blooms. A walkway curved to the entry. As they got out of the car, Krista came flying out of the house followed by Karen and a tall man who looked to be about Cliff's age. Krista gave Cliff and Lou quick hugs, and then looked in delight at Gandalf.

"You got a haircut," she said, kneeling as he enthusiastically washed her face. "You're not shaggy anymore. You're beautiful." She took Gandalf's leash as she introduced her dad. Anton stood a couple of inches taller than Cliff's six feet. His hair, cut very short, revealed the healing wound on one side of his head. He gripped Cliff's hand firmly and then leaned down and kissed Lou's cheek.

"Call me Anton, please," he said. "It's good to finally meet you. Thank you for what you did for Krista."

He looks a little like his cousin, Vidar, with his dark blond hair and blue eyes, but Anton's smile lights up his whole face, Cliff thought. I can really see the Nordic ancestry in both.

"Welcome to our home," Karen said. "Come on in." She laughed at the dog who bounced back and forth from a standing to a play posture: front down, butt in the air, tail wagging. "Gandalf, too. I can see those two won't be separated."

They entered a large, open space with a cathedral ceiling. A staircase curved up to the second floor and a balcony. Windows gave light to some huge colorful tapestries on the wall. To the right, Cliff saw a seating area with large, comfortable-looking sectionals. Cushions in rainbow colors rested on each sofa, picking up the hues of the tapestries. Bookshelves and cupboards lined one wall, and a grand piano dominated another seating area near an archway into a dining room.

Lou stopped in front of a tapestry, transfixed. "I've never seen weavings like these before," she said. "The colors...they're luminous, and the light! The light just draws you right into the piece."

"Mom will be your friend for life," Anton said. "This is some of her work."

Karen smiled. "Weaving gives me great joy. It's what I do. After a while, if you are interested, I can show you my studio. You might have seen some of my alpacas as you drove in. It all happens here—the shearing, the dyeing, spinning, and weaving."

"After Krista's mother died," Anton said, "we moved back here to be with Mom. We remodeled the old house where I grew up and added on, tripling the space. We needed to be together—Krista, Mom, and I. It's a good home for us—big enough for private and family space. After you've seen her studio, I can show you around if you like."

They all sat in the living room around a low table with a spread of hors d'oeuvres—pieces of fruit, veggies, cheeses, crackers, and pickled herring. Anton poured some chardonnay. Conversation focused on Anton's recovery, dealing with the aftermath of the kidnapping, and then easily drifted to the topics of people getting together for the first time—jobs and their love of Santa Fe.

"Cliff," Karen said, "do I remember correctly that you write mysteries for a living? Might I have read any of them?" She set down her wine glass, put a slice of cheddar on a cracker, and took a bite.

"They are a series of mystery books for kids. Upper elementary and young teens. They have a couple of young sleuths, and of course, a dog, whose name is Shadow."

Hearing that, Krista's astonished gaze shot to meet his. She jumped to her feet and pounded up the stairs and down the hall. She came running back clutching three books. "I love these books," she said. "Is Gandalf really the dog in these?"

"Shadow is partly Gandalf, partly other dogs I've known, and some I've just made up." Cliff took a sip of wine and tried the pickled herring, relishing the taste that was new to him. "I'm glad you like the books."

"Have you written others?" Krista said. "These are all I've seen."

"There are two more. Let's see. You're missing the second, and the last one." Cliff crunched into an apple slice, savoring the sweet crispness.

"Where'd you get those?" Anton asked her.

"Silly, you bought them for me." She looked at Cliff and Lou. "Daddy buys me lots of books. Goin' to the bookstore is one of my favorite things to do. Look, this book is where I learned about fingerprints." She held out one of the books.

Wow, Cliff thought, feeling warm inside. That's really neat—it did make a difference. Can it really be that my book helped Krista do something that might nail her kidnappers? A lot of kids are reading these—and they're learning. Maybe it's given them a little bit of power.

CHAPTER SEVENTEEN

"Anton, I've heard that your company manufactures drones," Cliff said. "I've never had a chance to see them fly. I don't know much about them, but I would love to have my characters solve a mystery using drones. That would be really cool."

"I've a prototype I'm testing right now. Want to give it a go?"

"That'd be great."

"I'll go get it while Mom shows you her studio and alpacas."

Krista got Gandalf's leash. "I'll take Gandalf. He won't bark at them, will he? They don't much like it when dogs they don't know come around. We have a new baby alpaca. He's a real pretty gray."

Karen led them down a hall near the stairs and into a large airy room where a half dozen looms sat with projects going in various stages. Shelves of colored skeins and spools of yarn stood by each loom. An array of spinning wheels formed a semicircle around a television screen. The pleasing scents of lavender and cedar filled the air.

"How do you get the design from your head translated into a woven tapestry?" asked Lou.

"A Peruvian weaver really inspired me," said Karen as she briefly went through the steps of painting the concept, sketching lines onto the warp threads, and weaving in colors and texture. "Maximo Laura—his work is marvelous. I took some of his technique and created my own designs—mostly from mythology."

"I'm fascinated by all your colors," Lou said as she moved by the cedar cubby holes filled with a rainbow of colors feeling the soft alpaca fibers. "You have a whole palette here. Do you dye all these colors yourself?"

"Pretty much, but I have lots of help," she answered. "Alpaca fiber has over twenty natural colors, and we dye it to get the others. I'm currently working on a commission of a New Mexico landscape." She paused in front of a partly-finished work showing Pedernal in the distance and wildflowers in the foreground. You can see the photo and sketch I'm working from."

"It looks like it might have been taken from near Ghost Ranch. They have a great view of Pedernal. Georgia O'Keefe loved to paint that mountain."

"That's true. It might have been."

"Cliff and I climbed it last summer with some other folks. I was surprised how narrow it is on top. You don't realize it when you see it from this angle."

"I bet the view was awesome—would have been fun to see. Anyhow, most of these looms have student projects. I teach weaving—actually the whole process, except for the shearing. We have a crew who comes in May to do that. We send the fleece out to be washed, carded, and prepared for spinning. I'd prefer to spend my time designing and weaving."

"I had no idea of all that's involved," Lou said. "It looks like some of your yarn colors are already blended before they are woven in. That's how you get the marvelous shading. I'd love to watch the process some time."

"You're welcome any time, but if you came during one of the class sessions, you might see more of the steps in process."

They went out the side door and toward the outbuildings. Cliff decided it would be prudent to put Gandalf in the car for the rest of their tour. He didn't want to tempt fate by parading Gandalf past the docile animals. The sun was disappearing behind high clouds, and the temperature had dropped a little even in the short time they had been here. He could see a buildup of storm clouds towards the southwest.

Krista came with him, chatting happily. As they passed the duplex on their way back from the car, she told him Diego lived on one side and Maria on the other. When they rejoined the group he met Diego, a dark-haired man of Peruvian ancestry who looked to be in his fifties. His face was dark with the sun, and the wrinkles by his eyes showed a face that was used to smiling. They went through a barn where the shearing and the dyeing took place. He showed them around, patiently answering their questions.

Diego broke off several branches from a fruitless mulberry tree that shaded one of the corrals before opening a gate into a pen of mothers and their young ones. "Come on in, and they will come right up to you. They especially like mulberry leaves—it must be like candy to them. Just feed them one leaf at a time. You can pet them. They don't bite or anything."

They went in, and the eager animals gathered around for their treat. "I'd heard that they can spit like a camel," Cliff said.

"They don't do that unless they are really annoyed, and generally it's another alpaca they're upset with," said Diego. Then he grinned, "When I'm holding one that is being sheared, I've learned the hard way to hold its head facing over my shoulder. Their spit is no fun." They laughed with him.

"Here's the new baby," said Krista as a mother with a furry gray baby came for her share of leaves. "I named him Misty. Feel how soft he is. I got to see him born. It was way cool."

"Oh, he is soft and such beautiful dark eyes. What kind of sounds do they make?" Lou asked. "I haven't heard any yet."

"They're really quiet," said Krista. "But if you listen real good, you can sometimes hear the mommy humming to her baby and hear him humming back."

Anton came to the fence, holding a drone and a control. He and Cliff left the rest of the group with the alpacas and went to a wide open space near the drive and the house.

"Drones are a rapidly-evolving industry," said Anton. "The explosion in hobby drones is unbelievable. The laws for using them are trying to catch up. Part of our business is to find developments to make drones more useful, safer, and to recommend regulations which benefit and keep folks out of danger. You can imagine these would not be good in the wrong hands."

He started the drone and demonstrated how to maneuver it up, down, sideways, and make it hover in one spot.

"It's a lot more complicated than I thought," Cliff said. "I was thinking of having the kids in my book use a drone to help them solve a mystery. Now I'm kind of leery about that. I don't want to create a monster."

"You could probably write it in such a way that the kid reading it would understand the responsibility. Actually I think it would be good to have kids learn about them—they are going to learn one way or another—either from a responsible source or by doing stupid stuff. Might as well have some common sense drubbed into them along with the learning and the entertainment."

"Could I consult with you on what I wrote?" asked Cliff. "I'd want to get it right."

"Be glad to help. Let's see if you can fly this puppy now. Take it up, circle around the house, back over the duplex, then the barns and the corrals. Don't let it get out of sight; that's never a good idea. That's right—take your time. Circle around and do it again. Try hovering every so often and then move it on again. This particular model is equipped with a video camera. It's downloading onto my computer."

Cliff flew the drone around the ranch several more times, practicing hovering, and moving in all directions.

"The weather is starting to move in. Let's bring her down before we get wet. Anyhow, I think it's time to eat. Maria will be annoyed if we aren't there when it's ready."

"That was really awesome, Anton. Thanks."

"Just wait until we get you using a drone with the first-person view goggles. You can see in real time what the drone camera is looking at. You haven't seen awesome yet," he said laughing. He instructed Cliff in making a safe landing and turning the drone off. The first few raindrops spit at them as they went back to the house. Cliff rescued Gandalf from the car and shut its windows.

CHAPTER EIGHTEEN

After a delicious dinner of salmon with pilaf and fresh, steamed vegetables, a warm peach pie appeared for dessert. Lively conversation accompanied the whole meal. After coffee, Cliff and Lou reluctantly said they should get going before it got dark and the storm really hit hard. The light rain was falling only intermittently, but the clouds were getting darker to the south and west, and they saw lightning off in the distance.

They said their thanks and goodbyes and started off down the drive. As they drove past the horse corral, Cliff made a sudden stop. Several alpacas bolted skittishly off the road and into the piñon.

"Whoa, that's not good," Lou said. "The alpacas are out. We didn't leave any gates open when we were in the pens, did we?"

"We'd better let them know. Maybe we can help getting them back."

Cliff turned the car around and headed back to the house. Karen accepted their offer of help and found some rain gear for them. Gandalf was left in the car. Anton called Diego, and they went to check on the corrals and to see how many and which ones were missing.

"Two corrals are empty, and their gates are open," Diego reported. "The mothers and babies, and a batch of yearlings. Something or someone spooked them and chased them out. It ain't natural for them to bolt in this kind of weather."

Diego gave everyone a broom or long branch. He, himself, took a large branch of mulberry leaves. "Let's go to where you saw them last. Their instinct is to stay together, so that helps." He opened the gates wide. "When they are frightened, their first response is flight. So we don't want to yell, chase them, or do anything that will panic them. Be slow, calm, talk softly to them if you want. Blanca is one of the ones who is out. The others have a tendency to cue off her. If I can tempt her close enough, I can lead her, and the others should follow."

Maria joined them and passed out flashlights. "Thank you, Maria," said Karen. "Be careful, everyone. The terrain is rough, and the ground will be slick."

Diego led the way down the road to where Cliff and Lou had seen them go off into the brush. They saw the two-toed tracks in the damp earth. Not long after that they spotted the white shapes in the gloom. They had indeed stayed in a herd. Diego gave directions.

"I'm going to circle around behind them. Krista, Cliff, if you'll follow, stay about ten feet apart. Anton, you take the middle, Maria, Lou, and Karen will take the other end. When we're all in place, we'll start forward toward the road. Hold your branch horizontally—act like a moving fence. Stay as even as you can between Anton and the end person."

Slowly they circled behind the alpacas and started funneling them forward. The terrain, gentle rain, and the gathering darkness provided the biggest problems. The sharp tang of wet piñon filled Cliff's nostrils. Balancing his long branch, holding the light, and maneuvering around the undergrowth resulted in a few slips and near-falls. His shoes squelched as he walked the uneven terrain, and he could feel the layer of mud his soles had picked up. The bobbing lights and the ghostly images of the alpacas painted a surreal sight. He saw the little baby, Misty, trotting next to his mother. They didn't seem to have the same footing problem as he had on the increasingly gooey soil. He welcomed the appearance of the road with a soft hooray. Keeping his eye on Diego and Anton, he moved ahead, the semi-circle gradually getting smaller.

Diego tried to catch Blanca's halter, but at that moment a crack of thunder spooked her and they scattered. They had to collect behind them again with their branches. At last, the alpacas headed up the road toward the pens.

The rain had now become a steady downpour, and it was totally black outside the range of their lights. Rain dripped from Cliff's hair down under his collar and inched its way down his back. His cold fingers gripped the branch and the light. He wished he could wipe his glasses off—not for the first time he wished that glasses came equipped with windshield wipers.

They herded the animals into their enclosure, their efforts lit by lightning. Thunder rumbled nearer. Diego stayed to sort them out, get them into their shelters, bedded down, and make sure the babies were dry and warm.

"Get Gandalf, and bring him in. I can find you something dry to wear, Cliff," said Anton.

"We'll find everybody something warm and dry to change into," said Karen as they walked out of the rain and into the house. "Kick off your shoes; we'll find woolly socks for you, too. Krista, I think you have a pair of clean sweats in the laundry room. Go get those, and then come with Lou and me to get changed."

"Bring me your wet clothes, everybody," Maria said as she collected the flashlights and put them on the kitchen counter. "I'll dry them while you warm up with some hot chocolate." She took off her rain gear and put on a pair of slippers that were under her desk in the kitchen and started to make the hot drinks.

While Anton waited for Cliff and Gandalf, he started a fire in the kiva fireplace in the family room. As he stretched forward with the logs, he winced. Setting the wood in place, he rubbed his aching left shoulder before holding his hands out to the growing warmth. Then he rose and went to find something warm to fit Cliff.

They gathered back in the family room as they got changed. Hands circled hot cocoa mugs appreciatively, and the inner chill began to melt away. Each fragrant brew had a dollop of whipped cream on top, and a dusting of cocoa. They sank into the comfortable sofa and chairs facing the cheery fire, smelling the aromatic scent and hearing the crackle of the piñon kindling Anton had used. Gandalf wandered away, sniffing at the new surroundings.

The storm raged outside. A bolt of lightning lit up the sky, followed almost immediately by a crash of thunder that rattled the windows before rumbling away. "That was close," said Anton. Just then the lights flickered and went out. "Uff da. Well, the good news is we don't have to look for the flashlights."

Gandalf came prancing back in to the circle of firelight. He carried something in his mouth which he dropped into Anton's lap. "Uff da!" Anton recoiled from the damp T-shirt, picking it up. "Hey, this is my shirt. Where'd he get it? Maria had all the wet stuff in the laundry room."

Cliff laughed. "She must have left the door open. Gandalf likes to get into stuff—especially dirty laundry. My folks had visitors from Scotland once, and we were all sitting around. The visitors had been warned to shut the guest room door because he likes to snoop. Anyway, they'd forgotten. Gandalf came waltzing out of their room with the lady's merry widow in his mouth. He went right up to her and dropped it in her lap, and backed up and sat. Very pleased with himself. She turned six shades of red and everybody laughed."

Krista said, "You had Shadow do that trick in a book, didn't you? I remember that it was a clue."

"That's right," Cliff said with a grin as Anton came back from hanging up the shirt. "It was too good not to."

Karen found some candle holders and lit some candles. "We'll be sure to shut our doors when he's around. I don't think you should go anywhere until this is over," she told Cliff and Lou.

"What does 'uff da' mean?" asked Lou.

Karen laughed. "If you are going to be around folks with a Scandinavian heritage, you are going to hear it a lot. It's just an expression like 'oops' or 'oh, dear.' It's very useful when you trip on uneven ground, drop something, or have a wet t-shirt dropped in your lap."

Warm and dry at last and sipping on the last of his hot chocolate, Cliff dreaded the thought of heading out to his car and driving through the storm. Through the family room windows looking out toward the Sangre de Cristo Mountains, they watched the lightning stretch and zigzag through the sky. The rain drummed on the roof and poured out of the *canales* spouts onto the patio stones below.

Krista had curled up against a big squooshy cushion on one of the couches with Gandalf. Her head dropped forward, and her hand that had been petting Gandalf lay still on his neck. Anton set aside his cup and roused her. "Bedtime, Honey. Take a flashlight and go get ready for bed. I'll come up in a bit and tuck you in."

"Can Gandalf come with me?" she asked while finishing her round of goodnight hugs.

"It's okay with me, if it's okay with your dad," said Cliff.

"Sure, I'll get him later when it's time for him to go home," Anton said as he gave her a light. His eyes followed her until she disappeared up the stairs with Gandalf.

"Do you ever use your horses to round up the alpacas?" Lou asked.

"Not really, "Anton answered. "Horses make the alpacas think they're being chased, and they will run like crazy. I wonder how they got…"

A series of sharp barks came from upstairs. "Daddy," Krista screamed.

CHAPTER NINETEEN

Gandalf barked again and then began an unremitting, deep-throated growling.

Anton and Cliff shot out of their chairs, grabbing flashlights, and ran up to Krista, taking the stairs three at a time. Karen and Lou followed closely. Gandalf stood firmly in front of a closed door, still carrying on with reverberating growls.

"He won't let me in my room," said Krista, now wide awake and looking apprehensively at the Airedale.

Cliff grabbed Gandalf's collar, feeling the bristling fur and the tension in his body. He pulled him away from the door, knelt by him, and took his muzzle, telling him to be quiet.

"Shh, everybody, listen," Anton said. He slowly opened the door a bit, and they heard a noise, like water rushing over little stones.

"Jesus, that sounds like a rattler!" He slammed the door shut, pulled his cell phone out of his pocket and gave it to Karen. "Call Diego. Tell him to bring the snake stick, pronto, and a container. I'm going to go get my boots on."

"Be careful. If one got up here, there could be another one." said Karen.

"God, I hope not." Anton hurried down the hall toward his room, sweeping the light in front of him. He returned quickly wearing cowboy boots and pulling on a pair of leather gloves.

"Daddy, when I came up to get the books, I didn't close my door. I always leave it open," Krista said. "When Gandalf and I got up here, it was shut."

"Somebody is playing a dangerous game," Anton said. "Here's what we're going to do. When Diego gets here, he and I will go in and catch the snake. Lou, if you and Krista will take Gandalf back by the top of the stairs and hold him tightly, that will keep him out of trouble. Cliff, Mom, we need you to come in with us to hold the lights. After I open the door, shine them around the room, so we know what we're up against. Stay by the door, but try to give us good light on the snake. Just don't get it in our eyes. I'd rather not be blinded."

They heard Maria and Diego come in downstairs by the studio. Through the balcony they saw Maria lighting the way with her flashlight sending grotesque shadows bouncing off the walls. She set down the big umbrella by the stairs.

"We're up here," Anton called. "By Krista's room."

"Upstairs? How in the hell…" Diego muttered as he came in sight, carrying a couple of long gadgets and a big rectangular storage tub with a lid. One gadget was a pole with a hook on the end. The other was the snake stick, a long metal pole with a handle to squeeze on one end and on the other, tongs that closed when the person tightened the handle.

Anton took the snake stick. He put his hand on the doorknob and looked at the group. Lou, Krista, and Gandalf retreated to their assigned positions. "Diego and I have done this before. This guy will probably be coiled and rattling. He's also going to be damn mad. They don't move all that fast—he'll probably just hold his ground—at least I hope he does. The last thing we need is to have him slither under the bed. We're going to move slowly and steadily. Ready?"

Cliff nodded. He had never seen anyone try to catch a snake before, and wasn't too thrilled at the idea. He didn't like snakes. Bull snakes, okay. Rattlers—he would just as soon not be anywhere near them. But then, Anton seemed to know what he was doing, and obviously they needed someone to hold the lights. If Karen could do it, so could he.

Anton turned the knob and slowly swung the door open. Karen's and Cliff's lights quickly focused on a huge diamondback, coiled near Krista's bed. Anton and Diego moved cautiously into the room. The snake stayed put. Diego set the bin down and took off the lid. They advanced toward the snake, Anton's pole extended, the tongs open wide.

Slowly, he teased the lower tong under the snake's body. It writhed and moved as he squeezed the handle and lifted the snake, making it thrash back and forth.

"I don't have it close enough to the head," Anton said. "I'm going to put it down and get a better hold. A little more light on his head. Stay back." He lowered the snake and slowly shifted the tongs to a place about half a foot from its head. The agitated reptile had coiled again, continuing its constant rattle. "Easy, slowly, steadily, come on, fella. This looks good…. Got him."

"You really got him? Good and tight?" Diego asked nervously.

"Yes, Diego, good and tight."

Diego picked up the lid. Anton lifted up the rattler to its five-foot length, and carefully lowered the thrashing snake into the bin still holding the tongs closed. Diego partially covered the bin bit by bit. Finally, at a nod from Diego, Anton opened the tongs and slid the pole out of the container as Diego shut it, and snapped the locks in place.

Maria came forward and produced a roll of duct tape, cutting off strips and handing them to Diego.

Diego added the strips to the closed bin. "I hate these critters. They give me the heebie-jeebies."

CHAPTER TWENTY

"Let's take a look to make sure that's all the trouble we have here," said Anton.

They checked out the room and all its corners with the flashlights. Diego used the pole with the hook to hold up the dust ruffle so they could look under the bed. They could hear the rain lashing the windows and coming down even harder on the roof as they searched. They checked Krista's bathroom and closet, too.

The snake still rattled furiously. Diego picked up the bin, shuddering as he lifted it.

"Diego, would you mind checking the road for flooding, too?" Anton set the poles by the back door.

"Sure, this rain is pretty heavy." Diego left, taking the noisy bin with him.

They went back downstairs to the warm, welcoming firelight. Anton added another couple of logs to the fire. Krista and Gandalf followed Karen down the hall toward her rooms near the studio. Krista said she'd rather not sleep in her own room that night. Cliff and Lou sank into their chairs and Gandalf settled on the rug near the fireplace.

"Gandalf has earned a big doggie treat tonight," Karen said as she returned. "He was really protecting Krista. Has he ever encountered snakes before?"

"We've seen them occasionally when we've been hiking. I usually give them a wide berth. I did take him through a snake training course. He's never gone after one," Cliff answered.

Diego soon returned and said, "The water's up. Too deep to get through."

Anton said, "I was afraid of that. Lou, Cliff, if you don't mind sleeping in a house where we have just caught a rattler, I think it's best if you spend the night."

Karen showed them to guestrooms. Since it was too early for the grownups to go to bed, they came back to the family room. The lightning and thunder display moved off into the distance. They discussed the snake and the other wild events of the evening.

"No snake is going to be moving about on a night like this," Anton said, "and they definitely don't travel upstairs and close doors behind them. Someone is still trying to harm our family, and I don't like it at all."

"I wonder if that's why the alpacas were let out," Lou said. "Somebody wanted everybody out of the way so they could plant the snake. But how would a stranger know to do all that and how to get in your house undetected? That's scary."

"We do have cameras and a security system," Karen said. "The cameras run most of the time, but we didn't even think of putting the security system on while we were rounding up the alpacas."

"I'll check the videos when the electricity's back on," said Anton.

"Have you any idea who would be trying to harm you?" Cliff asked.

"Pete asked us that, too. I can't believe that anyone wants to hurt my daughter. She is just a child."

"Unless it is you they are trying to hurt through her."

"That's just evil," Anton protested.

"I'm frightened," Karen said. "I thought it was over—that the kidnapping and attack on Anton was the end of it, that when it didn't work, they would stop. But it isn't over, is it? Not until we find out who is doing it."

"We will find out, Mom. Soon."

"Do you think it'd be okay if I called Pete this late, Lou?" asked Karen. "He will want to hear about this. And, would you be able to stay after breakfast? I think we should pool our ideas. Maybe together with the police we can figure out why this is happening. Maybe they can find something, although I don't know if any signs will be left after this storm."

"He won't mind, in fact, I'm pretty sure he'd prefer it. I should talk to him anyway, to let him know I won't be home tonight," said Lou.

"Do you still live with your folks?" asked Karen.

"Yes and no," Lou said with a smile. "My parents have a casita next to their house. It used to be where my grandparents on my dad's side lived when they came out for the winters. My mom's parents still live in Japan. One of my sisters and I live in the casita now. It has a good studio with a skylight, bedroom, living room, and small kitchen. Until I get my student loans paid off, I guess that's where I'll be, and I like it. I don't mind being so close to my folks. We're in and out of each other's space all the time."

The lights flickered and came on again, then went off again. After a few minutes they came back on and stayed on.

◆ ❖ ◆

"Cliff, will you help me check the house, now that we have light—for everyone's peace of mind?" asked Anton.

"Glad to," Cliff said. He knew he'd sleep better if he were sure there were no more slithery beasts lurking unseen in dark corners.

They searched with the hook in hand to lift up and poke under things. They checked not only the large rooms, but the closets and bathrooms as well. They began downstairs in Karen's suite. Krista lay sound asleep in the day bed in her grandmother's sitting room. Gandalf sprawled out on the foot of her bed. At Cliff's motion he obediently left her and went with Cliff and Anton. They checked Karen's bedroom, bathroom, and closet.

Then they went toward the studio. The downstairs hall ended with a large window near the door of the studio. A seat under the window with inviting cushions made an attractive nook. Gandalf sniffed at the new places but gave no indication that the spaces harbored any unwelcome visitors.

After a cursory search of the large open living room with the grand piano, they went through the archway into the dining room and on into the guest suite where Lou would be sleeping. They followed the back hall to the laundry room. When they came to the door into the garage, they opened it, listened, and walked past the three cars. Cliff saw an area with large, flat work tables and many storage cabinets. Crossing into the back hall again, they checked another bedroom, an office, and the breakfast room and kitchen.

They used the stairs on Karen's end of the house to get to the guest room where Cliff would be sleeping, and then went along the balcony to the playroom with its outside door onto the deck. The playroom was an open area located above the family room in the center of the house. Anton had been making sure all of the outside doors were locked as they came to them.

They checked Krista's bedroom, bathroom, and closet again. As they walked down the hall from Krista's room toward Anton's suite of rooms, Cliff stopped. "Whoa, is that what I think it is? Reminds me of *The Lord of the Rings*." Ahead of them stood a set of double, arched doors, flanked by pillars with an overhead arch. On each door, an embellished gold Celtic dragon guarded the opening.

"Cool, aren't they?" Anton said. "Almost like the doors from Edoras, but with a bit more Viking thrown in. They were commissioned as a Christmas gift from my mom when we were building the house. Not only because I love the movies and the art so much, but Mom said that every time I walk through them I should be reminded of my role in life. She firmly believes that with power comes the responsibility to use it wisely."

Cliff ran his hand over the carved Celtic knot designs on the pillars. "These are marvelous," he said. "The artist did a good job with the gold embossing against the brown-stained wood."

"I'm certainly not in the king category, mind you, but I am the CEO of my own company and have grown up with plenty. She knew I'd begun to find this power bit seductive and was becoming a self-righteous prat. I was attracted to the status, of having people defer to me, of enjoying the privileges too much. The doors are a not-so-subtle reminder to not lose sight of who I am. She wanted me to remember to care for others, and to realize there will be those who try to take that power from me, or the power could become an end in itself. It's pretty humbling to walk through them."

"It's a wonderful gift. Your mom is cool," Cliff said as they continued on their search of Anton's suite. Cliff noticed another outside door from Anton's suite leading onto the deck.

"I wanted to ask you—are you and Lou dating?" Anton asked.

"No, she and I are both dating other people," Cliff said as he peered into the corners of the room and shone a light under a bureau. "We're just good friends. Have been ever since we were in college."

"Then I wouldn't be stepping on your toes if I asked her out?"

"Not at all."

When he finally went to his bedroom, Cliff found some paper and started making notes about what he'd learned. He appreciated the chance to spend the night, and it had been enlightening to see the extent and beauty of the Bjornson home. Besides enjoying the pleasant company, he had more time to ask questions and get answers. He thought about who and how, and listed questions he'd like to ask Karen, Krista, and Anton. He'd also like to talk with Maria and Diego. He made another list of questions he wanted to ask Pete and Sam.

He yawned, set aside his glasses, and turned out the light. Interesting, Anton asking him if he minded about Lou. Surprising, and maybe just a touch annoying. He didn't really know if he could picture them together. Then he stretched out under the cozy comforter. The house, with its security system set, slumbered. Gandalf had long since gone to sleep, sprawled out over half of the queen-sized bed. As Cliff drifted off to sleep he wondered who knew the family well enough to skulk around with so many witnesses and be able to mess with the alpacas and plant the snake undetected.

CHAPTER TWENTY-ONE

Vidar hung up the phone, his mind going back to the problem that was troubling him when the call had interrupted. Pete wanted to let him know they were meeting at the Bjornsons' in the morning and he wanted him to be there, too.

Sometimes I think I'm losing my mind, he thought. *Blackouts. ... Don't remember what happened. Woke up in my truck miles from home, no idea how I'd gotten there.*

I hear voices. One's my father, speaking in a loud whisper. Urges me to seek revenge for him. He spits out hate, and rails on and on about how my Uncle Edvar stole his girl. He also says how worthless I am, and that he would love me if I would take revenge...always revenge. Sometimes the voices tell me to do horrible things. Sometimes they hint at terrible things I've already done.

Every so often I have snatches of memory, like being carried. I talked to my friend, Vinnie, about it and he said that I had drunk so much that I passed out, and he brought me home.

I don't dare tell anybody at work or go to a doctor. They'd report it, and I'd lose my job. Who can I talk to? I tried to talk with Aunt Karen, but we were interrupted. I should try again. But what could she do, except tell me to go to a doctor? Could I talk to Anton?

Vinnie says I should write down my feelings. What I hear the voices saying. I should keep a journal of all the strange stuff. He says that should help get it out of my mind, and it wouldn't haunt me as much. So I've been doing that. It seems to help.

I should quit drinking. Told Vinnie I was going to stop, but he said he'd watch over me, and when I'd had enough, he'd make sure I got home okay. I crave the drink, so I felt better about that. And he does get me home…. But I can't remember. Maybe the best thing to do is to have a little of the hair of the dog that bit me.

Is this what my father went through? Maybe I've inherited it, and I'll end up like him, sinking into a pathetic pit of impotence. I couldn't bear that.

CHAPTER TWENTY-TWO

Cliff stayed in bed the next morning until he heard someone moving downstairs. He'd worried he'd set off an alarm if he and Gandalf were the first ones out of bed. He quickly got up, dressed, and went down to the kitchen, inhaling the scent of fresh coffee as he entered.

"Mmm, that smells wonderful," he said. "Good morning, Maria."

"I'm surprised to see you up this early."

"The best part of the day." He took the cup she offered, added some milk, and sipped the hot brew. "Ahh, ambrosia." He and Gandalf went outside through the family room doors. The storm had cleared out and left everything smelling clean. A little breeze stirred the trees, scenting the air with a hint of piñon. The sun peeked over the shadowed mountains to the east, painting the landscape to the west with gold and promising a clear day. He heard the coo-OO-coo-coo-coo of mourning doves calling. Other than that, the quiet stretched, surrounding him with peace. What was different here? he wondered. Ah, no city sounds. No neighbor's cars, voices, distant commute noises, dogs barking. Just nature and quiet.

While Gandalf checked out all the bushes and new smells, Cliff looked at this part of the house: a covered deck with inviting chairs, small tables, and a kiva. Outside stairs went up to a second level. He figured that was how the intruder had gotten to Krista's bedroom. His eyes followed the roof line, stopped, and then he laughed. Rather than the plain canales that adorned most Southwestern-style homes draining the flat roofs, this spout was a gargoyle-type fish head, grotesque and charming at the same time. The fish had a human nose and a smiling mouth. Water still dripped out of the fish's mouth, which had teeth, no less!

He put Gandalf's leash on and took him for a walk. As he went by Diego's house, he heard loud voices in Spanish disturbing the quiet. He thought one voice sounded like Diego's. He couldn't place the woman's voice. He walked on to the corrals. The alpacas stood silently, eating their hay. Their adventures of the night before evidently left them unfazed.

He and Gandalf went back into the house, and he set down a bowl of water for his dog before pouring himself another cup of coffee. Maria was making a big batch of scones for breakfast and for the police who were coming later. He asked if he could help, and she put him to work grating orange peel for the scones, and cutting peppers and onions for the omelets.

"By the way," Maria said, "since you weren't planning on spending the night, I don't 'spose you have any dog food with you. Would it be okay if I boiled up a chicken breast and cut it up with some rice and carrots for Gandalf?"

"That'd be super. He'd really like that. Thanks."

"Well, then, I'll get that started."

"Do you have any idea who might be behind all of the trouble?" Cliff asked while he grated and chopped.

She frowned and said, "I've been trying to think. In my mind I've gone over all of the employees we've had here since Sonja died. That was Krista's mother. Both Diego and I go way back before that time. Can't think of one who'd like to harm Krista or Anton. Anton's a good boss, and so's Karen. He has high expectations, 'n doesn't put up with folks doing less than their best, but he's fair and pays well. It's hard to describe; I know we are employees, but he treats us like family, and that's how I see them. He and Karen really care about us."

"How about the Drone Tech employees?"

"I don't know about the folks at Drone Tech. I haven't met many and don't know any well." She wiped her hands on her apron and took the veggies he'd chopped, setting them aside for when the rest of the folks wandered in for breakfast.

The kitchen, now bright with the morning sun, was homey, spacious, and efficiently laid out. The cupboards, stained in the weathered Santa Fe blue color, had designs painted on them. He got up from his stool at the counter and wandered over to look more closely at them. He recognized the painting, done in antique gold and soft shades of red, yellow, and light blue, as the traditional Scandinavian rosemaling. He would make sure Lou noticed these. She'd appreciate the design and color.

By now in the oven, the scones began to smell wonderful. The delicious smell of bacon sizzling added to it all, and his stomach rumbled. One by one everybody gathered. Maria finished the preparations, and they sat down together in the sunny breakfast room.

Chapter Twenty-Three

After breakfast, Krista took Gandalf outside. Karen and Lou wandered off toward the studio to look more closely at the process of getting from drawings to woven tapestries. Cliff and Anton lingered over their coffee at the breakfast table talking about drones and how Cliff might use them in his book.

Maria came to the door. "Anton, Cliff, I think you should hear this." She led the way to the family room, put a finger against her lips, and pointed to the open window. They saw Krista curled up on one of the big cushioned chairs on the patio. Gandalf lay nestled next to her, enjoying her scratching his neck.

"Gandalf, I'm worried. I don't sleep so good anymore. I keep on having bad dreams, 'n when I get back to sleep, another wakes me up. I'm scared. What if they try to hurt me again? What if they hurt Daddy again, or Gramma?"

Gandalf reached up and began to wash her face, wiping away the few silent tears slipping down her cheeks. She hugged him and buried her face in his fur. "I wish we were all safe. I don't want anything more bad to happen. I wish there was somethin' I could do."

Krista jumped as Anton opened the door and came out, motioning Cliff to follow. They sat down on chairs next to her. Gandalf raised his head to watch, but showed no inclination to give up Krista's attentions.

"Honey, can I talk to you?" Anton asked. "You know, what's happening scares me, too. This morning Pete and some other officers are going to come out and talk with us. They're going to see if they can figure out who is doing these bad things and put them in jail so they can't hurt any more people."

"You're scared, too?" Krista asked. "What can we do?"

"Well, let's talk about that. First of all, we will work as hard as we can to stop them. I want you to know that you can come to me and tell me about your bad dreams and what bothers you. Maybe together we can think of things that make us safer. What do you think?"

"Okay. We can be very careful. Stay away from strangers. Even if they have puppies," she said, her lips quivering.

"That's one idea, but don't forget that most strangers aren't scary, or bad. Cliff and Lou were strangers before all this happened. And Pete. They turned out to be friends. Krista, you did something very right when they snatched you. You kept your thoughts about you. You did smart things like take the breath mint package for the fingerprints and turning off the dome lights so they wouldn't know you opened the car door. And you used common sense in picking the people you thought could help you. I'm proud of you."

Krista wiggled past Gandalf and scrambled into Anton's lap. He enveloped her in a hug and said, "The bad people can't take away the fact that we love each other and will fight to keep each other safe."

Krista lay contentedly in his arms, thinking about that. Then she turned to look at Cliff. "Can you teach us more about clues? I know they are important, but I don't know very much."

"Well, I can do that, but there's another important thing. Always be aware of what's going on around you. I'm sure you learned about the senses in school, didn't you?"

Krista nodded.

"Use all five. They are there to help keep you safe. Also, some people say there is a sixth sense—a feeling inside that something isn't right, and that you should be wary."

"Life is scary for everybody at times, Krista," Anton said. "Don't be afraid to do things with people you trust. Just don't wander off by yourself looking for clues, especially right now."

She sat up and looked at Anton. "Okay, but does that go for you, too?"

Anton laughed. "It should, shouldn't it. Now, is there anything else that we can do to make you feel safer?"

She settled back down against him. "This is a big house. I worry that if something happens in the night nobody will hear me. Gramma's room is a long way off—too far to hear. Could you hear me?"

"My rooms are right next to yours. I think I could. Sometimes I think parents have a special antenna for hearing their kids. I remember when I was little, if I woke up crying in the night with a bad dream, Mom would be there right away."

"Really? I miss my mom."

"I know, Sweetie. We miss her very much, but daddies have the special antenna, too."

"But would you hear me?"

"When you were really little, we had a baby monitor set up in your room with a speaker in our room. Do you think it would be okay if we set up that again, just to be extra sure that I would hear, at least until all the bad guys are caught?"

"I think that might be good. Just until they're caught." Krista lay quietly thinking, then said, "Can we be detectives and help the police find them? Solve the mystery?"

"What do you think?"

"We probably should let Pete or somebody search for clues, rather than doing it ourselves. We might get in trouble if we went looking for the bad guys."

"If you think of something that should be investigated, remember, sharing something makes a worry lighter. Tell me. Tell Pete. Use your head."

"Can I get a dog? I feel safer when I'm around Gandalf."

"Maybe. We'll see. We'll have to decide together. It would have to be just the right dog."

"Could it be an Airedale?" Krista slid from Anton's lap and picked up Gandalf's leash.

"Possibly," Anton said. "If we got a dog it would have to be trained to get along with the alpacas. There will also be work to do. Good dogs like Gandalf don't happen by accident. Somebody needs to love them, take care of them, train them, and they have to be protected, too, from the dangers they don't understand, like cars and snakes."

"In the meantime," Cliff said, "If it's okay with your dad, I think you could learn something from Gandalf and he would love it. I could teach you how to train him. Actually, if you are going to spend much time with him, he needs to know that you're in charge. You could also brush his coat. Some dogs love that, some don't. It's best and much easier if they are groomed from the time they are little puppies."

"That's a good idea," Anton said. "Maybe we can go to the library and find some good books on taking care of dogs and training them."

"Oh, yes, please."

"A dog is a commitment, Krista. They don't live as long as people, but they might be a part of a family for ten or fifteen years. That means if you got an Airedale puppy, it would probably live until you were ready to graduate from college. That's a long time. It's worth the wait to find exactly the right dog."

They heard someone playing a few chords on the piano. "Who's that?" Krista asked.

"Let's go see," said Anton, leading the way back in.

Lou was seated at the piano. "Who's the piano player?" she asked.

"I am," Anton said, "but Krista has started lessons, too. Do you play?"

"Not the piano that well. My instrument is the violin."

"Really? Then you might be interested in seeing this." He knelt and took a violin case out of the cupboard. "It belonged to my great-great-grandfather. He brought it with him when he came from Norway."

Lou opened the case and said, "Oh, it's beautiful. Look—the inlays," As she gently traced the marquetry, a swath of her hair fell forward teasing the strings on the instrument. Anton brushed the blue-black silk back over her shoulder as she looked up at him and smiled. "It's not a violin. I've never seen an instrument like this. Look at all the tuning pegs—there're nine. My violin only has four."

"How come ours has more, Daddy?" asked Krista.

"This has a set of sympathetic strings that go under the bridge. It's a Hardanger fiddle. It probably needs to be taken to somebody who can give it the care it needs, so it can be played again." He put the old fiddle back in its case and put it away.

"Cliff and I play in a little Celtic group," Lou said.

"Really? You play the violin, too?" Anton asked Cliff.

"No, when my folks urged me to learn to play an instrument, I was in an ornery mood. I decided to play the Scottish bagpipes. Then I graduated to the Uilleann pipes. Sometimes Lou and I have a piano player with us, and sometimes a guitar. Sam plays with us a lot."

"Sam? Who's he?" asked Anton.

"He's a policeman—probably will be here this morning. He works a lot with Pete."

"He drove one of the police cars in the escort on the way to the hospital, Daddy."

"Sam plays a mean guitar. I could lose myself in his playing or any good music for that matter," said Cliff. "He has another amazing talent, too. He can whistle anything."

"Can you play for us sometime, Cliff?" asked Krista. "I don't think I've ever heard 'em—those u…u-lean pipes."

"I heard them for the first time when I was about your age. My parents took me to a Riverdance concert, and I was hooked. I'll be glad to play sometime, if it's okay with your dad. It doesn't take much to talk me into it. Maybe we could hear you play for us. Maybe your dad, and Lou, too. What do you think?"

"That'll be something to look forward to," said Anton. He got to his feet and looked out the window. "Oh, I think Pete just drove up."

Chapter Twenty-Four

Anton and Karen walked out to welcome Pete and the other officers. Vidar and Sam were among them. Pete directed members of his team to check the perimeters of the corrals and to talk with Diego and Maria. They also would check the entrances to the house—especially the one next to Krista's playroom by her bedroom and the one next to Anton's suite. Both entrances were accessed by the sets of stairs to the back deck.

Two of his team went with Anton into the office off the breakfast room to look over the surveillance videos. Anton showed them the location scheme of the cameras in and out of the house. Pete spent several minutes talking with Krista and showing her some photos before she and Gandalf went off for a walk.

After organizing his team, Pete, Sam, and Vidar joined Karen, Anton, Cliff, and Lou in the breakfast room. A stack of note pads and a pile of pencils sat the middle of the table. Everyone helped themselves to scones and coffee.

"Pete, as we mentioned before, we all want to help—to join forces in catching whomever is behind these attacks," said Karen. "We hope that by pooling our knowledge and brainstorming possibilities we might be useful."

Pete looked around the table at the circle of interested faces. "This is an unusual request. I've studied it, and I agree, but need to lay out some ground rules. I can share some information. Some questions I may not answer. During an ongoing inquiry like this, much of what we know will not be shared outside our department. I'm sure you can appreciate that. It'll be helpful for me to listen to you, and I'm sure I'll have questions for you."

"I can understand family being here," said Vidar. "What I don't understand is why Cliff is included. He's only a writer. Besides the luck of being on the spot when Krista got away, what does he have to offer? Maybe he's just milking the opportunity to get an inside story and promote his books. Which, by the way, are only for kids."

Humph, only a writer, Cliff thought, raising his eyebrows. Like to see him write a book. He looked toward Pete. Cliff really wanted to be included, but it wasn't his call, damn it.

"Karen has specifically requested, and Anton agrees, that Cliff, and Lou when she wants, are included," responded Pete, looking at Vidar. "He does have legitimate reason, and it's my decision to include him. Vidar, I believe he will be a highly-motivated asset to us."

"Sorry, Aunt Karen, didn't know it was your idea," Vidar said, looking down and picking up a pencil and a pad.

Pete continued, "I want each of you to agree that you won't discuss what is said here outside this group—even to family, including Krista, friends, and employees, including Diego and Maria. If you have a question about sharing a specific piece of information with a particular person, ask me. I'll answer you on an individual basis. If you have concerns you don't feel comfortable sharing within this circle, you're welcome to talk to me in private. Those are the ground rules. Are we all agreed?"

They agreed. Cliff caught Lou's eyes and drew a breath of relief.

"I'm passing around a series of photos of the items and locations involved here. They might help you visualize where the action took place and come up with questions. Let's go over some of what we know," said Pete. "First, about the puppy left at the kidnapping scene. We got fingerprints on its plastic collar. The leash was just a thin, rough rope available at any home improvement store. No luck there. The puppy had been micro-chipped and had been reported stolen from a home in Española. Unfortunately, the alarm system cameras there were not functioning.

"Using the GPS, we did find Krista's cell phone where it had been tossed into the brush by the kidnappers. We got good prints from it." Pete looked down at his notes, ticking off the items as he shared them.

"Now for the ransom note. It was made up of letters and words cut from an issue of the *New Mexican Stockman* magazine, but it looks like whoever made it wore gloves and used tweezers to hold the letters as they glued them onto the paper. There was nothing special about the paper—just common copy paper."

"We subscribe to that magazine," said Karen. "I believe Diego keeps the old issues."

"Have you taken Diego's prints?" asked Cliff. "Or his wife's?"

"Oh, Diego's not married," said Karen. "He lives alone. He has one part of the duplex, and Maria the other."

"We've taken his and Maria's," replied Pete. "Next we come to the cholla incident—Cliff's encounter with the two kidnappers. We don't yet have the DNA information back on the blood samples. There were good prints on one of the smooth rocks used to pry off cholla. There were also several good prints on the cell phone they grabbed from Cliff. We already had Cliff's prints on file. We got lucky at Rosa's Diner. We picked up several prints from a large canister and some from cupboard doors."

Pete handed Cliff a pile of mug shot photos. "Can you identify any of these as the kidnappers, Cliff?"

Cliff looked through them and pulled out two, handing them back to Pete. "The older guy snatched my phone and ended up in the cholla. I'm positive about both."

"Good, I'll pass them around. I'm sure all of you will want to see them."

"How about on the breath mint package Krista took?" asked Karen.

"We did get matches. We know the package belonged to the younger of Krista's kidnappers, Alfonso. Those prints match some found at Rosa's, on one rock used at the cholla location, and some on the note that Krista used to wrap the breath mint container." Pete stopped to take a bite of his scone. "Alfonso's prints were on file with us from a drunk and disorderly arrest last May. His last name is Cruz. Vidar, what have you been able to find out about him?"

Vidar appeared to be engrossed in his doodling on the pad in front of him.

"Vidar?"

"Oh, I'm sorry. Trying to figure out something. What did you ask?"

"I asked if you'd been able to find out more about where Alfonso Cruz might be."

"Ah, no, not yet," Vidar replied. "I'm checking with a pile of his relatives up north of Tierra Amarilla. It's a pretty close-mouthed bunch."

"Well, keep on looking," Pete continued. "We know it was the older of the two kidnappers who snatched Cliff's phone. His prints were found on that phone, Krista's phone, and the envelope which held the ransom note. We've identified him as Juan Mendoza, a small time crook. He's Alfonso's uncle. They have addresses in Santa Fe, but they haven't been spotted at them since the kidnapping. Family members and those they know would be much more apt to talk to Vidar than anybody from Santa Fe. Soon we should have the make, model, and license plate of the SUV—if it was registered to either of them. We can't trust to the license plate, though. From Krista's story they have quite a collection."

"I'll head up there again this afternoon," said Vidar. "But folks in that neck of the woods keep to themselves and are pretty suspicious of outsiders in general and the law in particular."

"I talked with Krista this morning and showed her the mug shots I showed Cliff. She had no trouble identifying them," said Pete. "We've updated the APB and have a warrant out for their arrest."

The pile of location photos reached Cliff, and he began sifting through them. "Do we know yet which business the ransom grabber used to gain access to the catwalk?" he asked.

"We're pretty sure they used the bathroom of the restaurant to get up there, but we aren't positive. The team from Chimayo found some evidence on the catwalk. Sam and Cliff know about the red fibers, the sequins, and the long dark hairs we found. Some of the hairs were human, but some appeared to be from a hair piece or wig. Whoever was up there wore gloves and did a thorough job of wiping out prints from the walk and the ceiling panels and grids. Our team went through the trash in the various locations, but no gloves were found. That amount of cash would take a fair-sized tote bag or handbag to conceal. It's possible they used a sequined tote bag to haul it."

Cliff passed some of the photos on, but held back a couple that intrigued him.

"We followed up on the phone number they gave you to call, Anton," said Pete. "The number is one of those pay-as-you-go burner phones. No record, unfortunately."

"How about the location of the shooter?" asked Sam. "Where were they?"

Pete pulled out a map showing the layout of Truchas. "Anton was here. As near as we can figure, the shots were fired from here." He pointed to a spot on another road, with open fields between the two locations. "Not far from where you were, Vidar."

"You're right. My God, that's next to where I was on that burglary call."

"What's this?" Cliff said pointing to a logo showing a hawk on one of the photos of the laundromat windows.

"Oh, that," said Pete. "It's the logo of the V Hawk Alarm Company. They're a well-known security company in Española."

"If I ever get a security system, I don't think I'll choose them," said Cliff with a laugh. "They're in all of these locations."

"Pete, I'm optimistic because you have identified the kidnappers," said Anton. "Surely they'll be arrested soon, and you can find the others involved. I was hoping this would all be behind us before I go to D.C. in early October." He looked at Vidar, whose pencil point had snapped off mid-doodle and who had taken another pencil. "I am showcasing one of our patents there. I really can't get out of going."

"Anton, this might be important," said Pete, alerted. "What is it that happens on that trip?"

"Well, we've developed some new technology in the obstacle detection system for drones, or put another way, advances that will avoid collisions between drones and objects and people. It'll be unveiled there. There's a lot of interest in it—both commercial and military, and we're the first to make this particular advancement in the technology available."

"What happens to this development or to your company if something happens to you? Might it have something to do with the urgency to harm you?" Pete asked.

"The development would still come out, but I'm not positive who would end up with it or when. My Board of Directors would have to get a new CEO. It would take a while to sort all that out," Anton replied. "Nothing'd happen for a while."

"Is there division within the present board as to the direction your company is heading?"

"Yes, but I own the controlling stock."

"Would the company be sold if you weren't there?"

"Eventually—the company's my baby. Mom and Krista would inherit, but it's not their thing. Vidar would also get some shares, but he's never been involved in the business. Logically the company would be sold, gobbled up by a larger company."

"How about the people who help you run the company and shape its vision now? And how about those who're interested? Have you thought of anyone else who might want to do you harm?"

"Besides the names I've already given you, I only thought of one more. His name's Dan Wooten. He's a retired military fellow who applied for an executive job with us, but we didn't hire him. He's talented, but I got bad vibes from him. He's sharp one minute and spacey the next."

"Spacey how? Dementia, drugs, PTSD? What do you mean?"

"More like not being transparent, of having a hidden part of himself that he wouldn't allow anyone to explore. It felt almost like we were interviewing two people."

"While we're talking about possible suspects with business connections, I want to update you on what I've found out about Fisher and Cleason. We can take Fisher off our list. He's been in California shooting a film on location every day for several weeks."

"And Cleason?" said Anton.

"Now he looks more promising. He says he was attending a convention in Phoenix." Pete checked his notes on his laptop. "He flew into Phoenix on the twenty-first with several others from his company and came back with them on the twenty-seventh. I'm not convinced that he's telling the truth. We haven't yet been able to prove he stayed there or came back here to do some dirty work, using the convention as an alibi. We've contacted several of the convention leaders and some of the businesses with booths next to Cleason's in the exhibit hall. I should have those replies in a few days. We found out he served in the Gulf War. He was trained as a sniper, so he'd have the necessary skill. We haven't been able to find out if he owns any guns. None burp up that are registered to him. No one remembers seeing him at the gun ranges around Santa Fe."

"I remember Cleason," said Karen. "When we were building this house he came out a few times to meet with Anton. We had an employee Christmas party here once, too, that he was at."

"So he's been here on the property and knows the layout of the house somewhat?"

"He does," said Karen with a frown.

"What does he look like?" asked Lou.

"He's tall, thin build, blondish hair. Has a rather gaunt face. In good shape. He used to exercise a lot when he worked for me. He's about forty," said Anton.

"Neither Anton nor I have come up with names at all from the Foundation," said Karen. "I'm wondering—how about last night? With the alpacas and the rattlesnake? Did the surveillance cameras pick up anything?"

"The high one overlooking the yard has stopped working," said Anton. "Have to check out why."

"The one on the barn showed a figure, dressed in black, a bulky raincoat, with a black ski mask," Pete said. "He or she—couldn't tell—unidentifiable. He opened the gates and frightened the alpacas, chasing them out and down the road. Then he cut back out of camera range. Sometime later a camera in the back caught a figure, completely covered, coming at the lens with a spray can. They had it well planned."

"Uff da, they won't be able to get in again," said Karen. "All of the doors will be locked. Did they tamper with the circuit breakers, or did the storm knock out the power?"

"That was the storm. A good part of this area lost power last night," Sam said. "How about the other fingerprints—the puppy collar, and the ransom note?"

"No ID yet. They weren't from Alfonso or Juan," said Pete. "Now Sam and Cliff interviewed the two ladies from the beauty salon in Chimayo. Do you want to share those highlights?

"The first lady wouldn't notice anything that didn't come through her cell phone," said Sam. "We do think the second lady, Miss Bruton, saw the ransom grabber who must be the dark-haired woman from the restaurant. She described a non-feminine, big-boned, tall woman. She had just put something in her trunk before our witness saw her. We came to the conclusion the ransom grabber could either be a man in drag or a woman."

"Miss Bruton said that she could definitely pick her out of a line up," added Cliff.

"Where are we now, then?" Karen asked.

"I'm going around the circle again—what does your gut tell you about what should be followed up? Also, if there is any idea that you would like to work on, tell me." Pete looked to his right. "Karen?"

"For me, Anton's and Krista's safety is most important. I'll be the over-protective mama. I will be very interested in your checking on the names Anton mentioned. And I'm curious—do you think it's possible one might be a woman? I haven't a clue about that."

"Very possible," said Sam.

"Bringing in Juan and Alfonso might be the key to finding out who else is involved. We know there are at least two others," said Cliff. "May I keep these location shots for a few days, Pete? I want to study them."

"Sure. I have copies on my laptop. Lou?"

"If it's okay with Anton, I'd like to spend some time with Krista. She's already shown interest in my drawing and has asked me to help her learn more. That really doesn't help solve anything, though."

"I like the idea," said Anton. "Anything that helps move her past this is good. As for what I'd like to do…I agree with Cliff and Mom. It's hard to believe that any of the guys I mentioned have any connection with the kidnappers. Can't think of any who would shoot me. Competition in business is one thing, but murder?" Anton touched his scar. "I have been wracking my brain trying to think of a woman who might be involved. I don't know anything about the women in the lives of the men whose names I listed."

Vidar leaned forward, tossing his pencils back with the extras, tearing the used pages off his notepad, and tucking them in his pocket. "Don't under estimate the power of greed and what it can do."

"Well, that about does it for today," Pete said. "Let me know if you think of anything else."

Lou and Sam gathered up the cups and took them to the kitchen. The others chatted quietly.

Cliff gathered the photos together with his notes. We're missing something, he thought. And who was the woman arguing with Diego? I'll have to talk with Pete later.

Vidar turned to Karen, rubbing the back of his neck. "Can I talk to you for a moment? There's a problem—about something else, not what we've been talking about."

"Sure, Vidar. What is it?"

"Yo, Vidar, you ready to go?" called Sam from the door. "We're on our way."

"Never mind, Aunt Karen. It can wait. Later is fine." Vidar followed Sam outside.

CHAPTER TWENTY-FIVE

"Let me walk you to your car," said Karen as Cliff and Lou said their goodbyes. "I wanted to tell you a little about Vidar. Sometimes he can be prickly, but don't take it personally. He's had a rough life. His father, Walter, was a bitter, angry man. Jealousy played a big part, I think. When we were teenagers I spent a lot of time with friends who included Walter. He always tried to get more serious with me, but I only saw him as a friend. Then one day he introduced me to his brother, Edvar. Something clicked, and the rest, as they say, is history. Edvar and I fell in love and got married. Walter never spoke to his brother after that, saying Edvar stole me from him."

She paused to pick up a small branch the storm had brought down. "Not long after Edvar and I were married, Walter got a girl pregnant. Anita's parents were really rigid and controlling. Walter had to get married. In those days that's what happened—he had no choice. Poor Vidar—born into a family with resentment and anger, rather than love. When he was just a little guy—not quite three—his mother left. Just up and abandoned her husband and baby. We've never heard what happened to her."

"Did she just disappear?" asked Cliff.

"On purpose, I think. All the signs pointed to that. I never knew her well. With Walter feeling the way he did, I'm not sure I ever even talked to her. Certainly never spent any time with her. I'm sure she had cause to leave; he was abusive toward her from what people said. But to leave your child in that mess—I have never understood how she could do that. Edvar and I tried to help Vidar, but Walter wouldn't have any of it. Vidar grew up hearing all about revenge and hate. His father became an alcoholic and used to beat him. He told Vidar he should never have been born, and that not even his own mother wanted him."

"That's a terrible thing to say to a child," said Lou.

"You got that right." said Cliff.

"Occasionally," Karen continued, "Vidar would get away from his dad and stay with us for a few days, but then Walter would double up on the abuse. About the time Vidar graduated from high school, Walter died. Edvar and I paid for Vidar's college education and supported him through his police training until he got a job. He has turned out remarkably well, considering what he's been through."

Gandalf came racing toward the car pulling Krista at the end of his leash, interrupting them with his antics.

"Krista, it looks like the time for dog training is overdue," Cliff said. "I'll call your dad and schedule a time. A dog should be doing what you want, not the other way around. Would that be okay?"

"Oh, yes," she said, looking at her grandmother. "Then I will know how to train my own puppy when I get one."

Karen laughed. "That's between you and your dad. I'm not getting in the middle of that one."

CHAPTER TWENTY-SIX

Later that afternoon in his study, Cliff pulled out his boards. He flipped over the one with the maps to the dry-erase side and started jotting down what they knew. Alfonso Cruz and Juan Mendoza might be somewhere north of Tierra Amarilla.

He looked at his Suspects / Motives list on the other board which still named only Ransom Grabber and Shooter. He added Wooten and Cleason. He added Vidar, too, just because he stood to inherit, if only some shares. He sure had a chip on his shoulder. Cliff was still amused about "only writing kid's books."

After thought, he added Diego's woman. Who knew what part she played? It was possible she was one of the other employees on the ranch whom he didn't know, but he could always take her name off if he learned she was legit. Then he added Mystery Woman, noting her long dark hair and red jacket. Or was Mystery Woman really a man in drag? There had been hairs from a wig found, too. Then he added Diego's name. He looked at it for a while, then erased it and paused. "Oh, what the hell," he said and wrote it again.

He pulled out a third board, wrote Means and Opportunity, and thought about those. To access the catwalk, you'd need to be somewhat agile. Not just anybody could do that quickly, even with a rope ladder. And the shooter? Using a rifle scope over that distance and shooting well enough to come so close to killing Anton required skill. That person would need to have some serious weapon's training, maybe even sniper training in the military. Could an avid hunter pull that off? Are there shooting ranges in Santa Fe where a person could get that training? Of course, they might have learned that skill long before they got to Santa Fe. Would gun shops be a source of information? That was a world he was not at home in.

How about law enforcement? Wait—Vidar was there. He has a rifle in his patrol car. Really startled him when Pete mentioned how close he'd been. Bloody hell. I'll have to ask Pete if they got any bullets or casings from the sites. Wonder if he's thought of Vidar. Karen's comments on Vidar interested him. He had trouble visualizing Vidar hurting Karen. Was he jealous of Anton? Did Vidar want Karen's attention all to himself? What was the relationship between Vidar and Anton? He didn't remember much interaction between them at their meeting.

Cliff got an apple, sliced it, and took it back to his study. Gandalf, alerted to the possibility of mooching a snack, followed and sat next to him. As Cliff crunched on the apple slices, occasionally sharing with Gandalf, he reflected on the weekend.

He updated his computer documents from his notes and worked on his internet searches for all the names, copying and pasting what he'd found. He tried to find a picture of each of his named suspects to copy as well. He printed off a few of the pictures and added them to the location shots he'd borrowed from Pete. Couldn't do much with those yet—it would be interesting to see what Pete discovered.

Something niggled at the back of his mind, and then he remembered making a crack about a security company. Pete had named it; said they were popular in Española. Then Anton had dropped the comment about wanting to have the case solved before his trip to D.C. giving their sleuthing a new sense of urgency, and the thought had been lost. He went back to the computer and soon came up with the name, V Hawk Alarm Company. He added that name to the suspects. He didn't like coincidences —and it was just too convenient that V Hawk provided the common link with most of the locations. He found the website of the company, followed links to other articles, and found a good photo of the owner, Guido Vittorio, and his son, Vincent, standing next to some real estate agents at a Chamber of Commerce event. One of the agents reminded him of someone. Who, he couldn't think.

He spread out the location shots and looked carefully. Too many coincidences. The V Hawk could mean something important. He decided to call Pete.

"I've been thinking about coincidences," Cliff said when he reached him, "and there's a big one about the kidnapping that bothers me. Would it be possible for you to tell me what alarm company services the place where that puppy was stolen in Española?"

"Let me look at my notes," said Pete. The sound of papers shuffling reached Cliff's ears. "V Hawk."

"And how about the burglar alarm call that Vidar had been responding to when the sniper tried to kill Anton? Was that V Hawk, too?"

"Son of a gun. That is a lovely bunch of coincidences. Don't know how I missed that one."

"Also, there's something else I wanted to tell you. When I took Gandalf out yesterday morning, we walked by the duplex where Diego lives. I heard loud voices arguing. My Spanish isn't too good, but I did pick up some words. Don't know if it's important. I recognized Diego's voice. The other belonged to a woman. I guess that's why I assumed he was married."

"A woman? Could it have been Maria?"

"No, I'd just left her fixing breakfast. Anyway some of the words I caught from Diego were '*divorcio*' and '*matar*.' Whoever the woman was, she used the words '*dinero*' and '*policia*' and '*termino*.' I haven't the foggiest what they were talking about, but thought you should know."

"Thanks. Interesting set of words, considering what's going on. Wonder what the hell she was doing there that early? Did you see an extra car around?"

"I didn't notice any in that little lot. Do you suppose he might have been talking to an employee? I got the impression that they have other folks that work there. It's not just Diego and Maria that do all that."

"I'll ask. Thanks, Cliff."

CHAPTER TWENTY-SEVEN

On the following Monday, Pete decided to dig further into Cleason's story. Brian had said he worked his company booth on the twenty-second, the day of Anton's attempted murder. Pete made up a bogus story and called Cleason's company. He posed as a customer and said he'd lost the business card of the person who helped him at the booth that day. "I think it may have been Ryan, but I'm not positive," he said. "I know it was on the first day the exhibit hall was open."

"Might it have been Brian?" they said. "Oh, wait, he wasn't there that day. He said he attended some of the workshop sessions."

Hmm, Pete thought after he hung up. Not at the booth, and no one remembers seeing him on the night of the twenty-first. No one remembers seeing him until late night the twenty-second. I think I'll check with the airlines to see about quick round-trip tickets. Maybe the hotel doorman would remember something, too.

He got lucky with the doorman who remembered getting a cab to take Cleason to the airport. It happened shortly after he'd arrived at the convention hotel and checked in. The doorman thought it was odd and wondered if there had been an emergency in the family or something. Pete wasn't able to find any record of quick airline tickets to Santa Fe or Albuquerque and back, but that wasn't conclusive.

On Tuesday, Pete arrived at Cleason's company.

Cleason was jumpy and looked around as if to see who might overhear him when Pete confronted him. It was clear he didn't want to talk with Pete.

"I'm following up on a case of attempted murder."

"Murder? I don't know anything about a murder. Who was killed?"

"Attempted murder. It'll just be a few more questions," Pete said, deliberately leaving Brian's question unanswered. "We have learned that you were not at the exhibit hall on the twenty-second. Where did you go?"

"Oh, I'm sorry, I forgot. When we got in the day before, I felt whacked. I slept late the next morning. I was there. I attended a morning and an afternoon workshop session—both popular, well attended."

"Which ones?" Pete asked.

Brian grabbed the convention flier lying on his desk and pointed to two sessions. "Don't know why it slipped my mind."

"How'd you meet Alfonso?" Pete said.

"Who?"

"Alfonso. The guy you hired to do your dirty work."

"I don't know any Alfonso. And you're wrong. I didn't hire anybody to do anything." Brian fidgeted with a paper clip until it broke in two. He tossed the pieces into the wastebasket.

Pete looked at the basket where the clip had landed and looked back at Brian, who tugged at his collar as though it was suddenly too tight. Pete raised an eyebrow as he let the silence stretch, noting the sheen of moisture on the man's upper lip. Then he closed his notebook. "I'll be checking out what you've told us. Make sure you're available to talk again soon."

Not a very good liar, he thought as he left the building. It's obvious he's hiding something.

When he got back to the office Pete contacted the convention staff again and asked if it were possible to verify someone's attendance at two of their workshops. They could put him in touch with the leaders. They mentioned the second session had had a different leader than the one listed in the brochure. The original leader, Mr. Kohl, had fallen ill. That session had been led by a woman, Joy Green.

Pete called the first leader. He didn't remember Brian. The leader had gotten the names and email addresses of everyone who attended to send them information. He checked. Brian was not listed. After several tries Pete finally reached Joy Green. He got the same story. She didn't remember Cleason, and he hadn't signed in. Pete made an appointment to see Brian Cleason again.

When Pete got off the phone, someone handed him the fingerprint results from the ransom note. Well, now that's interesting, he thought. Besides Anton's and Karen's, which he'd expected, Diego's prints were there. Some were cut across, like prints that would have been made by a reader of the magazine before it was cut up to make the note. Of course that could have been deliberately done by Diego to make it look like he was framed. But it didn't make sense. Why would Diego, or someone, be stupid enough to go to the trouble of wearing gloves and using tweezers to paste together the ransom note using a magazine they had handled already without gloves?

Pete remembered Karen's comment about Diego keeping the issues. That particular one's probably long gone. Well, guess I'd better get a search warrant. Interesting to see if anything burps up.

◆ ❖ ◆

On the following day Pete, Sam, and another officer pulled up at the Bjornson's. They found Diego who had just ridden in on his horse and was unsaddling her.

"Diego, mind if I ask you a few questions?" asked Pete.

"Go ahead."

"Can you tell me what you remember about the day Anton was shot?"

"Can't tell you much. Already told you that I was out of town that day."

"Where were you? When did you leave and get back?"

"Left about seven in the morning," said Diego. "Got back at about ten that night. Was surprised as hell to hear about Anton bein' shot."

"Where'd you go? And, can somebody vouch for you?"

"Can't tell you where I was. Nobody knew me where I went. Don't think I have anything more to say on it."

"Wasn't that a bit strange to go off just after Krista had been kidnapped?"

"Couldn't help it. Already had plans. Karen gave me the day off, and didn't say I had to stay. Not goin' to say anymore."

"Do you mind if we take a look inside your place?"

"Yes, I do mind."

"Well, we have a search warrant, Diego. Here, this is a copy for you." As Pete handed him the paper, he noticed that the normally mild-mannered Diego was starting to sweat. He glanced periodically at his house and appeared agitated.

"I didn't have nothing to do with this stuff. I would never hurt this family." Diego's voice had risen almost to a shout as they walked toward his home. "I don't want you in my house. You've no right to go pokin' around."

"Sorry, this piece of paper gives us the right to enter and search," Pete said as he and the other officers went in followed by Diego. "You need to stay in that chair." He pointed at a chair not far from the door. "Officer Gonzalez will be keeping an eye on you while we look."

Diego sat, his brows drawn together in a mutinous frown.

◆ ❖ ◆

Pete was a little surprised by Diego's noisy, belligerent attitude. He was acting like he was guilty of something, and that made Pete even more determined to do a good search. They put on gloves and methodically started in the living room and worked their way through all the rooms to the front again. The living room and Diego's bedroom yielded nothing on their list and no suspicious evidence.

The second bedroom did prove interesting. "Someone's been staying here with him," said Sam. "There's definitely a woman been using this guest room. Clothes in the closet, cosmetic bag and so on in the bathroom. Brush with long dark hairs. It was on our list, so I documented and bagged it. No purse or ID so far that we found."

They continued working their way around the rooms. Diego's office was next. In magazine holders on the bookshelf they found several years of the *New Mexico Stockman*. Pete pulled down the holder of the 2015 issues. "Sam, look at this." The May issue resembled Swiss cheese with cut-out holes throughout. "I think we'll find this is where the ransom note letters came from. Now, why the hell would he keep this? What good is a cut-up magazine that'll just get you into trouble?"

The next door in the hall was the appliance closet, the furnace and cooling system tidily tucked away. Sam opened the door. The color red jumped out at him. "Pete, pay dirt." They took photos and carefully removed a red jacket. Sam sucked in a breath as he saw what it covered.

"*Ach, du lieber.*" said Pete. Under the jacket was a large black handbag, covered with shiny, silver sequins. He looked at Sam, who started making notes on an evidence bag. "Does this belong to our ransom grabber?" As long as Pete had been doing detective work, he always had mixed feelings about these searches. He felt satisfaction in finding something, but it warred with the pain he knew would follow for folks who'd put their trust in someone, only to find it betrayed.

When they finished their work, Pete and his two officers loaded several bags and boxes into their car. Diego was in a sour mood when they handed him the receipt for the items they took. He refused again to answer any questions about the mystery woman or where he was the day Anton was shot.

CHAPTER TWENTY-EIGHT

Vidar had spent the afternoon chasing leads for Juan and Alfonso up in northern Rio Arriba County. He talked again with the State Police and with his buddies at the Sheriff's Department. He flashed around their mug shots and finally got wind of their presence in the area. Tomorrow was his day off, but it was important to find them before they split or got bumped off. Just before his shift ended, he got his best lead of the day. He would be back tomorrow to check it out.

As he got back in his truck a light rain began to fall, and he turned the windshield wipers on. His stomach reminded him with a growl that it was time for dinner. He wanted to get back to Española because Vinnie was coming over with pizza. He'd gotten acquainted with Vinnie a couple of years back after a series of security alarm calls that he had gotten from V Hawk. Vinnie had offered him a really good deal on a security system for his own house, and since then they'd become good friends. They had plans to kick back and watch the NFL Preseason Hall of Fame Game with the Vikings and the Steelers. Football season couldn't come too soon for him. He'd missed it.

When he arrived back at his house, he only just had time to dump his keys and the folder with his notes and photos on the table in front of the couch. Vinnie followed close on his heels carrying a large, heavenly-smelling pizza box.

"Help yourself to the beer in the fridge. Get a couple of plates out of the cupboard. There's napkins on the counter. I have to change out of my uniform."

"Take your time. Kickoff isn't for a while yet."

After he changed and returned, the pregame hype blared forth from his big-screen TV. Vinnie, already through his first slice of pizza, handed him an opened bottle of beer with a piece of lime wedged in the neck.

"Saw you the other day," said Vidar. "At a restaurant downtown. You were with an older blonde. Looked like she had the hots for you."

"Oh, her. She does. Met her a coupla years ago when we put in her security system. She really came on to me. Now I've got a good thing going. Pay the dame a little attention, and she'll do anything for me."

"Isn't she a little old for you?"

"I don't care how old they are. She's got piles of dough and wants a good-looking man. Gets me lots of places, man. What is the saying? All cats are gray in the dark?"

"That's true." Vidar said with a laugh. "Say—they were talking about V Hawk in our meeting the other day."

"Really? What about it?"

"Just asked about the logo on the laundromat window. You know. The Chimayo one where the ransom money was dropped. The logo showed up on several location shots. That guy that brought Krista home seems to think it was significant."

"How come he's still involved? He oughta be long gone by now."

"Stupid writer. Too stubborn for his own good. Krista thinks the world of that damn dog of his, and now he's even teaching her how to train dogs. Seems like he's always over there." Vidar reached for another pizza slice and settled back, propping his feet onto the low table, jostling the folder.

"What's his name again?"

"Cliff McCreath. He writes kids' books, and just because he sees the logo, he thinks your company is involved. Your logo is on lots of windows."

"Good company. Bound to be. Speaking of your case—is this who you're hanging around with these days?" said Vinnie, gesturing to the photos of Juan and Alfonso which had slid out of the folder.

"Hell, no. Those are just some low-lifes I have to track down. They've got all the evidence they need to nail those two for that kidnapping. I've got to go to Los Ojos tomorrow to see if I can find and arrest them. I found out that they've been hanging around the Cruz In Bar."

"Monday? I thought you had Mondays off."

"Not with a slave driver like Lieutenant Schultz. My time's not my own anymore."

"Brown-nosing? Vidar, that's not like you."

"Actually it is. Anytime I can gain favors by sucking up to the big shots—why not? My time will come."

"Ah, finally. Kick-off."

The pizza was soon demolished. The line of empty bottles grew. By half time Vidar was yawning.

"Damn, can't keep... my eyes open."

CHAPTER TWENTY-NINE

Vidar's bright red Chevy Silverado crew cab pickup started up, pulled out of the drive and headed north. It stopped at a house a couple of miles away. A tall thin figure opened the door and got in.

"Got the guns? Gloves? Ammo?"

"Yes."

"You know where they'll be?"

"Pretty good idea. Here are their pictures."

The passenger took the photos. "Do you know what vehicle they'll be driving?"

"Yeah, a beat-up, black SUV."

Silence fell as they drove on. The passenger studied the pictures and the information. About an hour later they arrived in Los Ojos.

"Here it is—the Cruz In Bar. Busy for a Sunday night." They backed into a parking spot near the edge of the parking area where they could see the entrance and turned off the lights. "Good. There's their SUV."

"I'll see what's happening." The passenger got out and went into the bar, ordered a drink and looked around, ignoring the curious glances directed toward the stranger in their midst with a bother-me-at-your-own-peril attitude.

The Cruz In Bar was crowded, full of testosterone. Conversations in Spanish outnumbered those in English. Good-natured ribaldry and bursts of laughter came from the pool table area where balls clicked against each other. Away from the pool table area low-watt bulbs hung from the pressed tin ceiling, barely lighting the shadowy booths. Above the bar neon beer signs lent colored light to faces. Several elk and deer heads looked down from the walls. A few stuffed rattlesnakes and a moth-eaten bear rug mounted on the wall added to the dusty décor.

Juan and Alfonso with hangdog expressions sat by themselves at one of the booths. Alfonso slumped back against the high wooden support, a feverish look on his face. His hands clutching a mug of beer shifted restlessly. One of his fingers stuck out awkwardly with a stained bandage. Juan leaned on his elbows, cradling his mug and looking blearily around.

Finishing the beer and flipping some bills onto the bar, the watcher quietly left, opened the door behind the driver and got in the backseat. "They're in there all right. Getting plenty soused, too."

The driver handed the guns back to where the passenger loaded them with familiar ease.

They waited for the two, watching the coming and going of the patrons, occasionally turning on the engine to run the heater against the cold mountain air as the sky darkened. Finally, Juan appeared, helping the drunken Alfonso into the SUV. They drove away slowly, seemingly oblivious to the pickup that trailed them. A few miles down the road the SUV turned off the highway onto a lesser road. Pine trees shrouded the crescent moon. As they followed, they noticed Juan's driving becoming more erratic.

"Now," the driver said, depressing the rear passenger window button. The red truck drove up alongside the SUV. The gun spoke, and Juan fell forward. They saw Alfonso rouse momentarily, and then he, too, was shot. Their vehicle veered off the road, rolling over again and again until it landed upright and crumpled at the bottom of the embankment, its passenger door ajar.

The pickup turned around and stopped by the edge of the road; the pair waited until they were sure no one else was in the area. They got out, one holding a flashlight, and the other with gun in hand just in case. They made their way down to the crumpled vehicle. Juan lay propped against the door, sightless eyes staring, blood covering his face. Alfonso's body lay twisted, half in, half out of the door. Neither moved. The pair turned and climbed back to the red pickup.

"That went well."

"I'm impressed—two shots, two varmints gone."

"We aim to please."

They drove off, the only witness a great horned owl in a pine tree, turning his head around to an impossible degree and hooting as he watched the tail lights disappear down the road.

Back at the apartment all was as it should be. He dumped the keys on the table, put the guns down, and kicked off his shoes, satisfied with his evening.

CHAPTER THIRTY

The call had reached Pete in the early afternoon, and he had gone right away to Los Ojos. Vidar reported that he'd been trying to track down Juan and Alfonso. A rancher had discovered the wrecked SUV with two deceased gunshot victims. It hadn't taken long for the local officials to figure out that they were the guys Vidar had been looking for.

Pete stood by the wreck surveying the scene bordered by yellow crime tape and the team at work. Damn, he thought. I could have been an insurance agent. Something nine to five, no weekends. None of this dealing with gunshot victims, murder, and mayhem on your day off. *Ach du leiber.* They'd been so close. He'd so wanted to talk to Juan and Alfonso about who else was involved in this mess. Now it would be much more difficult to find out who the ransom grabber and the shooter were.

Maybe Vidar's asking around provoked the attack, he thought. Going to be interesting to see what the ballistics and any evidence found here showed. Well, now they'd have to do it the hard way—trace back Juan and Alfonso's actions over the past couple of weeks, ferreting out their friends and contacts. Who would their mourners be? What was the tradition here? A wake? Viewings? It would be too easy to have folks sign a condolence book. Dream on. He sighed. They did have tracks of two individuals who had descended the slope after the wreck, stepping in the wet soil where the vehicle had gouged out the grass. One person had large shoes with ordinary soles similar to his own uniform shoes.

The other, with smaller feet, had worn some type of athletic shoes. They should be able to find that brand and both sizes. Chances were good of estimating the heights and weights of the individuals, too, from their tracks. There were also tracks of the rancher who had discovered the wreck, but since the ground had dried a lot in the intervening hours, those appeared quite different. An interesting set of tire tracks ran by the edge of the road, too, crossing those of the SUV after it had veered off the road. It showed the vehicle had stopped. Was that the killer's vehicle? If the tires were original, they might luck out and know the make and model of it.

The sound of the tow truck arriving interrupted his reflections. He went up to talk to the driver, wanting to impress upon him that the vehicle should be taken to where it could be thoroughly searched. It was certainly the one in which Krista had been held. It might contain clues that could push the case forward still. Vidar came up the slope to join him on the road, stumbling on the uneven turf, rubbing his temples and frowning.

"You okay, Vidar?" Pete asked.

"Yeah, headache—hangover actually. Didn't sleep well last night. I'm sorry. I keep thinking that if I'd stayed up here last night, we'd have those two in custody now."

"Their days were limited—they screwed up and then got themselves identified. Whoever the culprits are, they would try to take them out to save their own hides."

Chapter Thirty-One

I blacked out again last night. Don't know how much I had to drink. Sure were enough bottles on the table. Can't remember what I did. Where I went.... God, did I kill Juan and Alfonso? Who was I with? There was somebody else.... I was watching football. I remember being so tired.

When I woke up this morning I was still on the couch. My guns were on the table. My handgun had been fired. And I'd been out. My shoes were all muddy.

I heard voices again, too. Saying they had to be killed or they would tell—tell that I had planned the kidnapping and had shot Anton. Had to be silenced forever. I don't remember. Time gone. I feel horrible. Hung over. I'm going to have to quit drinking.

Vinnie asked me where I went last night. He said I was acting strangely. Left in the middle of the game, got in my truck and drove off. He said he waited until after the game finished, then left. Don't know where I went. The gas gauge in my truck registered almost empty.

I heard my father whispering, "Good, good for you. It had to be done. They couldn't live.... They would tell and stop my revenge." Over and over again. God, I'm losing my mind.

CHAPTER THIRTY-TWO

Cliff looked up from his chair in the family room as Anton welcomed Vidar, the last of the group to arrive at the Bjornson's. "Hi, come and join us, the Sleuths in a Circle."

Vidar tossed his jacket onto a chair and came to sit next to Cliff on the couch, putting his notes on the low table in the center of the group.

"I like that—the Circle Sleuths," Lou said.

"What a gang!" Cliff said with a grin.

Anton looked at Krista. "It's time you and Gandalf went outside to play now."

"Can't I stay, Daddy? I want to help, too."

"This is just for the grown-ups, Honey."

"I hate being ten. Nobody lets me do anything," she grumbled as she took Gandalf's leash and led him outside.

Pete chuckled and then said, "Let me bring you up to date. You may have heard that Juan and Alfonso were killed up in Los Ojos. That ruined our chances of bringing them in to find out who else might be involved in this. We're following up on the evidence from that scene, but it did set us back."

"We'll get 'em." said Sam.

"We have had another development. Maybe you've wondered about the fuss surrounding Diego this morning. It may be distressing for you." He looked at Karen and Anton. "We have taken him downtown for questioning."

A chorus of dismay and denial arose from the circle.

"Before you say impossible, hear me out," said Pete. "First, the prints on the magazine cut-outs on the ransom note belonged to Diego. After we learned that, we got a search warrant and went through his house. One of the issues of the *Stockman* magazine in his file had been used to make the note. We found a red wool jacket and a glitzy handbag decorated with sequins tucked in beside the furnace in the appliance closet."

"You're kidding," said Cliff. "Seriously?"

Pete nodded. "The jacket fibers and the hair found in a brush in the bathroom look similar to what we found in Chimayo. They will be tested to see if they match. We got a warrant to check his bank account. Large sums of cash were withdrawn recently, including the day before the kidnapping. There have also been several large recent deposits. Diego has not been cooperative. He refuses to say anything about a woman living in his house and heard arguing with him, or the sums of money, and even more serious, he won't account for his whereabouts on the day Anton was shot."

"Who could have told you about an argument with a woman?" said Karen.

"I'm afraid I can't give you that information."

"I'm shocked, but he had the perfect opportunity to let the alpacas out and plant the snake," Vidar said. "I wonder why, though?"

"Diego had nothing to do with the snake. He has a very healthy fear of them," said Anton. "He screws up his courage to help me get them when he must, but he certainly wouldn't go looking for them. Anyhow, he'd never want to harm Krista—or me."

"Oh, for goodness sake," said Karen. "It's not Diego. He would never hurt us. He won't say anything either. He's protecting his daughter."

"I thought you said he wasn't married, that he lived alone," said Cliff.

"His marriage ended a long time ago," Anton said. "His daughter, who goes by a different last name, contacted him recently. She lived in Albuquerque, is married to a cop there who has insane jealous rages. He beat her—more and more often and each time worse. The last time she feared for her life. Her husband doesn't know about her father. Diego withdrew the money for her. He took her to Denver to meet with a lawyer the day I was shot. We knew his plans. He wanted to be here after the kidnapping, but we knew how important it was to him to get his daughter away safely. We told him to go. He wouldn't tell you because he didn't want any possible way that information could leak back to her husband."

"What an awful quandary for him," said Lou.

"The deposits are easily answered, too," said Karen. "He owns quite a few of the alpacas living here. He sold several a couple of weeks ago. He got a good price for them."

"His daughter was pretty badly beaten up," Anton continued. "We knew she was living with Diego—even Krista knew."

"She's gone now," Karen said. "The Foundation helped get her a job in Minneapolis through one of the nonprofits we support there. We have a lawyer who's sorting out the legal issues and getting her a divorce."

Cliff said. "Somebody could have framed him by planting the hairs and stuff."

"This isn't one of your books," said Vidar. "It would be almost impossible to do that. It would take several trips in and out of Diego's house. First they'd have to get the magazine. Then put it back. No, it was the right thing to do—take him in for questioning."

"I agree with you, Cliff," said Anton. "We've become too complacent about locking doors and so on here. It would've been quite easy for somebody to have gotten in and out unnoticed."

"I still say Diego is in on it," said Vidar.

"What would be his motive?" asked Cliff. "I can't see it. It's a big stretch of imagination to see him being involved with Juan and Alfonso, too. What would he have to gain? He'd lose his job. His freedom, too, if he were caught."

"I'm sure he had a reason," responded Vidar. "Greed makes people do strange things."

"The stuff must have been planted," said Cliff. In the back of his mind he remembered that Vidar stood to gain if something happened to Anton. Those shares of the company would have to be worth a pretty penny, if you are talking about greed. He didn't mention it though, as he could see Karen was visibly upset.

"Children, children, enough," said Pete. "You have answered a lot of our questions, and we will certainly take another look at Diego. There seems to be good reason for his silence. We'll be needing more information from you, Karen. I will personally ask him about his daughter, and if you or Anton want to be present at that private meeting, I'd welcome that. I assure you and him that nothing will leak back to Albuquerque. I wouldn't mind talking to his daughter either. None of this will be mentioned outside this meeting. Is that clear?" Pete made a point of meeting everyone's eyes around the circle, not moving on to the next until he had gotten acquiescent nods from each.

"I'm sure Diego is innocent," said Karen. "We will be glad to get him a lawyer, too. Anton and I will talk with you later about this, Pete."

Lou brought the coffee over to the table and sent the plate of goodies around again. She sat next to Anton, and he smiled at her.

"Now, Cliff brought up an interesting idea to me the other day," said Pete. "He called to find out what the security company was for the folks who had the puppy stolen. I checked, and it was the V Hawk Alarm Company. I've taught Cliff to distrust coincidences. This might be a big one. Most of the locations involved in this case keep on burping up a connection to V Hawk, including the home with the burglary call that brought Vidar to Truchas the morning the sniper shot Anton. We're going to check these connections thoroughly. We can't conceive of any possible motives for V Hawk's involvement, so it's possible this might be a true coincidence. They do have a very large client list in that area."

"My friend works for them," said Vidar. "Actually, he's the son of the owner. His old man isn't doing well now. Vinnie is carrying all the work load."

"Here's another interesting fact," said Pete. "The security camera overlooking your yard, Anton, had been shot out. Another interesting bit for the ballistics folks."

"How close would they have to be to do that?" asked Cliff.

"Depends. Until we can figure out what kind of weapon they used, could be anywhere from a few feet from the pole, to about a mile away. We already know that one of them is a good shot with a rifle."

"Does Diego have a gun?" asked Vidar.

"Vidar," said Karen. "Diego did not do it."

"Sorry, just asking."

"One of these crooks knows their way around security cameras," said Sam. "On the day of the kidnapping the gate camera only showed a gloved hand coming toward the lens with a spray paint can. Now this."

"I think I'll have to monitor our cameras more frequently," said Anton. "How about Brian Cleason? Were you able to verify his alibi? And Dan Wooten?"

"Not completely," said Pete. "Cleason either lied or conveniently forgot that he didn't work his company booth on the twenty-second. Now he says he attended workshop sessions that day. We are trying to verify that. We're also looking into the possibility that he zipped back here and then back to Phoenix. By the way, I did find out the source of his wealth. He married into it. He wife is quite wealthy."

"I don't think he was married when he worked for me. I wondered how he could suddenly afford to own his own company," said Anton.

"Dan Wooten is retired military," Pete continued, "but he lives in Florida now and has been attending a drug-rehab facility. He hasn't missed any days, and has been behaving himself from what they told me. He has a rock-solid alibi."

"So he's off the list," said Anton.

"I'm in favor of more frequent monitoring of our cameras, Anton. Maybe we should set up a schedule for checking," said Karen. "Diego and Maria can help, too."

Cliff glanced at Vidar as he heard quiet muttering about the fox and the hen house. Karen did not seem to hear it, he noticed with relief.

"Good idea. Anything else?" Pete asked. No one responded. "Guess that's it then. Thanks, folks."

Chapter Thirty-Three

Krista poked her head in from the patio door looking at the circle of grownups. "Can we come in now?"

She and Gandalf came in, and she started chattering to her dad and Lou about their plans for the next day. Anton and Lou were going to take her to Taos to several of the art galleries. Gandalf greeted everyone and then wandered off snooping around. They weren't paying much attention to him.

Suddenly, he came prancing into the circle trailing a blue scarf from his mouth. He went directly over to Vidar and dropped it in his lap, stood back and gave him a doggie grin.

"Hey, what's this?" Vidar said.

Karen leaned forward, her eyes riveted on the scarf. "That's *my* scarf. The scarf we wrapped the ransom money in. Where did that come from?"

Vidar sat there, a shocked expression on his face.

"Let me see," Anton said and took the scarf from Vidar. "This *is* it. Gandalf, where did you get it?"

They all looked back at the direction he had come from to see Vidar's jacket on the floor, the inside pocket showing traces of dog spit.

"Cliff…" Krista began, but then Cliff caught her eye. He shook his head slightly. She didn't finish.

Krista might be in danger if she tells about Gandalf's trick, Cliff thought. Vidar's beginning to bother me. I don't think I want him knowing the significance of what just happened. I'll tell her not to say anything before I go.

Pete picked up the jacket and took the scarf from Anton. "Vidar, do you know where this came from?"

"I never saw it before in my life, I swear. Are you sure it's the same scarf? Maybe it's another just like it. I don't know where it came from."

"I marked it before we put it around the money," Karen said. "Look at the tag in the corner. I wrote Krista's birth date with a marker."

Pete looked at the tag. "Here's the mark. This is the one. How the hell did it get here?"

"Where did your damn dog get it, Cliff? Can you tell us where it came from?" asked Vidar.

"I've never seen it. I didn't even know about it. We weren't told about any scarf. It looks like it came out of your pocket, Vidar." Cliff reached out and took Gandalf by the collar, holding him by his side.

"Stupid dog must have already had it when he started nosing around my jacket. Do you suppose Diego hid it here somewhere?"

Pete looked around the circle. "Did anyone see where Gandalf got it?"

"I did," Krista said in a small voice. "He was snoopin' in the jacket, knocked it on the floor, and pulled it out."

"It's silk, not bulky," said Pete. "It could have been in the pocket for quite a while and not be noticed. Where have you had the jacket lately, Vidar? Have you left it anywhere where someone could have planted it?"

"God, I don't know. I think it's been in my truck; it's been hanging at work when I'm wearing my uniform jacket. I never look in that inside pocket." Vidar's face was white, his eyes dark with apprehension.

"Karen, can I trouble you for a bag? I'll note what happened, and put it with the rest of the evidence. Vidar, retrace your steps. See if you can think of how it got there," said Pete. "This is one for the books."

Chapter Thirty-Four

I'm at my wit's end. Maybe I have some terrible disease. I feel lousy— my hangovers are worse than they ever used to be. I feel nauseous and have beastly headaches. I'm losing weight. Not sleeping well.

The blackouts are more frequent. Once I had stuff in my car that must have been stolen. I freaked out and chucked the stuff in a dumpster. My rifle has gone missing sometimes, too. Then I find it in my house somewhere, like under my bed. I don't remember putting it there. It always smells like it's been fired. Where had I been? What was I shooting at?

Crap! Keep thinking maybe I had something to do with Sonja's death. I can see her in her car, see how it balances on the edge, see how easy it would be to push it over. I start to rock the car; she screams, and then it goes over, crashing so terribly down the cliff....
But I remember being with Anton all day the day his wife died. How could I have killed Sonja? Maybe I just don't remember it right. Maybe I wasn't with Anton. I don't know what to believe.

Maybe I could tell Anton that I had this nightmare, and he could tell me I was with him. But to bring all that up again would just be hurtful. Maybe I could ask Karen? She'd remember where I was. But every time I try to talk with her, someone interrupts us.

And now this scarf from the kidnapping. How the hell did it get in my pocket? Did I have something to do with Krista's kidnapping?

I don't remember anything about it. And yet... and this terrifies me. I found a stack of money, hundred dollar bills in my drawer where I keep my ammunition. I have no idea where it came from. Is that part of the ransom money?

Hearing voices more and more often. I should talk to Pete. But I'll lose my job. I must be going crazy.

CHAPTER THIRTY-FIVE

Later that week after Cliff finished a dog-training session with Krista, he spoke with Anton. "I was wondering if you could fly a drone up to check the damage to your yard camera. Would it be possible for you to determine which direction the bullet came from? And, then could the drone turn around to show us where the shooter might have been located?"

"It's worth a try." Anton got one of his drones with a first-person view and set it up to show and record the video on a tablet. He flew the drone up, and they looked at the tablet screen.

"It looks like they dug the bullet out of the post here. Let's note the GPS coordinates." Anton told them to Cliff who jotted them down. "Now if I turn it around facing the other way. What do we see? It looks like it's a possibility somewhere on that ridge. Let's fly this baby on that coordinate and see what we find."

They flew it slowly along the straight line, checking the ground below. About half a mile away Anton had to bring it back. "This model can't go much farther—limited by battery power and the control. I have one at work I can bring home that would let us explore all the way to the ridge and even beyond."

"Would it be possible to do that tomorrow?" Cliff asked. "Sam and I had planned to go hiking that day anyway. Could you join us with the drone?"

"Sure. As long as we're through by five o'clock. Lou and I are going out tomorrow night. Want to take a look at what we got today on this drone video?"

"Oh, sure. I want to see it." They have a date? Cliff thought with a frown. That's twice this week. Wonder where they're going.

They went into Anton's office to see the video. "That's interesting. There was already some video recorded on this card. I bet it's from when I was showing you how drones work on the day the alpacas got out. Do you want me to skip through this bit?"

"If you don't mind, let's take a look at it." They watched as it went around and around the ranch. "Not too steady, was I?"

"Uff da, look! Who is that?"

"That must be the culprit with the rattlesnake! Pete will want to see this. Who knew we caught them on camera?"

They saw a figure dressed in black walking below the trees on the slope beyond the ranch buildings. The action was interrupted by Cliff's clumsiness at the control and his circuitous flight path, but they saw whoever it was carrying a bucket with a lid, setting it down a hundred yards or so from the house, and then continuing on past the duplex, before the video ended. They replayed it several times.

"I can't make out who it is. Can you, Anton?"

"I don't recognize them. Hard to tell looking down at them. But, I'm positive it's not Diego."

CHAPTER THIRTY-SIX

On Thursday Pete went back to Brian Cleason for a third interview. This time he brought Sam with him, in uniform. When they were seated in Brian's office he said, "There are still some questions that we have about your whereabouts on Wednesday, July 22. You told me that you were attending some workshop sessions."

"I thought we covered all the questions about where I was." Brian picked up a pen and twisted it in his fingers.

"Not quite. If you can just tell us about Mr. Kohl's session, when it began, how long it lasted. Did you know any of the others who were there? Can they vouch for your attendance?"

"I believe they were strangers to me. People come from all over the country to that convention."

"The subject of the second session—the one with Fred Kohl—sounds pretty dull to me. What did you think of him?"

"Oh, I know the topic sounds dull to the layman, but to us in the business it is very interesting and timely. And, Fred is a good speaker. He can make any topic come alive. Yes, I took several new ideas away from that session with him."

There was a commotion outside. The door opened slightly. They heard the frantic voice of the secretary trying diplomatically to dissuade the visitor from entering.

"It's okay, Stevens. Brian won't mind." A small woman wearing a tiny hat with a cascade of feathers curled over her brow pushed her way in and shut the door smartly in the secretary's face.

Brian got to his feet. Pete and Sam also rose. Brian moved out from behind his desk to buss her cheek. "Hello, Darling."

"Who're these people?" she said.

"This is Lieutenant Schultz and Sergeant Martinez from the Santa Fe Police Department. They've been asking about one of our employees."

The hell we have, it's you we have been asking about, thought Pete. What a little Banty rooster she is. And I do mean rooster—all feathers, petite size, and an attitude as big as a gorilla. "Ma'am," he said nodding to her.

She sat down in the other chair. "Well, do go on."

"I'm afraid this is a private conversation, Ma'am," Pete said.

"Nonsense. My husband and I have no secrets from each other."

"Dear, this isn't anything that would interest you—it's just a petty little thing."

"Who is it about? I want to know. We can't have troublemakers working here."

Pete imagined the Banty wings fluffing feathers. "Police inquiries are often private," he said.

She swung to pin Brian with her gimlet gaze. "I don't think these men need any more of our help."

"Please, Dear, wait outside."

"Well, I never. You *will* tell me when you get home." She strutted out. Pete found himself looking for feathers wafting through the air.

They all sat again.

"I'm …I'm sorry," Brian said. "She does run things here. Sometimes I could wring her neck." Then he colored, remembering who he was talking with. "I didn't mean that. Just a figure of speech, you know."

"You were telling us about the convention workshops." Pete was starting to see the whole picture. The source of the stress didn't seem to be the law asking questions, but the little Banty rooster.

"She watches me, keeps track of everybody I see, every penny I spend, everywhere I go. I strayed…. Once. She has never let me forget."

"Mr. Cleason. She is not your biggest trouble at the moment. You have been lying to us about where you were on July 22."

"Oh, no, I was at the convention."

"I don't believe you. The leader of the first session has no recollection of your presence there. You did not sign in with the other attendees. Fred Kohl, who was supposed to have led the second session, was taken ill. His session was led by a woman, Joy Green. You weren't at either session. What's more, the hotel doorman says he got a taxi for you to go to the airport on the evening of July 21st. Where did you go, Mr. Cleason? Did you come back here and try to kill Anton Bjornson?"

Brian looked at him, stunned, then rested his head on his hands, elbows on the desk.

"Mr. Cleason. Wouldn't it make a whole lot more sense to tell us where you were and what you were doing that day? We don't need more lies."

Brian sat back in his chair, leaning his head against the leather padding. "I did leave the convention. I got there that night, made a big splash, so they'd remember me. You were right. I took a taxi back to the airport. There's this woman, Rhonda…. God, this won't get back to my wife, will it? I can't leave her. She controls me, the business. Anyhow Rhonda and I are having an affair. We spent that night and most of the next day in one of the airport hotels…. We'd finally found a way to snatch some time together…. I didn't come back here. I had nothing to do with Anton…. Oh, God. She'll find out. My life is over."

"Mr. Cleason. I'm not interested in your domestic drama," Pete said. "But I am conducting an attempted murder and kidnapping investigation, and it'll be a whole lot better if you stop lying to me. I'll need her name and number. If she can corroborate your story, I don't see that it has to go further."

Brian scribbled a name and a number on a slip of paper and pushed it across the desk toward Pete. He read it and passed it to Sam. Pete took out his cell phone and gave it to Brian. "Call her now. Tell her it is okay to tell me the truth, and then hand the phone back to me." Brian did as he said, and Pete asked his questions of Rhonda and hung up. He told Brian he didn't think he would need to trouble them again, but was making no promises.

On their way back to the car Pete said, "Well, Sam. Another suspect gone. Where does this leave us?"

"Still looking for at least two bad dudes. Damn, Cleason seemed to be the one, what with his sniper training and all."

"*Ach du lieber.* I should have been a barber. Work by appointment, don't have to think about it after hours or take your work home with you."

"You'd hate it. You'd be bored out of your skull," said Sam. "You thrive on the puzzles and the chase."

Pete's phone rang just as they were getting into the car, and Cliff's number showed up. Cliff told him about what the drone saw on the shot-out camera and the direction the shot must have come from.

"Hold on a minute, Cliff. Sam is here, too. Let me put you on speaker phone."

"Good, I think it would be interesting to hike up there and see if there's anything to be found. Are you up for a hike, Sam? Do you still have tomorrow off?"

"Sure do. Sounds good. Will Anton be joining us?"

"He says yes. Come by my place a little before noon. Before we hike, we'll show you the video, too."

"Make me a copy of that video," Pete said. "Maybe we can do some magic with enhancement and find our villain."

Later, at home, Cliff checked out the area on his computer. He pulled up maps on the internet and digitally explored the area between Anton's home and the ridge where they expected the shots to have come from. He used both the road maps and the satellite views. He looked at the terrain and tried to picture what it would be like on Friday when they hiked. He widened the view and looked at the roads in the area. There was very little development, and the roads looked mostly like unimproved fire-access roads. He wondered what they would find and if the villains had been kind enough or stupid enough to leave clues.

CHAPTER THIRTY-SEVEN

An eddy of dust and leaves whirled across the driveway as Karen opened the garage door. Some blew into the garage as she backed out. "Uff da. I forgot the books," she said, putting the car in park. "Just enough time to go to the library before I pick up Krista, and make it back before Sam and Cliff get here."

She went back in and picked up the pile of books and movies. Balancing the stack, she opened the car door. A breeze caught her scarf and blew it over her eyes. Reaching up with one hand she pushed the scarf away from her face. The stack tilted and several of the movies fell. She bent over to pick them up, and her side mirror exploded with a bang, stinging her with shrapnel. She jumped back, falling to the ground with a scream. Books and movies scattered. The car window shattered with a second explosive sound, sending little cubes of glass flying. Rolling, crawling, whimpering, she scuttled around to the front of the car. My God, I don't believe it. Someone is shooting at me! she thought. A bullet slammed into the driveway just past her head, gouging a furrow into the cement and sending up a little spurt of gray dust. She ducked back behind the front end of the car.

"Oh, God, I hate this. Why? *Why?*" She crawled on hands and knees into the garage, being careful to keep the car between her and the direction she thought the shots were coming from. Once inside she reached up and hit the remote control, flinching as she heard another bullet slam into the garage door as it started down. She cried out as another struck the house with a crack.

"Anton! Maria!" she screamed as she stumbled down the hall.

"Mom, what happened? You're bleeding!"

"Karen, did I hear shots? Are you hit?"

"They're shooting at me. I was just getting into the car," she said with a sob. "Dropped some movies; bent over to pick them up. Shot hit the car mirror. Bits got me. I don't think I'm hit." They heard one more loud crack as yet another bullet hit the house and Karen ducked her head, scrunched her shoulders, and flinched, putting her hands to her temples. "God, make them stop."

"I'm calling 911," said Anton. "Maria, call Diego. Tell him to get inside." He punched in the numbers and pulled his mother to him as he put the phone to his ear, alerting the dispatcher of the shooting. They told him a police unit was on its way. They put him through to Pete.

"I'm going to send up a drone," Anton said to him. "Maybe I'll see them."

"Anton, don't go outside. You'll be killed!" cried Karen. "Please don't. We don't know where they are. We're not safe anywhere."

"They must be shooting at us from the ridge again," said Anton. "I'll be sheltered back by the family room. I was outside with a drone there already when I heard the shots."

"Anton, no." Karen's eyes were wide with terror.

"Mom, I'll be okay there. Calm down. Take a deep breath."

"But, Cliff and Sam are going to be here soon. They will be walking right into danger. They don't know about the shooter," said Karen. "Oh, God, this is a nightmare. Will it only end when we're all dead?"

"Pete, did you hear all that? Here, Mom, talk to Pete. Tell him to call Cliff. Have him tell them to park on the studio side. I'm going to get that drone up." Anton pushed the phone into her hands and hurried off.

Karen followed as far as the patio door, still on the phone. She relayed Pete's message to Anton, "He's going to call Cliff and Sam and have them pick up Krista. Should I call her and tell her to go with them?"

"Good idea, Mom."

♦ ❖ ♦

Anton sent up his drone and flew it in the direction of the potential sniper vantage point they'd discovered. Near the top of the ridge he saw someone walking with a rifle.

On his first-person view goggles, he saw the figure stop, glance up and point the rifle toward the drone. He immediately maneuvered it through tricky moves to make it difficult to hit, seeing fire bursts from the gun. He brought the drone to hover safely behind a tree. A few seconds later, he sent the drone high again and watched as the person ran over the ridge down to a truck, got in, and drove away. He got footage of the vehicle until it rounded a bend and was lost.

Karen watched anxiously from the door, her knuckles pressed into her lips. "Call Pete again," Anton said, "it's a big white pickup going south on Mitchum Road. Whoever it is has a rifle. Maybe they can cut him off."

As she told Pete, he brought the drone back and took off his goggles. He pulled Karen into his arms. "Are you better now? Okay? Your cheek and arm are still bleeding."

Maria came to them with a wet cloth, a bowl of water, some antiseptic, and small bandages. They began looking over the cuts and brushing the window-glass cubes out of her hair.

"Anton, this has got to stop. I can't *take* it anymore. Why are they doing this? *Who* is doing this?" Her voice rose.

Pete called Anton back shortly. "By the time we got units in the area the pickup had disappeared. I'm going to take a team up to the ridge spot and see what we can find. We're getting really close to nabbing them now. We have to hurry."

"Sam, Cliff, and I will hike up there from the house. They'll be here shortly. I'll bring the drone, too, just in case we need it." He replaced the spent battery with another one. "I can see one improvement Drone Tech should look into is more efficient use of battery power," he said to Karen. "I think Cliff just drove up. Good, they are parking on the studio side."

"Be careful, Anton. Why do you have to go? They might shoot again."

"Pete and his team will be up on the ridge. I saw the person drive away. I'll be okay, Mom. Krista and Maria will be here with you. You'll all be safe inside." He gave Maria an imploring look, needing her help in keeping his mother calm.

"It's just… just too much. We can't live like this. They have to be stopped," she said with a sniff.

Maria enveloped her in a hug. "There, there, Lamb. They'll get them. You'll see."

Sam, Cliff, Gandalf, and Krista burst into the family room. Anton filled them in. He sent Krista to get his binoculars and compass, and then to stay with her grandmother. He called Diego, told him what had happened, and asked him to come and stay in the house. "Diego will be here in a jiffy. He'll take good care of you."

❖

With the drone case in Anton's hands, they set off toward the ridge. Sam carried the binoculars. Cliff had the compass in one hand and a tight hold on Gandalf's leash with the other. Anton was tense as he told them about the sniper, evidently more unnerved than he was willing to let on. He seemed glad of their company and for something to actually do in the face of the attack.

"Pete should be there by now," said Sam. "I believe you're right. The danger is over for now. This may have been a big mistake for those jerks. By the way, we should probably watch where we step. If they have been moving around here much, there might be some evidence or tracks we don't want to disturb." He began to whistle the theme song from *The Andy Griffith Show.*

"I noticed several no trespassing signs as we drove in today," Cliff said, hoping the mundane topic would further calm Anton. He adjusted his cowboy hat to keep the sun from his fair skin. "Do we have to get permission from anybody to hike around here?"

"All this is our land," said Anton. "We own about a thousand acres around here. My grandfather bought it years and years ago."

Sam broke off his whistling. "I was looking at your horses the other day when we were here. One of them looks like it has a lot of Andalusian blood."

"It does," said Anton. "You must know your horses."

"I should," replied Sam. "My dad raises Andalusians. There was also a fine-looking, bright-bay mare."

"That's Diego's. She's a Peruvian Paso. Has a wonderful gait. We have a good trail that goes around the ranch boundaries. Would you and

Cliff like to join us someday? We have enough horses. Karen and Krista are good riders, too. Lou could come, too. Does she ride?"

"She does," said Cliff. "Sam has had us out many times, riding up into the Pecos."

"Let's plan on it," said Anton. "Especially after our sniper pals are caught."

They hiked, using the compass to keep them on track when they couldn't see the ridge. They passed a rocky area where a rattler lay basking in the sun.

"Anton," said Sam as he noticed the snake. "Do you want me to get rid of him for you?" He put his hand on his service weapon.

"God, no, not right now," he replied. "If Mom hears another shot, she will freak out. He's not bothering anybody way out here."

They kept on, not disturbing the rattler. The sun shone relentlessly, but the breezes cooled their skin, occasionally sending up a whirl of dust. After a few detours around obstructive land formations and growths of juniper, they arrived below where Pete and his team were busy with cameras, evidence bags, and notebooks. Crime tape, looking incongruous in the wilderness, stretched around the area.

Pete came down to talk to them as they waited beyond the yellow tape. "Look back at your house, Anton," he said. "I would venture a guess that somebody has spent a lot of time up here spying on your family. They'd know when you came and went."

They turned and passed around the binoculars so each could look. They could see the driveway by the garage, the yard light where the camera had been shot out, and the landscaped area leading up to the front door. They saw Anton's upstairs windows, partially screened by a trio of desert willows.

"Son of a bitch," said Anton. "It's enough to make your skin crawl. That sniper is damn good. We're almost a mile from the house. But for today's capricious wind blowing, and Mom's dropping the movies and bending to pick them up, she would have been killed."

"What are you finding up here?" Sam asked.

"Two sets of footprints," said Pete. "Not made today. It's too dry. But fairly recently. One bigger, one smaller. Going to be interesting to compare these with the ones we got at Los Ojos."

"Anything else?"

"Some empty water bottles. Cigarette butts. Shell casings. There's a fairly well-used path over the ridge to the road. There was a pen lying on the path. Might have been dropped when they were running. One of those give-away, realtor advertising pens. Got some tire tracks that look like they are a couple of days old. Our sniper might not be the only one using this hidey-hole, though. There are some food wrappers and trash here, too."

"Terrific view up here—you can see forever," said Cliff.

"We'll be here a while," said Pete. "They're just finishing photographing and documenting now. Then they'll start bagging the stuff for the forensics folks to have a go at them."

"Gandalf, what?" The dog was pulling off to one side. "Probably sees a squirrel." Cliff followed Gandalf along the ridge to a patch of low-growing piñon outside the crime tape. Sam followed along.

"Pete, more tracks," Sam called. "Look out, Cliff. Watch where you and Gandalf go."

Pete joined them and said, "Well, what do we have here? How'd we miss this?"

Near a boulder that would make a good place to sit, a small black lunch tote rested under some brush, its lid unzipped. A half-eaten peanut butter sandwich sat in the top, already being explored by ants. They could see an empty baggie, an apple, and a water bottle inside.

"Gandalf has a nose for peanut butter," said Cliff. "He can smell it a mile off. It's even better than a squirrel."

CHAPTER THIRTY-EIGHT

As Cliff drove into his cul-de-sac Sunday night, he noticed a light on in his house. That's funny, he thought. Must have forgotten to turn it off. Oh, well, it was daylight when I left, maybe I didn't realize it was on.

Just then the light went off. "Somebody's there, Gandalf, where they have no business being." He pulled to the curb and parked down the street, turned out his lights and watched, while snapping on Gandalf's leash. They got out of the car and walked slowly toward his house. He pushed on the front door, knowing that he had locked it. It swung open quietly. He heard the sliding glass door at the back open and saw two figures in dark clothing run out. The hair on Gandalf's neck bristled, and he growled deep in his throat. Gandalf pulled the leash out of Cliff's hand, and went tearing across the room, his nails clicking as he sought traction on the polished wood. He slipped through the door and gave chase. Cliff heard the familiar metallic clink of the side gate latch shutting. Gandalf, now barking fiercely, pawed at the gate, then dropped his nose to the ground and followed a scent trail. Cliff caught up to him and grabbed the leash, hearing running footsteps, car doors slamming and the sound of someone leaving in a hurry on the next street over. He pulled out his cell phone and called Pete, who lived a few blocks away.

When Pete answered, he told him what'd happened.

"Don't touch anything," Pete said. "I'll meet you out front. Don't let Gandalf loose. I'll call this in, too."

Cliff went back through the dark house and waited with Gandalf out front.

"It might have been kids," Pete said when he arrived. "Might be someone looking to steal stuff to feed a habit, but somehow I don't think so. It's more likely to have been one of our villains up to no good." He set down his fingerprinting kit, took out his flashlight, and put on gloves.

"Which light was on—could you tell?" he asked.

"My study."

Pete flipped on the light switch by the outside door with the edge of his flashlight. Through the study door they could see the ghostly blue light of the computer screen. The beam of Pete's flashlight shone on papers strewn all across the floor as they entered the study. Pete turned on the study light, again with the edge of his flashlight.

"These are all my bills and stuff, my to-be-filed pile," said Cliff.

"Can you tell if anything is missing?" Pete asked.

Cliff looked around. His house was messy, but organized—he knew where stuff was. He didn't notice anything missing. Koda still looked down wisely from his home on the shelf. His bagpipe cases were still where he'd left them. He pulled open a drawer using his pen, and saw with relief that his back-up hard drive and his flash drives all seemed to be untouched. Then he frowned and said, "The notebook with my passwords—I keep it in this drawer. It's on the floor now."

Gandalf pulled on the leash, his nose to the floor. "Where does he want to go?" asked Pete. "Maybe he will show us where the guys went." As they followed, Gandalf sniffed his way along the floor, from the front door, to the kitchen, where he seemed especially interested in the refrigerator, to Cliff's bedroom, spending time sniffing the nightstand drawer, to the study, around to the desk and then to the back door.

"Now that's interesting," said Pete, opening the refrigerator door. "Anything missing, out of place? You aren't one of those that keeps their valuables in a fake soda can are you?"

"Not this kid." Cliff stood there looking, and then sucked in a breath. "The hamburger, Pete. It hadn't been opened. There's some missing."

"*Mein Gott.* Hang on to that leash." Pete went to the sliding door and spent some time sweeping the patio and the yard with his light. Near Gandalf's water bowl was a ball of hamburger. "Get something—a baggie to put it in, and a couple of spoons to get it up with. I'll take a sample of the water in his dish. Don't touch anything else yet, but when we're done, clean out his dish good, too. I want pictures. When the team gets here, somebody will take evidence."

Cliff got his car, put it in the driveway, and locked a disgruntled dog inside. "It's just until Pete is finished," he said. "Then you can come back in." Pete went to work, snapping photos, and dusting for prints. They scooped up the meat to be analyzed.

The team from the Crime Investigation Division soon joined them. They did a thorough search of the yard, looking under bushes and plants, but found no more booby traps for Gandalf. "Let me take the rest of the hamburger," said Pete. "They can weigh it with what we picked up to see if any is missing—just to be sure."

"Good idea. I wouldn't eat it now anyway. I'll keep Gandalf on lead when he's outside until I hear back." He sighed. "Damn, this is unsettling. Now I understand why people say they feel violated after a burglary. Sure how I feel. Bloody hell, that's a nasty thing to do to Gandalf."

"I think Gandalf's gotten in their way once too often. These are vindictive, dangerous people we're dealing with. What I'd like to know is, why now? It's been quite a while since you and Gandalf helped bring Krista home. Why the interest still? Do they know you are still involved? And how?"

CHAPTER THIRTY-NINE

Cliff was getting ready for their Celtic band practice at his house on Tuesday night. He shelved the stacks of books which were piled on the chairs and floor. He arranged three chairs and set up the music stands. As he was tidying up he thought about his tickets to the Santa Fe Opera. Because he'd broken up with Ashleigh, he now had an extra ticket. Not that opera was his favorite thing, but the open air venue with its view of the mountains and the excellence of the productions made the tickets highly prized. Lou and Sam would be here soon for their practice. Maybe he'd ask Lou to go with him. If she didn't want to, maybe Sam would.

Lou arrived before Sam, so as soon as she came in and sat down he asked, "Would you like to go to the Opera with me on Thursday? I have an extra ticket."

"What happened to Ashleigh?" She took her violin out of its case and started tuning it.

"We broke up."

"Good. Somebody finally got wise."

"Well, do you want to?"

"I'm already going."

"With whom? Your folks?"

"No, it just so happens I have a date." She shot him an annoyed look.

"Really, who?"

"Not that it's any of your business, but with Anton."

"Well, he didn't lose any time." Cliff put some music on the stands.

"What do you mean by that?" She lowered the violin to her lap. "Sometimes, Cliff, you can really be a pain."

"Isn't he a little old for you? He already has a ten-year old."

"Watch it, Clifford. What's wrong with that? He's only thirty-three. I'm old enough to be Krista's mom. I'd like to be a mother—and anyone would be glad to have a child like Krista. Anyhow, no one has said *anything* about marriage. I have a date, that's all."

"Isn't he a little out of your league?"

"Out of my league? I'm certainly out of *your* league—blond bimbos that you know won't last, and yet you do it all again, time after time. You never learn. Pretty soon there'll be another, and she won't see the real you, and... enough.... Just forget it. I'm going home." With jerky movements she put her violin back in the case and snapped it shut.

"What? Sam's not even here yet. Tonight we're working on the new piece."

"Tell him I have a headache."

"You can't just leave."

"Watch me." She stood and went to the door. "I got a real job offer with a publisher in New York. I think I'm going to take it. Find another fiddler. I don't want to do this anymore."

"What? Oh, come on, Lou!" Cliff said as he followed her. "You're blowing this all out of proportion. We've always kidded each other about our dates and having kids—it's all in good fun."

She whirled to face him. Her eyes looked moist. "Is it? You call this fun? You don't even see that it hurts, do you?"

The phone rang. Cliff stood there, looking at her. It rang twice more.

"Answer your damn phone. Goodbye." She shut the door firmly.

Cliff picked up the phone.

"This is Antoinette from the bookstore. You were supposed to do a book signing on October third. We have a scheduling conflict, so we'll have to cancel."

"Just a minute. I'll get my calendar."

"Sorry, Mr. McCreath. We'll give you a call if we want to reschedule." She hung up.

"Mr. McCreath? Bloody hell. Since when have we been on a formal basis?"

The phone rang several more times, but Cliff stood there, making no move to answer it, letting it go to message. "Hi, Cliff. It's Sam. Say—I won't be able to make it tonight. They've changed my shift. Tell Lou I'm sorry, okay? Gotta go."

"Oh, fine. They all cut out." Cliff sat down on the couch and leaned back, closing his eyes. This is turning out to be a crummy evening. What the hell got into Lou? And why had he said what he had about Anton? He knew before the words came out of his mouth that it was a mistake, something just prodded him to say them. Even as the words tumbled out he knew that Lou would be hurt. Bloody hell.

CHAPTER FORTY

The doorbell rang. "What now?" Cliff got up and opened the door. "Pete, this is a surprise. We're still on for the Circle Sleuths tomorrow, aren't we? Anything new happen?"

Pete didn't say anything. Cliff noticed his serious face and then saw the other officer behind him. "What's wrong?"

"Cliff, this is Sergeant Gonzalez. There has been a development, but not one you're going to like. We've gotten a serious allegation about you sending out pornographic pictures of children."

"What?" Cliff looked at him in disbelief. "You're kidding. No way!"

Pete's face didn't lose its grave look. "We have to take a look at your computer. You can let us, or we can get a warrant."

Cliff moved aside so they could come in. "Take a look. I've got nothing to hide. What's going on?"

"We got emails that appear to be coming from you."

The sergeant sat down at his computer in the study and began clicking away. When Cliff saw the series of pictures he brought up, he felt sick. "Pete...I'd never...I have no idea where this came from. That's gross, and... God, that's awful."

"We'll have to take your computer. When did you last back it up?"

"About a week ago. I try to do it regularly, more often when I'm on a roll, but I haven't written much this week."

"We'll need your backup drive, too. And your tablet."

"Pete, tell me what's going on. How did this happen? My God, who would do this? Who got this shit?"

The sergeant clicked a few more times and printed out a list of a couple dozen or so recipients of the emails and handed it to Cliff.

Cliff looked at the long list with growing horror. "The bookstore—that's why they called. They canceled my book signing. Sam got it, you, Anton, and Karen got it…. Shit, Vidar? I'm sure he'll say plenty. Mike Nelson. Bloody hell, he's on the school board. And Lou, oh, my God." Cliff sat down heavily. "How in the hell can I fix this?"

"I'm sorry, Cliff. but the Chief wants me to stay clear of you until we've gotten to the bottom of this."

"I can't come to the Circle Sleuths, can I? And you probably can't keep me in the loop."

"Afraid not. And Sam's schedule changed. The Chief laid on him, too. He knows you're friends."

"You think that's why somebody broke in here? To do this?"

"Yes, I do. Or at least to get what they needed to pull it off. If there's one good thing about all this, it's that we are getting close to the truth, and they are lashing out like any cornered animal fighting to survive. I told the Chief that, too, but he said we still had to go through the process. Watch your step, Cliff. And keep an eye on Gandalf. These are nasty folks who don't care who they hurt."

CHAPTER FORTY-ONE

Late the next morning Cliff was in the kitchen about half way through his sandwich when the doorbell rang. He was supposed to go out to the Bjornsons' that afternoon to give Krista a dog-training lesson.

I wonder if I'll be welcome, he thought. Maybe I should call first.

The doorbell rang again insistently. "I'm coming. Hang on," he called. When he opened the door he saw a belligerent-looking Anton.

"I thought I knew who you were, but I was wrong. You are contemptible. How could you immerse yourself in such filth?" Anton spat the words out like icicles.

"I didn't do anything. I have no idea how that stuff got on my computer," said Cliff. Actually, he thought he did, but it didn't seem like the right time to launch into the explanation about the break-in with Anton.

"You are no longer welcome at my house or anywhere near my daughter again. For that matter I never want to see you again. I hope you rot in jail."

"I didn't do it. I was framed."

"Yeah, right. Like I believe that."

"Anton…"

"You're a pervert." Anton grabbed him by his shirt, pulled him up to his toes, and said, "So help me, God, McCreath, if I ever see you anywhere near my family again, I'll pound you into the ground." Then he shoved him forcibly back, turned, strode to his car, slammed the door, and roared off down the street.

Cliff straightened away from the door frame he'd hit and rubbed his shoulder. He glanced next door to where his elderly neighbor was looking at him with wide brown eyes. He went back in, slammed the door, and went to his study. Bloody hell. That's the thanks I get. If Anton is that upset, I can just imagine how the other people who got that email are feeling. Damn!

Spotting his dry-erase boards on their holders with all of the suspects, means, and motives, he reached out, grabbed first one and then the other and sent them crashing hard to the floor. Gandalf jumped, looked at him warily, and went to stand by the back door. Cliff sat down at his desk and glared at the computer monitor that was no longer attached to a computer. He snatched off his glasses and threw them onto the desk. He ground the heels of his hands into his eyes, before resting his face on his hands, elbows on the desk. He sat motionless, and felt the rage gradually drain away, leaving hollowness behind.

Minutes passed by before he finally looked up and saw Gandalf waiting by the door, his tail down. Gandalf looked uncertainly at him and tentatively wagged his tail a couple of times.

"Come here, boy," he said. Gandalf came to him and buried his head against Cliff's chest. "I'm sorry," he said, rubbing the wiry fur. "I don't know what to do. I think I have to get out of here for a while."

Cliff decided he should go see his parents and tell them what was going on before they heard it from somebody else. He folded the list of the email recipients and tucked it into his pocket. There was a good chance his folks would be home even mid-day. Both of them were teachers, and neither of them were involved in summer school this year.

As he picked up his car keys, he noticed his half-eaten sandwich. No longer hungry, he dropped it in Gandalf's dish as a gift to make up for his bad humor. Leaving Gandalf in the house he got into his car. The neighbor he'd seen earlier was talking with her neighbor on the other side. They both turned to look at him, shaking their heads as he drove away. "Fine," he muttered. "That ought to get the neighborhood going."

◆ ❖ ◆

He found his parents in their familiar, homey kitchen just finishing lunch.

"This is a nice surprise," Lynn said. "Can I fix you anything to eat? I made plenty."

"No, I've already eaten. I will have some coffee, though." He poured a cup and added some milk before sitting down. "I have a problem that I should tell you about."

"A problem?" said Andrew, glancing at his wife.

"Yeah. I told you about the break in last Sunday night at my house. Well, they got my passwords, and somehow got into my computer and yesterday sent out some really awful pornographic stuff to a bunch of people in my contact list. The police came and confiscated my computer, and they're trying to get to the bottom of it." Cliff looked into his coffee and swirled it around a bit. "I wanted you to hear about it from me, not somebody else." He looked up at them. "I had nothing to do with that crap. It really was sick and awful. I hope you never see it."

"I'm glad you came by," said Andrew. "We were going to come see you this afternoon. We got a call from Mike Nelson just a bit ago."

"Already? The school board? My God, the grapevine sure works fast in this town. I'm sorry, Mom, Dad. I didn't want you to be dragged into all this." He set his coffee cup down, put his elbows on the table, and buried his face in his hands.

Lynn got up and went around the table to hug him.

"We know you didn't have anything to do with it. We *know* you, Cliff."

"You are innocent, and we told Nelson that, too," said Andrew.

"Pete thinks it might have something to do with the Bjornson case. He thinks we might be getting close to solving it, and that the villains are lashing out." He wiped a hand over his eyes and sat back and looked at his parents. "I'm sorry. Will this hurt your jobs?"

"It's not your fault," said Lynn. "You've done nothing. It will be okay. We'll get through this. The police will find what happened with your computer and email. They're good at that."

"Do you know who else got the emails?" said Andrew. "Maybe we should know. Maybe we can do a little proactive work in slowing down the grapevine."

Cliff pulled out the list and showed it to them. They looked it over and shared some thoughts on damage control and how they might approach the different folks.

"By the way," Cliff said. "I have tickets to the opera for tomorrow night. I don't really want to go. Would you like to use them, or do you know anyone else who might?"

"I think we should go, Andrew," said Lynn. "First, I would love to see the opera, and, second, I think it would do folks good to see us out and about. It's a good strategy to counter any gossip."

As he stood to leave, Cliff gave them each a hug. "Thanks, Mom, Dad. Your support means everything to me. I love you."

"We're proud of you. Hold your head high, Son."

"I'm making lasagna. I'll bring some over later. You can't make just a little bit of lasagna."

"You know I love your lasagna. I'd never turn that down. Thanks."

After leaving his parents, he ended up at the grocery store. The supportive, embracing world of home seemed to evaporate as he left it. There was a different feel about being back in the outside world. Walking down the aisle pushing his cart, he saw people looking at him and turn away to talk quietly. Feeling like they must be gossiping about him, he glared at the offenders, and they scurried to other aisles with their carts. At the checkout, he silently dared the clerk to say something. She scanned his purchases and hurried him through. He bagged his items, not caring how they got thrown into the bags and quickly left. It seemed to him when he walked by people there was a hush. Then when he passed, the voices started again. Talking about what a terrible person he was probably.

When he got home again, he felt like he had his own personal dark cloud above his head. Who could he talk to? Certainly not the Bjornsons. Pete and Sam had been told to stay away. Lou wasn't speaking to him. Probably even Koda wouldn't listen this time.

He sat down at his desk again. Damn. He couldn't even work except with pencil and paper. If he wanted to check something over the internet, he couldn't. Bloody hell. He grabbed a book he'd been reading, went out to his patio, sat down in a cushioned chair, and opened the book to where he'd left it before. He stared at the words, lost, not seeing, just feeling misery.

CHAPTER FORTY-TWO

With Cliff's and Lou's absence, the Circle Sleuth group was smaller for their third session. They were meeting in Anton's office where they had better privacy and where the drone videos could be seen.

"Everyone here knows why Cliff is not present today," said Pete when they were settled. "But some of you may not know that there was a break-in at his house Sunday night. Nothing was taken, but his papers were searched. They did get access to his notebook where he kept his passwords, and they got into his computer. I believe there is a good possibility they did that in order to sabotage him with the porn. He called me right away. We dusted for prints and took a good look around. One thing the culprits did try to do was to poison Gandalf."

"Oh, no," Karen said. "Is he okay?"

"Yes. We found the poisoned hamburger before Gandalf did. He's very lucky. There was certainly enough poison there to kill him several times over. An ordinary burglar would have no reason to hurt the dog, so I'm fairly certain that attack was connected to this case."

"Are you serious?" asked Anton. "He might not have had anything to do with it? I threatened to pound him into the ground."

"It really bothers me about Cliff," said Karen. "He needs someone to stand by him."

"He's a predator, and he's created an environment that lets—even encourages kids to be around him. That's evil," said Vidar.

"That's enough, Vidar," said Karen. "I don't believe he did it. Look what happened to Diego—he was innocent and they damn near succeeded in framing him. They were diabolical. Brazen, too, getting into his house like that."

"I find it troubling. It's very hard to believe that Cliff knew anything at all about the porn," said Pete. "But the Chief is under pressure from some of the folks, like the school board member who got the email. I've been told to back away. The department doesn't need any scandal. I did talk with our computer guy—he should be able to get to the bottom of it. I should hear soon."

"It's just too convenient," Karen said, her voice shaking with emotion. "He just happened to send kiddie porn to his friends at the police department, his publisher, and bookstore? Now, really. Give me a break. And, school board members and the district? He was set up. He was helping us, and now he is being harmed."

"Mom. you can't say for certain that it's connected with us."

"Oh, come off it, Son. Krista is already questioning why he's not here, and why can't he bring Gandalf for dog training."

"Because when this spreads, and you know it already is, she'll be tainted and teased. Gossiped about." said Anton, his voice rising in frustration. "She's been through too much already."

"I'm not saying she should see him. What I *am* saying is that his adult friends are not standing by him when he needs us."

"Look at it objectively, from the outside, if you can," said Pete. "We know they got into his computer. We know they got his passwords. Look at who the emails went to—obviously not those you would send the bad porn stuff to if you were that kind of person. Karen's right. The people to whom it was sent are the people who have the most power to destroy Cliff—law enforcement, the school board, his bookseller, his friends. This attack damages his reputation, his ability to make a living, his supportive community. I really feel for what he's suffering, and I hope that our computer forensics guy can get to the bottom of it soon, but, *damn*, until then, my hands are tied."

"Oh, my God," said Anton. "But I *need* to know. I need convincing evidence that he is innocent before I let Krista have anything more to do with him."

"And you should feel that way about your daughter. My daughter has been good friends with Cliff for ten years. Do you think I would let that continue if I didn't believe Cliff is innocent? No way."

"Cliff and I have been friends since we were in high school," said Sam. "Not once have I ever sensed anything but revulsion from him for anyone who would hurt a child. He is haunted by what may have happened to Johnny. It would be completely out of character for him to be involved in that crap."

Anton sighed. "When will you know, Pete, about the results of the computer forensics?"

"Soon, very soon."

"This is a nightmare," Karen said. "It just keeps getting worse. We've been fortunate so far, but they won't stop. We *have* to find out who's behind all this before someone is hurt again or killed."

"Have you thought of any possible suspects who may be connected with your Foundation? Or from among your alpaca business contacts? Is there an area that we haven't considered yet?" Pete asked.

"Mom and I have wracked our brains; we've pored over the grant applications—both successful ones and those who didn't get grants. We even considered all our board member connections. Nothing raises red flags," said Anton.

"I was afraid of that. Well, let's look at who we have left for suspects," said Pete, looking at his laptop. "We did look some more at Brian Cleason. He had told us some lies, but he didn't come back here. He was trying to cover up a little bit of personal drama."

"Any more connections to V Hawk?" asked Vidar. "I'm curious."

"Not that I've seen." Pete replied. "I'd like Anton to show us the videos that he captured with his drone. The first ones are taken the day the alpacas were let out and the rattlesnake planted. The first one will be from the drone, the second from the security system for what it is worth. Then, on the day the sniper shot at Karen, he sent up the drone to capture the guy fleeing from their hidey-hole on the ridge top. Take a good look. Do you know the person, do they look familiar, or can you think of who it might be? If you want Anton to back up, or use slow motion, that's okay, too."

They watched carefully. "I've been over these a thousand times," Anton said. "I've no idea who it might be. I can't even tell if it's a man or woman. It does concern me they seemed to know how to find Krista's room."

"On the other hand, if they came in that door on the deck, whose would be the first room they'd find?" asked Sam. "They needed to get in and out quickly. Maybe she wasn't the primary target. Just convenient."

"Good point," said Anton. "The figures were completely covered in the first videos. Now, up on the ridge, the culprits were not as prepared." They saw the figure shoot at the drone, and then from a farther distance the figure running toward the pickup.

"Cowboy hat, loose clothing, no hair showing. Fairly tall—look at the car for size. Were you able to figure out the make or model?" Karen said. "I'm not good at cars."

"It's a Cadillac Escalade EXT," said Sam. "I know cars. Too bad New Mexico doesn't have front plates. That would have been helpful here."

"Run it again, Anton," said Vidar. "I want to make sure…."

"Do you recognize him?" asked Pete.

Vidar shook his head, some of the tension draining out of his posture as he watched. "No, haven't a clue."

They gathered up their things as Anton turned off the monitor.

"I've been thinking," said Karen. "Until the computer geek has finished the investigation, I think Anton's right in keeping Krista from Cliff. But on the other hand, Cliff needs friends. He must feel terribly isolated. Anton, I want you to do something for me."

"Do I have a choice?"

"Of course. I want you to deliver a package, if you feel you can."

"I can see where this is going. I suppose it has to do with a certain project I've seen underway."

Karen smiled.

"Oh, all right. Guess I might have to do it. I get to pick the time, though. And don't be surprised if he slams the door in my face."

CHAPTER FORTY-THREE

Thursday wasn't an improvement on Wednesday. The black cloud which had formed over Cliff just grew bigger and more dense. He didn't venture outside his house—not even to walk Gandalf, rationalizing that if he threw the ball for him enough he would get exercised that way. He didn't know what to do, trapped in his misery and wondering how the geek was getting along with his computer and why it took so long to get results. He found himself wondering how the Circle Sleuth meeting went, and if they were any closer to finding the villains. Then he grew angry at himself for wondering, for caring about those folks who certainly didn't care about him. Or believe him. God, that hurt.

The violence he'd felt the day before had dissipated. It had moved into a state of depression where nothing tasted good, nothing was interesting on TV, and no book held his interest. He had taken to screening his calls after the first one, in which an angry lady shouted in his ear something about being a degenerate beast, not fit to live.

Gandalf knew something was wrong and tried to cajole him into games. When he didn't succeed, he flopped at his feet and kept him company. He stayed constantly by Cliff's side, seemingly the only being in the world, other than his parents, who cared about him.

His mother called that evening after they'd come home from the opera, using the tickets he'd given them. She wanted to know how he was. He appreciated their belief in him and their concern. True to her word, his mom had brought over some of her lasagna. She'd even added some salad and a batch of brownies. It was all still in the refrigerator, untouched.

They were sorry he'd missed the performance of *The Daughter of the Regiment*. His mom went on about how much they'd enjoyed it. The weather was perfect. Then she'd dropped the bombshell he'd been dreading. One of her friends had snubbed her, and his mother had confronted her, telling her it was a frame up, and she'd better not be spreading any more nasty rumors. He hated to see them dragged into this mess.

And, then to cap it all off, his mom told him that they'd seen Lou. He hadn't told them about his fight with her. Why would he? She'd been there with Anton Bjornson, his mom told him. He seemed such a nice young man. They made a good-looking couple. It was about time Lou found somebody. She was a special girl. They didn't have opportunity to meet her young man, but Lou had waved to them across the crowd.

CHAPTER FORTY-FOUR

When Anton brought Lou home from the opera, she invited him into her casita for coffee. He sat on the couch while she was in the kitchen, and began flipping through her sketch book which lay on the coffee table. He saw first the sketches she had done of Krista playing the piano and some of himself and Karen. He was impressed. Her ability to capture the likeness and have the personality shine through was uncanny. As he flipped further into the book, he came across a series of Cliff playing his pipes.

◆ ❖ ◆

"You found my doodling," said Lou as she returned, gave him a cup, and sank down next to him on the couch.

"What you call doodling shows a remarkable feeling for the subject," he said still looking at the sketches of Cliff.

"Sometimes I feel that subject is a blockhead."

"Do you think he's telling the truth?"

Lou knew immediately what Anton was thinking about. "I've known him for ten years. We've had lots of discussions about lots of things. Everything in me says he would never do anything to hurt a child. Yes, I think he's telling the truth."

"I think I over-reacted. I didn't know about the break in. Mom thinks he's innocent, too. She's already lectured me. Sometimes she makes me feel like a thirteen-year old, grabbing me by my ear."

Lou laughed. "Did she really?"

"No, just metaphorically." He smiled back. "It's hard to be thirty-three and still have your mother chew you out."

"Can you see yourself doing the same to Krista when she's thirty-three?"

"Humph. Probably. Maybe you never get done parenting. Uff da."

The words came out of Lou's mouth before she could stop them. "Tell me about Sonja."

Anton looked at her, surprised. Then he frowned, closed up the sketch book, settled back, and sipped on his coffee. "Sonja...we were high school sweethearts. There was never anyone else for either of us. We were so young, so happy, so much in love. There's a lot of her in Krista. That makes me feel sad and wonderful at the same time. Krista needs a mother, but Mom has stepped into that role better than I ever dreamed would be possible—kind of takes the pressure off. We are lucky that way."

"She's great with Krista. You've worked it out well between the two of you," said Lou.

"I started dating again the last couple of years, but haven't found anyone I want to invite into my life, into my home and family. I'm not willing to share that last little bit of me yet, honestly—maybe partly because I'm afraid it will be snatched away again, but maybe that I just haven't been motivated, haven't met anyone I've wanted to share the whole me with yet. To tell the truth, I'm not really ready to let Sonja go, even though it's been five years. I've thrown myself into my work. That has taken up my energy."

"That can be very satisfying, too. You light up sometimes when you talk about it, especially the development challenges. You thrive on that, don't you?"

He smiled, "I do. The down side of being successful is that there are too many out there who want to get close to you for the wrong reasons. They enjoy basking in one's wealth and status, but they don't have warmth or staying power." He looked at her. "You're easy to talk to, Lou. You're a good listener. Sometimes I've thought about getting married again, and even more often since I met you."

"Hold on," she said. "It's too soon to go there."

"I know. My thoughts aren't clear.... It's not time yet. A wise person once talked to me about settling for less than your dreams, and I don't even know what my dreams look like yet. Maybe dreams are unfolding and we just don't see how. You've become very special to me. Lou. I'd like to get to know you better. Time may show us more. We haven't known each other all that long." He paused, and raised one eyebrow. "But I think you're holding back that little bit, too? There is someone you truly care about, isn't there?"

"I didn't know I was that easy to read." She ducked her head; a curtain of hair hiding her face. "There is someone else, but he doesn't see me that way. It isn't going anywhere. And I'm tired of waiting."

She leaned back into the corner of the couch, tucking her feet under her. "Does love grow... from friendship? Or do you think there's a soul mate for each of us somewhere? Does one find them by choice... or by chance? What happens if we do settle, and then find that special one later? Can a couple decide to make it work, work at it, and not let anyone else come between them? I don't want anything less than a lifetime, Anton, not with anyone."

"Commitment is a choice. Working at a relationship is a choice. There are far worse foundations for marriage than friendship. There's time, Lou." Anton glanced at his watch. "And it is time I left." He put down his cup, stood, stretched, and slid into his coat.

Lou walked him to the door, where he turned and tilted up her chin, kissing her lightly on the lips, then on her forehead. He shut the door softly behind him.

Lou hugged her arms. What just happened? she wondered. Time, time to grow. Odd that he is talking about settling, and I have been thinking about it, too. I do feel better... see a little hope, for what— not sure. He's a good man.

She flipped off the porch light, touched her lips, and thought about Anton. We've spent a lot of time together since we met. He's fun, easy to talk to. Is he looking for a wife... or a mother for Krista? If we did get serious, what would my role be in that house? To carve out a place in that family as Anton's wife, to have any kind of equality or standing—it's overwhelming. Really hard to see. I'd never want for any-thing...except.... Sonja is still there in his life.... And I wonder if Anton has guessed how I feel about Cliff.

Damn it, I really miss Cliff. I wish we hadn't argued. That I hadn't been so angry. Yet, what else could I do? How many years have I been in love with him? How many times have I heard about his blond bimbo *du jour*, wishing he'd see me as somebody he could love? How many nights lying on my pillow, feeling tears crawling down to my ears? Is our friendship over? Is another door opening as that one closes?

CHAPTER FORTY-FIVE

The last couple of days had been hell for Cliff, feeling blamed for evil he had no part in, isolated from friends. Feeling like everybody was pointing fingers at him. Hearing about the opera hadn't helped. How could he stay here? His writing, his music, his friendships—he'd forged a good life here in Santa Fe, but now it seemed so fragile. Cliff started thinking about leaving, of moving to Scotland, wondering how he would fare during the winter months when the wind swept off the Atlantic and the hours of sunlight were so very brief. Would his cousins welcome him again? As a short-term tourist the Scots had accepted him, but how would they treat him over the long haul? That's supposing he could even get a visa. The thought of all of the disruption and the very thought of moving was depressing.

Sitting still-clothed on his bed and full of miserable thoughts, he fell asleep.

♦ ❖ ♦

He was back at the park again. He saw the big sausage fingers wrapping themselves around Johnny's arm, saw him lifted, and slung over the broad shoulder. Cliff tried to run, but his feet were mired in molasses and as fast as he ran, he never got closer. Then the child thrown over the shoulder changed, and it wasn't Johnny anymore. Now Krista was in the clutches of the man, her blond hair flying. She was screaming, "Daddy, Daddy," screaming, out of reach, getting smaller, and then she changed into a little red-haired toddler. Somehow Cliff knew it was his own future child—moving farther away until he was sucked down into a black vortex with Juan and Alfonso, spinning away, never to be seen again. Cliff couldn't move. He couldn't stop it. He struggled....

He woke up, shaken.

◆ ❖ ◆

There was no point in even trying to get back to sleep. The images wouldn't leave his mind and his head began to ache. He turned on the light, filled a mug with milk and heated it in the microwave. He swallowed a couple of aspirin and sipped the milk slowly, holding the warm mug in both hands, staring unseeingly ahead of him. After finishing the milk, he took out his pipes and began to play, losing himself in dark thought and music. Playing from memory, he chose the plaintive laments that suited both his mood and the Uilleann pipes.

I *could* go to Scotland, he thought. They seemed to appreciate my talent. I could go back to Eilean Donan Castle. I loved it there. I've wanted to write a book set in Scotland. Maybe this is the time for that project. I love it, steeped in history, battles, color, mystery, scenery…, highs and lows. And passion—maybe there I can heal.

But that would be giving in, running away. Well, people wouldn't be looking at me like I was some horrible creep. I wouldn't have to run into Lou. Wouldn't have to watch her relationship with Anton grow. I'm pretty sure they have something going. I could leave it all behind. No one would know me. I could start again. But, what to do with Gandalf?

I've had it with sick people in a battle that wasn't even mine to begin with. I was sucked in because I had the big idea that I might be able to help. They will have to solve the mystery themselves. I don't want to do it anymore.

He started another lament, the one he loved so well from Riverdance. It always soothed him. He missed not having other musicians to join in with the harmony part, but then he became lost in his music. At first he didn't even hear Gandalf barking, and then he realized that someone was knocking at the door. Still holding the pipes, he looked through the peep hole and saw Anton.

Now what? Go away. His thoughts tumbled back and forth. I wonder if something has happened. I don't want to see you. Is everyone okay?

He slid the dead bolt back and opened the door. "Go away, I don't need any more dumped on me. You were pretty clear when you told me to stay away from your family. I heard you the first time. Go away."

"I need to talk to you. May I come in?"

"I guess you're going to." He stepped back. "Nothing has happened, has it?"

Anton shook his head and gestured at the pipes. "That sounded good. I saw your lights and heard you."

Cliff unstrapped the bellows from his arm, set his pipes down, and sank into a chair. Anton looked around, set down a bag he was carrying, picked up a pile of books from a chair, put them on the floor, and sat.

"Tell me, truly," Anton said. "Did you have anything to do with that stuff?"

Cliff erupted to his feet, fists clenched. "Bloody hell, no! I told you already. How can you even ask? Disgusting crap. How could anyone hurt a child that way?" He turned away from Anton and began pacing. "I hope to God somebody like that didn't steal Johnny. It gnaws on my mind." His pacing took him by the shelf where Koda stood watch. He took him and held him against his chest.

"I had to ask. I'm sorry. Krista has to come first."

"I understand." Cliff straightened Koda's blue jacket. "She should come first."

"That's not why I've come."

"Yeah, you just happened to be driving by. It's two a.m. I'm not on your way home. I'm not in the mood for company. Especially if you are coming to gloat." He continued pacing.

"Hey, man, I'm not here to gloat."

"I'm going to leave...go away. I think it's for the best. I'm going back to Scotland, to the Highlands. Maybe this'll all blow over." Cliff spoke slowly, as if each thought came from a long way down. "I know several folks there—and my cousins. I can write...I can play music...I could be at home there." He paused and rubbed his temples. "This isn't my battle, Anton. It's yours. I thought I could help, but I've butted in where I wasn't welcome. I think I've made it worse. Pete will figure it out. He doesn't need my help. I don't know what I was thinking—what I could possibly add to what the professionals do."

"And your folks. Will they lose another son?"

Cliff's head jerked up, and he glared at Anton. "Damn you," he swore. "I resent that. That was below the belt, and it's none of your business."

"And Lou will lose a friend?"

"Enough. She's not even speaking to me. She won't care I've gone. I'm sure you'll keep her mind off me," he said nastily. "You can leave now."

"And Krista? And the other kids who read your books?"

Cliff clutched Koda to him and sat down heavily in his chair. "It hurts. It hurts so bad." He swallowed. "I had just come to the place where I thought I could make a difference in their lives. I don't want to stop writing for the kids, but my publisher, the parents, the schools, the bookstores, the kids will run scared. I won't be able to. They'll drop me like a hot potato. It's gone. Pete and Sam should stay away before they get tarnished, too. Why don't you just leave?"

"So you can crawl in a hole and pull it in after you?"

Cliff didn't answer, just rocked a little on his chair, bent over Koda. Gandalf came over, sat by his side and leaned against his knees.

"I had a long talk with Mom this afternoon. We think you need our support. I don't believe you would do anything so stupid." Anton paused and cleared his throat. "I'm sorry I reacted like I did and threatened to pound you. I didn't know about the break in. I came unglued. Lou and I talked tonight, too, after the opera."

Cliff looked up when he heard that, almost afraid of what he might hear next.

Anton leaned forward. "Listen, Cliff. It *is* your battle. It's mine, my family's, Pete's, and everybody's. If you give in to those bullies and run, they win, and pretty soon they will be hurting another family, and crushing someone else's dream into the dust. You might have thought you inserted yourself into the Bjornson battle, but you were already fighting. It has *always* been your battle, since they took your brother. Don't give up the fight." Anton reached down and picked up the bag he had brought with him and handed it to Cliff. "I have something for you."

Cliff took it and looked in the bag. He lifted out a wrapped package, looking questioningly at Anton.

"Go ahead. Open it."

Cliff slowly untied the bow, opened the ends of the wrapping, and slid out a box. He lifted the lid and unfolded the tissue and looked. Nestled in the paper was a needlework bell pull. He touched the design, done in golds, greens, and white—a triangular Celtic knot interwoven with a heart.

"Krista has been working on this for quite a while for you. Mom helped her design it and finish it."

Cliff lifted it out of the box and held it up to its full length. The bell, attached to the ornate brass fittings, tinkled softly. Moisture filled his eyes. "Oh, my God… She couldn't have done anything that pleased me more. Tell her thank you for me. It's very special."

"You can tell her yourself, Cliff. We want you to come over Wednesday. We amateur sleuths are meeting with Pete. We want you to be there, too. I'll call Pete and make it right with him. It's our house. We'll invite whom we please."

"Damn," Cliff could feel tears well up in his eyes again. He blinked rapidly and took a few audible breaths, before he could get out the words. "Are you sure…" he started and then brushed the soft alpaca yarn again, tracing the knot with his finger, swallowing a few times.

"Please, Cliff. Come back. We will fight this together."

"This means so much…. Scotland might have to wait," he paused, and when he could speak steadily, continued, "I know I can't run. I can't give up. I have to stop them. There is no other way. Even if I can't get the computer mess cleared up, I have to try. If I'm ever to have power— I have no choice if I'm ever to live with myself."

"The Circle Sleuths are riding again?"

Cliff chuckled and met Anton's gaze. "I guess we're riding again. You know, Pete thinks that the bastards planted the stuff on me because they are getting nervous, that we know something that they're not happy about. What is it? I keep on thinking about the last Circle meeting when we went over what we know. I don't know what made them so nervous. And how do they even know what we are thinking?"

Anton laughed. "And, he's off and running."

173

CHAPTER FORTY-SIX

On Saturday Cliff got his computers back. The computer geek had found a remote access program which the intruder must have installed from a flash drive. With the passwords, the villain had made easy work of planting the porn and taking control of his computer. The task ahead, convincing the folks who'd received the emails that he was innocent, was challenging. At least now he had the proof.

When Cliff woke up on Sunday, he was drained, but feeling like there was light, that the clouds might roll back, and the sun emerge. Lou filled his waking thoughts, and he knew he had to make peace with her. Her absence left a raw sore in his life. He wasn't at all sure how to approach her without being ignored. An honest apology along with a gift seemed like the best idea. Not something ordinary like chocolates or flowers, but something that would make her laugh. He made a quick trip to the grocery store.

Back home he found scissors and went to work on his creation, snipping and sticking. Then he put it in a paper bag and went to see her.

The little boy looked up out of the watercolor, celebrating his triumph as he took his first steps alone. Lou smiled back, pleased with the joy in his eyes and the life she had created on the page. A knock on the door interrupted. She swished her paintbrush in the water and laid it down. "Just a moment," she called.

When she opened the door, Cliff stood there holding a small paper bag. Pleasure at seeing him was immediately followed by an urge to shut the door in his face. Her intention must have showed as a movement caught her eye. She glanced down and saw that he'd stuck his foot into the door opening.

"Lou, I came to say I'm sorry. I'm sorry that I said what I did. It was stupid, and I was wrong. Can we talk? Can I come in?"

She looked at him. Now what? He looked sincere. She'd missed him, too. But she wanted to make him work for it.

"Okay, just for a minute," she replied, checking her watch like she had places to go and things to do, even if she didn't. She didn't even invite him to sit, just stood with him a few feet inside the front door.

He handed her the bag. "This is for you—well, not really. It's something I have to eat for you."

"Eat for me? What on earth?" She took the bag, noting the strong smell of anise. She peered down into it. "Licorice?"

"It's made out of licorice, yes, but that's not the point. Look at it. Please."

She pulled the crude, sticky shape out of the bag and held it on the palm of her hand. "It's a bird. A black bird." Then she laughed. "Cliff, are you telling me you're going to eat crow?"

He nodded. Giggling, she pulled a piece off and held it up to his lips. He opened his mouth, took it and dutifully chewed. She followed that piece with another, and another. He held up his hand and stepped back to finish what he had in his mouth.

"This can't be much of a hardship," Lou said. "You like licorice."

"I know. The hard part is convincing you to forgive me for being so insensitive and hurting you. I'm sorry. The crow is symbolic. And it did make you laugh."

He accepted another piece she held out to him. "Want to share?" he asked.

She moved back and looked at him warily. "Depends on what it symbolizes."

"For you, nothing. The symbol part is on my side. I just know you like licorice, too.

"In that case, I think I'll have a piece of the wing."

"I am sorry, Lou. I missed you. These past awful days were even more awful because you weren't there to talk to. I like to hear your perspective on things. I treasure our friendship. What you have to say is important."

"I missed you, too. And I knew you had nothing to do with those pictures."

"I was all set to run, to chuck it all, and move to Scotland."

"You were?"

He nodded.

"I'm still thinking about New York," she said.

"If you decide to go, then they'll be lucky to have you. That publisher will have gained a wonderful illustrator. I'll miss you, though. We'll have phone bills from hell."

"I haven't decided yet."

"Will you come back? Be a part of the band? We've an opening for a fiddler," he wheedled. "At least until you decide you want to move, that is?"

"I'll think about it…. Maybe…. I suppose."

One of Lou's sisters came in, looking strangely at the unrecognizable remainder of the licorice on Lou's hand. "What's that? Ooowweee. There's black stuff all over your teeth. Gross."

They laughed as she went on by muttering about some people being really strange.

"Thanks, Lou," Cliff said. "See you Wednesday at the Bjornsons'? Riding with your dad?"

"If you want, you can pick me up."

"I'd like that. See you then."

CHAPTER FORTY-SEVEN

Cliff felt a rare burst of energy for housework. He didn't want to do anything as drastic as cleaning or filing, but it was the perfect day to get out and do yardwork. He opened up the garage door, got the clippers and a rake, and pulled out the yard-waste toter. It was time to do a little trimming. The rosemary looked as though it was trying to take over the blanket flowers. The Russian sage plants were well into their first flush of blooming. A breeze wafted through them, making an undulating lavender wave across his front yard.

He tackled the plants, trimming them away from the walk and dead-heading blooms. As he worked, his mind went to the mystery of who had it in for the Bjornsons. Vidar's role in this whole thing mystifies me, he thought. So many things point to him and tell me he's guilty. But it's like a jigsaw puzzle. Some of the pieces won't fit no matter which way you turn them. It's almost like two puzzles have gotten mixed up and the Vidar pieces form a perfect edge, but the middle pieces have been switched.

He cleaned up his clippings and tossed them into the toter. He drew in a deep breath of the herby rosemary scent. I can tell Pete's worried, too. He's included Vidar in the Circles, but many things seem to bother him. About the kidnapping—Vidar knows the family. He knows their schedules, knows when Krista gets home from school, knows about the security system and the surveillance cameras. It would be easy for him to come around and plant stuff in Diego's house. He could always come up with an excuse for being there.

After picking up the few branches that had fallen during the last wind, he got a broom and cleaned the walk. I don't think Vidar knew about Diego's daughter. They didn't want anyone in law enforcement to know about her. They were probably right. It could have been leaked quite innocently and made it back to that SOB husband of hers. That was kept very close to the family and Maria. For the most part they trust Vidar.

Cliff moved to the back yard and grabbed the pooper scooper. He thought about the ransom spot and the shooting site in Truchas. Both in Vidar's beat. He was in Truchas at the right place at the right time. He has a rifle with a scope in his patrol car. I wonder about the ballistics reports. Pete has never shared that with us as far as I know.

Vidar's in the loop. Knows what we're doing, Cliff thought as he picked up the green windfalls under the apple tree and tossed them. He straightened and surveyed the lawn. The turf grass only needed mowing a couple of times a season. Might as well do it today. He pulled out the lawn mower and plugged in the long bright orange extension cord tethering it to the garage outlet. As the buzzy-hrumm of the mower started, his mind went back to Vidar. We've wondered sometimes how they know what we're thinking. He was up in Los Ojos the day the kidnappers were shot. Could he have gone back again? Said he was watching football with a friend. Vinnie, I think. I haven't heard much about the vehicle, the tire tracks, or the foot prints. And I wonder about the ballistics again. Pete never said.

Cliff flipped the cord out of the path of the mower and started another swath. Motives. That's troubling. Vidar stands to gain financially big time if the family is wiped out. Karen told us about his unhappy childhood. What if Vidar had adopted his father's bitterness and desire for revenge? Could be. Sins of the father and all that. Vidar certainly gets a five out of five on the motive scale. Cliff finished mowing and rolled up the cord. He took off his cowboy hat and wiped the sweat off his forehead.

The rattlesnake? Once again—the knowledge. The figure in the drone video when I was flying it, could have been Vidar, but Anton didn't recognize him, or find any mannerisms that were familiar. Basically all the video showed was an active, thin person in black. Can't tell how tall, how old. Could have been a man or woman. Not even their hair showed.

Some patrol cars carry snake sticks. Probably Vidar's does. I wonder about his schedule—was he on duty? Was he with friends? Who are his friends? All I know is that he watches football with the son of the V Hawk owner. That connection bugs me.

What really bothers me is the scarf. That's about the fifth time I've seen Gandalf pull that or something similar on someone. He's never given it to the wrong person. Vidar wasn't there when I told the Bjornsons about that trick. He was sure upset when Gandalf gave it to him. Sweating. Of course, if it had been stuck in his pocket and left there, it would pick up his scent. Was Vidar supposed to plant it on Diego? That wouldn't do any good now, though. And if that's what he had planned to do, he would have gotten rid of it sooner. I wonder what Karen and Anton think. Hope Krista didn't say anything to Vidar. They've already killed to cover their tracks. And who is 'they'? If Vidar is one, who is the other?

Cliff looked with appreciation at his home, glad he no longer was thinking about going to Scotland and being there for a dark winter. A squirrel, Gandalf's nemesis, scolded him from a tree. Gandalf always chased him, never came within a mile of catching him. The squirrel seemed to know exactly how far away he needed to be, and then he just taunted the poor dog.

Cliff scoured out Gandalf's water dish and refilled it. He let out Gandalf, who promptly found his ball under the apple tree. Cliff threw it for him a couple of times. I wonder if Vidar will be there next time with the Circle Sleuths. Maybe there will be another new development and the missing piece will finally let the others fit.

He went back inside, dropped his hat on the counter, filled a glass of water from the refrigerator door, wandered into his study, sat down, and stared at the photos tacked up on his bulletin board. His eyes went to the picture of Guido Vittorio and his son, Vinnie, talking with the realtors at the Chamber event. I've been to a few of those Chamber events. Networking. Schmoozing. Making contacts. Stand around nursing a drink and being bored-out-of-your-skull events. I'm not good at that kind of thing. Ashleigh had been.

Cliff looked at the blond realtor in the picture and wondered what she and Vinnie found to talk about. He remembered his overheard conversations at the bookstore and wondered if she were that same lady. Probably Vinnie was trying to convince her to put in a V Hawk system. Couldn't have been he was trying to hustle the blonde. She looked almost old enough to be his mother. Actually, she didn't look like the mother type. She looked hard and aloof; maybe that's what'd made him think of Ashleigh. He was well out of that relationship.

He turned on his computer. This real estate connection intrigued him. He brought up an internet map system and began searching the earth map version, looking at the terrain, pinpointing where they had hiked, and getting a better idea of the roads in the area. He remembered the view from up near the hidey-hole. He typed in the address of Anton's home, and looked at the results that came up. Idly he clicked on a lot advertised for sale near that area. He was astounded at what they were asking for it. He checked out other land for sale in the area. Bloody hell! They're sitting on a gold mine. Here's a motive that I hadn't thought of. If someone could get their hands on all that land, that would be a juicy motive for murder. I wonder if Pete's thought of that?

CHAPTER FORTY-EIGHT

Pete leaned forward in his chair, elbow propped on the desk, chin cupped in one hand, slowly flipping the papers in front of him from the contents of the Bjornson case folder. He looked at the ballistics report from the murder of Juan and Alfonso and set it next to the forensics report on tire tracks and prints. The growing suspicion of a bad cop in their midst niggled at his mind. *"Mein Gott,"* he muttered. "To betray the trust placed in you. Can it possibly be true? Abominable. *Scheisse."*

He slammed his hands against the edge of his desk, rolling his chair back. He stood, thrust his hands through his hair and stretched. He turned to the window behind him and pressed his forehead against the glass. His shoulders slumped. "I hate this," he whispered.

Thoughts marched insistently through his head. The footprints at the murder scene were the right size for Vidar's shoes. The tire tracks on the edge of the road could have come from Vidar's Chevy Silverado pickup truck. A truck matching that description had been seen by several people outside the bar where Juan and Alfonso had been. The scarf wrapped around the ransom money had ended up in Vidar's pocket. And, damn it all to hell, the bullets that killed the kidnappers were fired from the same type of 9 mm weapon the police used.

Now what? Can't ignore it. Arrest him? Confront him? Tell the sheriff? Don't tell him? Feed Vidar a lie and see what he does? Warn him? Don't warn him?

Pete straightened and picked up his coffee cup. He went to get a refill, still thinking. *It doesn't seem right. Whoever these blasted jerks are, they have already framed Diego, and now Cliff. Just too pat. But how could they do all this to Vidar? How can he be innocent in the face of all this? And he stands to benefit big time if the Bjornsons are wiped out. Every time I turn around in this case, I keep tripping over Vidar.*

The jangle of the phone interrupted him, and he turned back to answer it. "Schultz, here."

"Pete, I've been thinking," said Cliff. "Poking around on the internet, and I might have found something. I think there's the possibility of a real estate connection. You know the Bjornsons own a big bunch of land by the ridge where the sniper was? That land with its views is worth a tremendous amount of money. That's a big motive for doing away with the owners."

"A real estate connection?" Pete was glad for anything that took his mind off his Vidar quandary. "How would that work?"

"I have no idea how they would get their hands on the land, but it's worth batting around. When you were up on the ridge, didn't you say something about finding a give-away real estate pen? What company was on it?"

Pete sat down and ruffled through the pages on his desk. "Giordano Real Estate. In Santa Fe and Chimayo. Oh, *mein Gott*. That's the name of the real estate business in that strip mall. That's certainly worth looking into." He did a search on the internet. "Owned by Helene Giordano. Elegant blonde, bit cold looking."

"Pete, when I was searching for sites related to V Hawk, I found a picture of the owner and his son talking to a blond realtor at a Chamber mixer. I'll bring that picture when I come to the Bjornson's meeting tomorrow. In the meantime, is there any way you can find out more about this lady?"

"Good idea. We have our ways of snooping into the past." Excitement raced through Pete as he thought, *Yah. Like driver's license, car registration, marriage license, realtor's license, job history. If she's ever been in trouble with the law, we'll know. We need to find some way of getting her prints.* "Thanks, Cliff. See you tomorrow."

Maybe I'll send one of my gals out to hand her a photo and ask if she's ever seen this guy. Then we'll check out the prints on the photo. We'll say he has been involved in a real estate scam, renting properties he doesn't own to folks. Pete pulled up a picture of his cousin, Karl, who lived in New Jersey and printed off a copy on glossy photo paper, slipping it into an envelope.

Now, I think I'll have to bite the bullet and talk to Vidar. Damn.

Pete settled back in his chair, watching the nervous Vidar standing on the other side of his desk. The man really didn't look well. He'd lost weight, even in the short time he'd known him. Pete had stunned him with the few forensic test results he'd selected to share with him. He wanted to see what he would do.

"I think I'd like to be transferred off this case," Vidar said. "I've got a problem... It's just too close to me...very stressful."

"I think that would be a good idea. Actually, I was about to talk with the Sheriff about booting you off the case, anyway. Is there anything that you want to tell me, Vidar?"

"I... Do you.... Please don't say anything to the Sheriff, yet. I can't answer...not yet...soon."

"We will be watching you, Vidar. Don't go anywhere near the Bjornson family or property. That's an order. I have some more results coming in soon. Don't do anything stupid. Someone may be framing you. I want to talk to you again on Friday."

After agreeing, Vidar left the office. Pete's brows drew together as he collected the documents on his desk. He tried to put his thoughts in order for the Circle Sleuths tomorrow. What would he tell them? For that matter, would there be another bombshell waiting for him?

CHAPTER FORTY-NINE

"Vidar won't be attending our Circle Sleuth meeting today. He's requested a transfer off this case, finding it too personal. He has a lot on his plate right now."

"Uff da. Would it be good for me to talk to him?" Karen asked. "I'm sure it's been tough for him."

"I think it would be best if you and Anton let it rest for a couple of days. Okay?"

Karen nodded, "Okay…. I guess."

"I'm bothered by Vidar's connections to the events," said Cliff. "He rates too high on the motive, means, and opportunity scales."

"Vidar would never hurt us," protested Karen. "Don't even think of suspecting him."

"I'm not saying he did it or helped someone do it, but …I don't know," said Cliff. "Diego was framed. I was framed. Could someone be framing Vidar?"

"It's crossed my mind that Vidar may have something to do with it," said Anton. "But I can't see it. What do you think, Pete?"

Karen gave Anton a surprised look. "How can you even…," she said and then trailed off at the look on his face.

"It's just unreal, the way his name keeps turning up in this," Anton said. "Pete?"

"I think Vidar is a troubled young man who is stretched near his limit, like a rubber band. Be careful. If he contacts you, I think it would be good to let me know right away. Be cautious. Rubber bands can snap. Circumstantial evidence doesn't always point to guilt. Some things concern me a lot." Pete paused to sip his coffee. "But we know our villains are very good at framing people. We also know there are at least two people we are looking for. Let's move on.

"First, there is some very good news from our computer forensics guy," Pete said. "He's found proof that Cliff's computer was hacked, and that the porn stuff was planted. We're now able to reassure all of the folks who got that email and those anonymous calls, that Cliff had nothing to do with it. He was a victim. I'm sure that there will be some that can't let go of what they see as a juicy story, and will still be convinced that he was guilty, but we'll do our best to get the truth out."

Karen went around the table with the coffee pot. "That's good. I'd like to string that person up and leave them there until everything important falls off."

"Hear, hear," said Cliff. "I agree with that."

Lou sipped her coffee, and said, "I've been curious. What were you able to determine from the ridge top where the shots came from?"

"We found some interesting evidence. They weren't so careful there. Didn't think they had to be. Didn't wear gloves, or tidy up any evidence they'd been there. Foot prints, tire tracks, fingerprints on several surfaces including the peanut butter sandwich bag, water bottles, and shell casings. When we know who these belong to, then we're going to be very close. First—we haven't found anything up there that tied Vidar to the scene. Some things, like the smaller footprints matched the smaller footprints at Los Ojos. Those two scenes now are tied together. The shell casings are the same caliber of the bullets that were shot at you, Anton."

"Do you know whose prints they are?" asked Anton.

"Not yet," replied Pete. "By the way, do you know if Vidar smokes? We found quite a few cigarette butts up there. Some with lipstick, some without. Forensics should be able to pull information from those soon."

"Vidar never has, to my knowledge," said Karen. "In a way he is very fastidious and health conscious."

"Cliff brought up a very interesting idea to me yesterday," said Pete. "May be a possible motive that we hadn't thought of. We'd been so busy chasing Juan and Alfonso's connections, and the business connections, that we overlooked the fact that your family is sitting on real estate worth enough to make any greedy murderer salivate. Then, we discovered another connection that reinforced it. We found a give-away pen up there from the same business in the Chimayo strip mall—the Giordano Real Estate company. Cliff, show us the picture you found."

Cliff brought out the picture and passed it around. "This is of Guido Vittorio and his son, Vinnie, from the V Hawk Alarm Company. The blonde is the woman, Helene Giordano, who owns Giordano Real Estate."

Sam asked, "Have you had any inquiries about selling any of your land? Any developers knocking at your door?"

"Occasionally they come around," Anton said. "I just tell them we're not interested. How about you, Mom?"

"I don't remember any this summer, and my answer would be just like Anton's."

Lou got the picture, looked at it briefly, turned to pass it along, then hesitated and studied it more. "I've never seen the guys before, but the blonde looks familiar. Right now I can't think of where I might have seen her."

Anton took the picture, looked at it, shook his head and passed it to his mother. She looked and passed it on.

Pete took a head shot photo of the blond realtor from his stack of notes, handed it to his daughter and said, "Does this help?"

"Very distinctive face. Beauty in a kind of cold way. High cheek bones. I've sketched this face, I know," she said. She passed the picture along. "Wait, I remember." She took out her cell phone and scrolled through her photos. "I like to take pictures of interesting folks so that I can sketch them later. This was when I was waiting outside the hospital on the day we brought Krista back." She found several shots and showed them to her father.

"I've seen her before, too, I think," said Karen. "Those eyes. Blue that you could ice skate over. Very unusual. The name doesn't ring a bell, though."

"So, she was at the hospital on that day?" said Pete. "That's very interesting. There were several folks who inquired if they might visit you, Anton, but we didn't let anyone in. Thought you might still be in danger from the shooter—or they might be press looking for a scoop. Maybe we were right to be cautious. We should have her prints this afternoon. We tried yesterday, but the office was closed. Finally, progress. At least, I hope."

"How about the guys in the picture?" asked Anton. "Do you have their prints?"

"Vinnie's father is pretty well out of it and bed-ridden now from what we can find out. We'll get Vinnie's prints as soon as possible," said Pete.

"Do you know if Vinnie has a rifle? Does he have the skill to pull off shots like those?" asked Karen.

"Or do you know if Helene has the skill?" asked Lou.

"A woman?" asked Anton.

"I'm learning to not underestimate what women can do," said Cliff. "A woman would be a possibility."

Karen caught Lou's eye and gave her a thumbs up sign. Lou smiled back.

"Speaking of the woman, something just occurred to me," said Cliff. "On the day they shot at Karen, and Anton sent a drone up to the ridge, the sniper got away in a white truck. Do you know what kind it was?"

"It was a Cadillac Escalade," said Sam.

"Pete, do you remember all the white trucks at the strip mall in Chimayo? One of those was an Escalade."

"Ayeee, I know what you're thinking," said Sam. "Miss Bruton said the realtor had a Cadillac that she took her clients around in."

"Hot damn," said Pete. "I think another piece of the puzzle just got placed. Good work, guys. We seem to be narrowing in on the villains, Everybody, please take special care right now. Since the sniper attack we're getting closer. They're on the run and very dangerous. When criminals like this know they're cornered, expect them to turn and fight back viciously."

Anton followed them out, maneuvering Cliff and Lou aside, speaking to them quietly. "I volunteered to deliver a tapestry and pick up some stuff for Mom at the Ohura Lavender Farm tomorrow and wanted to know if you'd like to come along. It's a pretty drive. I'd really like your company. Gandalf can come, too"

His request met with enthusiasm, and they made their plans.

Chapter Fifty

Vidar put his journal down on his desk and rose to leave for work. Stunned by what was unfolding, he thought about the last few days.

Damn, if that wasn't an interrogation from Pete, I don't know what it was. My boots were shaking. Probably sounded guilty as hell, stuttering and all. I'm glad to be off the case. The whole world seems to be imploding in on me. I didn't know about all of the forensic evidence pointing at me. I'm surprised Pete didn't arrest me. Good thing, 'cause I have a job to do.

Ever since that call I went on last week with that hysterical woman. That floored me—the feelings she described when somebody slipped a roofie in her drink at a bar and then assaulted her. The lethargy, confusion, the blackout, the inability to remember what happened—hell, she could have been talking about me. She was right on.

I'd begun to wonder if Vinnie was doing something to my drinks. My blackouts seem to be happening most often after I'd been drinking with him. Of course I also had problems with drinking Scotch out of my own bottle at home. Vinnie said he didn't like Scotch and wouldn't touch it. Yeah, right, that bastard. Now I know why.

A few days ago I decided to find out. Still hadn't cleaned up from the last time when Vinnie was over. Took an almost empty beer bottle and my bottle of Scotch and gave them to the lab guys to have them tested. Got the results emailed back today with a positive result for a date rape drug. When I read that, I could feel myself boiling inside until I was ready to explode. I'm on duty today, but I'm going to Vinnie's office on my lunch hour. Confront the bastard and find out what the hell's been going on.

Have to tell Pete this afternoon. Damn, it rankles to be used like that. I thought Vinnie was my friend, the little piss ant.

CHAPTER FIFTY-ONE

Anton felt preoccupied and edgy Friday morning as he, Lou, and Cliff drove to the farm and accomplished their task. I'm probably not very good company, he thought, yet they aren't saying anything.

As they left the serene beauty of the lavender fields, Lou buried her nose in her newly-acquired lavender bundle. "Mmm, I love this. Now I know where your mom gets all the sachets she tucks in with her yarn in the studio."

"Actually, I had an ulterior motive for inviting you along." Anton finally marshaled his thoughts into order and now was ready to share them. "I wanted to bounce some ideas off you away from Mom and Krista." He turned onto a side road rising up from the valley.

"What is it?" asked Cliff.

"Let's stop here for a bit. It's one of my favorite spots for sorting out stuff in my mind," he said pulling off into an overlook. Scrubby piñon trees and huge rocks circled the edge of the small parking area. They could see the valley spread out below them, the distant purple of the lavender farm, the bosque with the green of the cottonwoods and willows lining the little creek, and the glint of sun on water as it joined the larger river. Beyond, red and gold sandstone mesas rose from the valley. The sun warmed their skin against the freshening breeze. Off to the southwest they saw a bank of puffy, dark clouds that promised wet weather coming their way soon.

Cliff sat on one of the boulders, tugged his hat lower on his face, and called Gandalf away from his exploring. Gandalf came obediently and sat by him, looking around like he hoped to see a squirrel or some little critter. Lou brought out her phone and snapped several pictures. They waited patiently for Anton to speak.

Glancing from one to the other, Anton stifled a grin, distracted for a moment. After my conversation with Lou the other night, he thought, I have finally seen the light. Cliff is so smart about figuring things out and connecting the dots, yet he is totally blind when it comes to Lou and her feelings. She's a beautiful woman. I'm almost tempted to give him a nudge or a slap upside the head, but some things he'll have to figure out for himself. I hope he does soon, otherwise I just might *have* to do something. He frowned, forcing his mind back to the situation at hand.... Vinnie and Helene....

"I see myself as the protector of my family," he finally began. "I hate these attacks. I want it over. I'm tired of playing their game. Can we do something to bring it to a head? Can we bring them out into the open?"

"Don't do anything rash," said Lou. "I'd hate to see you putting yourself in harm's way."

"I can't stand it. I'm a doer. I can't wait like...like a tethered goat in a lion's cage. They have been too close. Next time they may succeed."

"I'd like to take action, too," said Cliff. "They tried to kill Gandalf, and they threatened me—my career and my reputation. I've wondered if we can find a way to make them dance to our tune, rather than waiting for them to attack again."

"We're pretty sure Vinnie and Helene are the culprits, and it's something to do with the land," said Anton. "I hate to think that Vidar might be involved. Maybe he just talks too much—Vinnie is his friend. Hell, maybe that is even why Vinnie hangs around with him, just using him for information. I've wondered if that's why they always seemed to know what we were up to, or how they found Juan and Alfonso."

"I don't think Pete has told us all he knows about Vidar," said Cliff. "But he really meant it when he said he was like a rubber band ready to snap. You know him well. Do you have any ideas?"

"Something's going on with Vidar that's odd. The tightness is new—not like him. In a way I wish Mom could talk to him. He has a special rapport with her. She's always been there for him in the dark times in his life. His dad tried to pit him against me, so that's colored our relationship. We got along; we did stuff together, but were never what you'd call good friends." Anton picked up a small pine cone and hurled it at a boulder, taking satisfaction in it being smashed to bits. Gandalf picked up another cone and brought it to Anton, hoping for a new game to play.

"What does Vinnie get out of all this?" asked Lou. "What motivates him?"

"Money? Power?" said Cliff. "He's a dark horse. He does seem to use the V Hawk customers as a private resource he can tap into. His own little kingdom. That won't last long if word gets around."

"What are our options?" asked Anton. "Can we set a trap for Vinnie and Helene? Draw them into a net?"

"Setting a trap implies bait. What are you thinking?" Lou asked.

"The bait they would come for is me or one of my family, and I won't risk them."

"Don't even think of setting yourself up as bait," said Lou. "I don't like where you're going with this. It wouldn't be smart to put yourself in danger just to draw them out."

"Cliff, if you were setting a trap, what would you do?" Anton paced back and forth, stopping every so often to hurl another pine cone. Gandalf was very interested.

"Listen to Lou. She's right. The bait doesn't have to be you or one of your family," said Cliff. "There's also the land. What if you made it known that the land was going to be given to the Foundation or something? It wouldn't have to actually happen. Just a rumor that it was. What would that do to Helene?"

"God, I didn't think. It could push her into mistakes. You could be right. It's worth considering."

"They have to be getting rattled," said Cliff.

"I have a feeling that something is going to happen soon." said Anton. "They should know they'll be identified now. They've got to worry about the possibility of a drone video, but they don't know what it might show. They know they left evidence all over the ridge."

"I feel something's imminent, too. There's a closeness in the air," said Cliff.

"That's the storm moving in," said Lou. "It's supposed to be a big one. Didn't you guys see the forecast?"

"No, I wasn't in the mood to sit and watch the weather this morning," said Anton, exhaling a deep breath. He finally stopped his pacing and sat on a rock. Gandalf went over and pushed his head into his lap, and he obliged by scratching his neck. "Thanks, guys. You know, when you choose people to bounce ideas off, you probably already know pretty much what they will tell you. That doesn't mean it isn't helpful. I really wanted to stomp right over to Vinnie's and pound somebody. I guess I knew you would reason with me and calm me down."

CHAPTER FIFTY-TWO

When Vidar came into Vinnie's office, the secretary was out to lunch. With no one to challenge him, he walked softly toward Vinnie's office. The door stood ajar. He saw a blond woman seated in Vinnie's chair watching a bank of screens. With a shock he recognized his own voice talking in a video. He was talking to himself, in despair about why he couldn't remember, and thinking he may have done something horrible. Vidar stood there aghast listening and slowly pushed the door open. The woman looked up in alarm.

"Vidar," she said as she switched to another screen. "I'm sorry. Vinnie is out." She reached for her coffee mug and knocked against it. Some sloshed over, but she caught it before it tipped and spilled it all. She grabbed some tissues to wipe up the little puddle.

"I don't remember meeting you. What is your name?"

"Helene Giordano. I feel like I know you. Vinnie has told me so much about you."

"I bet he has. What was that video?" he asked. "Turn it on again."

"Just an old movie," she replied. "It was boring. I don't wish to see any more of it."

Vidar heard a slight sound behind him. He whirled, but too late. Vinnie clobbered him over the head with a bronze statue of a hawk. Vidar sank bonelessly to the floor.

♦ ❖ ♦

"Now what should we do, Anita Helene? How can we explain this to him?" Vinnie asked.

"Don't call me that." Helene said. "You know I hate that name." She came up to Vinnie with a handful of tissues, taking the statue from him, and wiping it off. Then she set it back on the secretary's desk and tossed the tissues into her hand bag before continuing. "I think we should go ahead with our plans. It's just a few days sooner than we expected. Almost all of the ground work is in place."

"How about the documents?"

"I picked them up from Tony this morning. They really look authentic. Never know they aren't. He did a good job. We just need to add the dates and signatures. All that lovely land was owned by my late husband, Walter, not that traitor, Edvar." She gave a sarcastic laugh. "Imagine that."

"And if they won't buy the fact that his lovely widow now owns the land?"

Helene shrugged. "Plan B. His late son had arranged to sell through Giordano Real Estate, recommended by his good friend, Vinnie. And the developer—in our pocket. We will be rich, Vinnie. Rich beyond dreams. I can take you all over the world. Now, Darling, why don't you run along and get that bitch, Karen. I can hardly wait to finish her off. Thanks to you, it's all coming together. I've waited a long time for this day." She slipped her arms around Vinnie's waist.

He grabbed her by her butt and pulled her against him, rolling his eyes behind her back. Then he leaned away, kissed her, and smiled. "We have work to do. I'll help you move this idiot into our van in the garage. He should be out for a while—until his suicide. You can drive the van out to the crossing. I'll take his truck and meet you there with Karen. Leave the stuff on the desk. It'll be okay. You're right. All our good plans are paying off." He bent, took Vidar's gun from its holster and handed it to Helene, who tucked it into her bag. He reached down again, took Vidar's cell phone, and put it in his own pocket.

CHAPTER FIFTY-THREE

Vinnie drove Vidar's truck into the Bjornsons' yard and parked near the studio, but away from the window. Diego's truck was gone from its usual spot. A quick look around showed no one about. He got out carrying an empty beer bottle he'd found in Vidar's truck and went into the studio, leaving the door open. Karen was alone, listening to some kind of classical choral music turned up to a good volume and working on one of the big looms. Vinnie stood for a few moments watching her rhythmic movements as she worked the weft colors into her design. He grasped the bottle by the neck and crossed the floor silently behind her. He slammed the bottle down hard on her head, and she fell onto the floor, not moving. Grunting, he bent and picked her up with her midriff over his shoulder. A noise stopped him, and he turned; then held motionless, listening, but the music was the only sound. Noticing one of her shoes on the floor and figuring that must have been what made the sound, Vinnie carried her out the door and dumped her onto the floor of the back seat of the truck. With another quick look and a satisfied smile, he got in, pulled out past the corrals, and was gone.

Krista's eyes grew huge as she saw him leave from her vantage point behind the curtain of the window seat in the hall. Then, pulling her cell phone out of her pocket, she sucked in a big shuddering breath, and ran yelling down the hall to the kitchen and Maria.

❖

Before he reached the highway, Vinnie pulled over and punched out a text message on Vidar's cell phone. "That should do the trick," he said as he finished. Glancing into the back to see Karen still lying quietly, he drove on.

CHAPTER FIFTY-FOUR

Anton's phone chirped and vibrated, signaling a text message received. He looked at the screen. "Oh, oh, Vidar. Wonder what he wants…. What the hell? Look at this! My God!" He read the message out loud, feeling like the blood was draining from his head.

> "sorry just cant take more. going crazy. done terrible things. I killed Sonja - was no accident. missing chunks of time. Blackouts. think I shot u. just woke up and I have shot Karen. think she's dead. going to shoot myself. Don't let us lie here - at Gomez Crossing. Sorry. Vidar"

"No, is it really Vidar?" Lou said. "Can it be true?"

"It's wrong. Vidar was with me all day the day Sonja died. That's burned into my memory. This is all wrong. It says Gomez Crossing, but you can't get cell phone coverage there—something about the valleys and peaks—so it didn't come from there. But it's coming from Vidar's number…. How the hell? This must be a set up. Damn. They built the trap first."

His phone rang. "That's Krista's ring." He answered it.

"Daddy, Daddy," her frantic words tumbled over each other. "A man took Gramma. He hit her, carried her out 'n put her in a truck that looked like Vidar's, and drove off. I was just coming into the studio and saw him take her. I hid, just before he saw me."

"Who was the man? Was it Vidar?"

"No, never saw him before. He was dark-haired, tall, about as old as Vidar, I think."

"Was Vidar with him?"

"No, didn't see Vidar at all. This man was alone."

"Where are you? Who's with you?" Anton asked.

"I'm home. Maria is here with me."

"Stay there. Go to the safe place we talked about. Don't either of you let the other out of sight. Don't let anybody in, unless it's Pete or one of us. We'll call first. I'm going to call the cops now. Love you, Honey. Do as I say."

"Daddy, don't go after them alone." Krista sobbed.

"I'm not alone. Cliff, Lou, and Gandalf are with me. We'll bring Gramma home." He hung up.

◆ ❖ ◆

Cliff was already dialing Pete.

"Schultz, here."

"It's Cliff. It's an emergency. Anton and Lou are with me. I'm going to put you on speaker phone."

Anton told Pete briefly about the text message and Krista's call.

"I'm on my way. I'll radio Sam. He's closer, should arrive first. Be careful."

They all got back in the car. "Should we drop Lou someplace?" Cliff asked.

"Bite your tongue. I'm not baggage. I'm part of this group. I'm coming with you."

"Ouch. I guess you're coming with us."

"Is this crossing the place where the road goes through the arroyo— that floods when it rains in the mountains?" she asked.

"Yeah. Vidar and I used to go there all the time. We even flew a drone over it once when it flooded. Got some wild footage."

"I don't like this, guys. Look at the sky—how quickly the clouds are moving in," Lou said.

The sun had disappeared behind the changing clouds. Off to the southwest the sky was dark and foreboding with rain streaks slanting down. They turned off onto a gravel road. An idle thought came to Cliff about how amazing it was to have such a lonely wilderness so close to a metropolitan area. The road went over a series of ridges, up and down, through scrubby brush and piñon pines. Anton, tense and focused, drove his four-wheel drive as fast as he dared.

"It's hard to make a plan when the script is dumped in your lap," said Anton. "We didn't know this scene had already started."

"They're making mistakes," Cliff said. "They don't know they messed up about no signal being there for cell phones. And they probably assume you're alone. They don't know where you are or how long it will take you to get to the crossing. They don't know that Krista saw them take Karen, so they lost the advantage of that surprise. Also, Krista's a witness that knows Vidar didn't do it. They underestimate our determination and working together."

Lost in apprehension of what might await them, they were silent, hearing only the sounds of the car bumping over the rough road, the rain beginning its patter on the roof, and the intermittent swish of the wipers.

CHAPTER FIFTY-FIVE

When Vinnie got to the crossing, Helene was waiting by the van, which she had pulled off into an open area not far from the bank of the arroyo near where the road dipped to cross the wash. He pulled up next to her and pulled Karen out onto the ground. Then he pulled Vidar out of the van. Helene moved the V Hawk vehicle around the bend, past the wash. Karen, lying in the cold rain, moved, groggy and groaning, but waking up. Vidar was still quiet. Vinnie parked the red truck in the crossing.

"It's coming together perfectly," Vinnie said. "There's a lot of rain in the mountains and the wash will flood and complicate matters. The law won't be able to figure out this wasn't the simple murder - suicide that it would appear to be." He wiped all of the surfaces in the pickup that he may have touched.

"Even if the flood doesn't come, it will be successful," Helene said, adjusting her latex gloves. "When he gets here I'll kill him first, then Karen, then Vidar."

"Why wait to kill Karen? She is waking up. Do it now. It will just make Anton crazy."

Vidar moaned and moved. Karen rose up onto one elbow. "You—I remember who you remind me of—Anita, Vidar's mother. Those cold blue eyes, they're hers."

Helene laughed. "Took you long enough, Sister," she said sarcastically. "No longer Anita Bjornson. Now I'm Helene Giordano."

Vidar rolled over, lifting his head and blinking the rain out of his eyes. He stared at Helene. "What?... My mother? No…. You left me with that drunken…. You framed me for murder? Why?"

"Her," Helene pointed at Karen. "She dumped your father for that holier-than-thou Edvar. I got trapped into a hell of a marriage and had you, the miserable spawn of that devil, Walter. It's all her fault—making Walter crazy. I could have been happy if it hadn't been for her. Because of her, Walter beat on me. I couldn't take it anymore."

"You left me," Vidar said, "Not my mother…" He shook his head as if to clear it. "I'm still out of it…dreaming…. Why am I seeing her? Hearing her? Why can't I wake up?"

"You are awake, you idiot. I never wanted you. I didn't want any of it. He never appreciated me. It was always her. She made him crazy. He never cared if I lived or died. Rotten son of a bitch. Yes, I got out of there. Good riddance. I wanted to make something of my life, not be a slave to a sniveling brat."

Helene glared at Karen. "It's *your* fault. You took everything from me. I wanted to make you suffer. And I did. I saw my chance with that goody-two-shoes, Sonja."

"Oh, my God! But that was an accident," cried Karen.

"No, I was the first one by after she blew that tire. She begged me to help. I pushed her off and laughed while the car bounced down that cliff. I hated all of you. I wanted to see you lose everybody and everything— and then kill you. I want to see you all dead."

Fascinated by all the vitriol spewing from Helene's mouth, Vinnie didn't hear the car coming at first. Then he ducked and moved out of sight behind the red truck.

The afternoon sky grew ominous. Dark, heavy clouds and rain obscured the mountains. Lightning flashed and distant thunder rumbled.

Chapter Fifty-Six

"Here goes." Anton said as they neared the crossing. "For Krista, Mom… and Vidar."

"For Johnny. So help me God, we'll stop them this time," said Cliff.

"Amen to that." said Anton. "Get down out of sight now."

Anton slowed as he got to the clearing and parked on high ground. Ahead the road descended through an open space in the brushy scrub before going down the bank and crossing the arroyo. Vidar lay propped up on an elbow on the ground in the clearing. Karen sat nearby. A tall blond woman stood by them. Anton told his passengers what he could see. "Mom is there, and Vidar. Helene has a gun. I don't see Vinnie."

The rain began to fall steadily. Thunder rumbled nearer.

Anton got out of the car and began walking down the slope.

"Anton, no!" Karen called, touching her hand to where she'd been hit on her head. "She's got a gun. Vinnie's here, too."

Cliff and Lou threw open their doors and stepped out leaving Gandalf in the car. Thunder rumbled closer. God, Cliff thought, this is not a good place to be. It's been raining hard in the mountains. What rain falls up there is all going to rush down. This arroyo won't be dry for long.

Helene aimed the gun at Karen, who struggled to get up. Anton began to run.

Cliff started toward Helene. A noise in the brush startled them all. He paused, heart pounding, not knowing what was coming. The crashing through the undergrowth grew louder. The dark afternoon sky sizzled with blue, surreal light; immediately thunder cracked overhead. Several deer shot out of the bushes and bounded by them. Gandalf pawed at the window of Anton's car, barking sharply with displeasure at being left behind.

As Helene was momentarily distracted by the deer, Vidar exploded into life, clumsier than usual, but filled with rage. Karen had been more of a mother to him than this woman ever had. He sprang toward Helene, knocking her arm just as she pulled the trigger. The shot went wild. They struggled over the gun, and she pulled the trigger again. Desperately Vidar wrenched the gun away from her and threw it into the wash where it lay amid a growing stream of water. Standing there frozen, Vidar stared at Helene. Then, in slow motion he crumpled over and collapsed onto the ground. The rain ran red down his uniform shirt.

Anton reached his mother and pulled her into his arms. Lou ran toward Vidar.

Where the hell was Vinnie? The thought fleeted through Cliff's mind as he threw himself at Helene, grabbing her and taking her to the ground with his momentum. The angry, angular body, spewing obscenities, writhed beneath his in the mud and rain, aiming for vulnerable parts. He tried to get her face down, struggled to capture her hands to force them behind her back. She flung her head back, catching his chin. Damn, she had a hard head. He heard a scream ending abruptly, followed by a voice that stopped him cold. Oh, shit! he thought. I think we found Vinnie.

"I'll kill her. Let Helene go. Stay back!" Vinnie had snuck around the truck and come up behind Lou as she bent toward Vidar. He'd grabbed her and held her tightly against him with one arm. With his other hand he held a knife at her throat. He backed toward Vidar's truck in the arroyo. Cliff rolled off Helene.

Sam arrived on the scene, stopping next to Anton's car. The flashing red and blue lights lent a bizarre dimension to the tense tableau. He jumped out of his patrol car, pulling his gun smoothly. "Officer down at Gomez Crossing," he said into his radio. "Suspect armed with a knife, has a hostage. Need back up. Now!"

Gandalf pounded his paws on the window again. With one hand Sam opened the door, letting Gandalf free. He burst out of the car and came to a stop at the clearing's edge just past Sam.

"Throw that gun away, or I'll slit her throat. Stay back," Vinnie shouted.

"It's over, Vinnie," Sam said. "Let her go." With steady hands he aimed his gun at Vinnie.

"No. Drop that gun, or I'll kill her. Helene, let's go."

"You really *don't* want to hurt her." Sam's voice was calm and firm. "In a minute this place will be swarming with cops. Don't give yourself more trouble than you already have."

"No, we'll take her with us. Drop it, or she'll die. Helene, now!"

Cliff watched Vinnie carefully, his muscles tensing as he readied to spring at him when he had a chance. He's dead if he hurts her. Murdering creep destroying lives, he thought. He won't get away with it.

Helene got to her feet and headed toward Vidar's truck, but even as she started, the stream of water running across the road in front of her rapidly expanded. Suddenly a wall of water, pushing trees, brush, and rocks burst upon the road, startling them all with its explosive power. The water filling the wash with churning debris hit the truck, sweeping it sideways down the arroyo.

"You... Anton, your car keys," Vinnie screamed over the roar of water. He panicked as the odds changed, and the loss of Vidar's truck narrowed their chances of escape. The rushing turbulence had risen rapidly. "Helene, get his keys. Gotta get the hell outta here." A small rivulet of blood appeared on Lou's chin, running down to be diluted and washed away by the rain.

"Let her go," yelled Sam. "Too many people know it's you, Vinnie. Give it up. There's no way you can escape. Stop, before you dig your hole even deeper."

Unexpectedly Gandalf sprang into the fray with a ferocious growl. Vinnie's grip on Lou loosened as he turned to face the new threat. Lou picked up her feet and let her weight pull her out of Vinnie's slippery grip. Gandalf leaped and latched onto Vinnie's arm. Vinnie swore and cried out as strong teeth ripped his flesh. He swung the knife at Gandalf, and they heard a yelp of pain. Gandalf fell near the swirling water.

Anton grabbed Helene and brought her to the ground.

"Hands behind your back, Helene." Sam tossed his cuffs to Anton who snapped them on her wrists.

As soon as Vinnie lost his hold on Lou, Cliff lunged, knocking him away from her and tackling him to the ground. Vinnie's arm hit the ground, and he lost his hold on the knife.

Anton dragged Helene none too gently away from the edge of the arroyo. Sam darted in and kicked the knife into the water, keeping his gun on Vinnie, waiting for a clear shot.

Lou rolled away from the water's edge, but she was still too close. Cliff noticed with horror that the arroyo curved here and that the bank Lou lay upon was being eaten away by the water careening below it. That bank a little upstream began to crumble into the water. The crumbling came closer and closer, reminiscent of a curling wave.

Forgetting Vinnie, Cliff scrambled forward and grabbed Lou's hands in a desperate grip. He heard her frightened whimper and saw the terror in her eyes. She struggled to get up, but the filthy, foaming water swirled around her legs, sucking away her shoes. The ground shook; he knew it was from boulders moving along the arroyo. Cliff slipped and went down on one knee, then flat. He felt the power of the flood tugging Lou and struggled to hold onto her wet hands.

An uprooted piñon spiraled near the bank and scraped over Lou. She screamed and choked in a spray of water as one of her hands was torn from his. More of the bank crumbled away. Frantically she reached back toward him. Cliff caught her wrist, digging in and locking on with desperate strength, feeling the bones in her wrist. He felt her hand close about his wrist in return. "Hang on, hang on!" Cliff felt his body sliding slowly toward the flood. Then he felt Anton grab on to his feet and dig in, pulling back, adding his strength to drag them away from the water. They inched back. Cliff's muscles strained, protesting against the pull of the current on Lou's legs. He felt the gritty, wet scrape on his stomach as his shirt rode up in the mud.

Vinnie wasn't giving up. Out of the corner of his eye, Cliff saw him grab a branch. Arm bleeding and face ugly with rage he swung the branch up over his head aiming to bash Cliff with all his might. A shot rang out, and the momentum of Vinnie's swing was arrested. Red blossomed high on his chest.

Cliff felt Anton grabbing his belt, lifting up and back. The leverage was enough to get him to his knees again. Sam, still pointing his gun at Vinnie, added his strength to the chain. Gandalf scurried, bleeding, toward them.

Vinnie screamed, teetering as the undercut bank gave way beneath him. He toppled backwards into the dark, swirling water. A fallen tree raced by, hitting Vinnie and ending his scream abruptly. As they watched from their backwards scramble, powerless to do anything, the tree rolled and forced Vinnie under, entangling him in its branches. It hung there for a moment, then moved on, out of sight. The human chain pulled Cliff and Lou and struggled to firm ground beyond the reach of the rushing water. A thunderclap broke overhead and rumbled away into the distance. As that sound diminished, a police siren came closer.

Karen had pulled Vidar a little farther away from the water. She was now cradling him in her arms. Her hand, pressed against his chest was red with blood. With every beat of Vidar's heart his life ebbed away. Anton knelt beside them. Sam came over, his shoulders slumping in defeat when he saw there was little he could do.

Vidar opened his eyes. "You ...more a mother...she made me... think I was... crazy. Search... Vinnie's office ...my place." He gasped as he struggled to breathe. Red trickled from his mouth. Karen leaned over him, shielding his face from the rain. "Aunt Karen.... Love you." His eyes closed as his head turned toward her breast. A few seconds later his tortured breathing stopped. Karen started a keening sound, rocking Vidar's body slightly back and forth. Anton put his arms around them both, resting his head against hers.

Then Sam went to where Helene sat cuffed, looking old and gaunt, the starch taken out of her spine. He moved her to his car, searched her, and then shoved her into the back seat. Handcuffed, belted in, she still muttered and cursed. Sam tucked a blanket around her and moved back to Vidar. Pete's car pulled up, lights flashing. They could hear the siren wails of more patrol cars coming closer.

Taking in the situation with a glance, Pete noted the immediate danger was over and the water seemed to have stopped rising. His sight fell on his daughter, now standing surrounded by Cliff's arms, held tightly against him. Then he strode to Vidar and Karen, his face somber. "Sam, what happened?"

The rain was diminishing somewhat. Nature's fury still rolled down the arroyo, a little quieter now, a dark, menacing mass following the first roiling onslaught of trees, brush, and rocks.

Gandalf hauled himself over to Cliff, trembling violently and whimpering. Cliff looked him over and found the cut on his shoulder. He pulled off his shirt and pressed the cloth against the wound. "Hush, fellow. Good brave dog."

After a bit, he checked to see if the bleeding had stopped. "It's a long cut, but I don't think it's deep," he told Lou.

The patrol cars, whose sirens they'd heard, arrived. After a quick briefing by Pete, the officers began checking the arroyo for Vinnie. Sam and Pete eased Vidar's body away from Karen and covered him. From there Pete turned to his daughter, pulling her into his arms with a long, thankful hug.

Sam checked out the goose egg on the back of Karen's head. "Karen, did you lose consciousness?"

"Yes, I woke up just after we got here."

"Anton," Sam said, "She should get to the hospital and be checked out. You don't want to mess with a concussion."

"I don't want to go to the hospital."

"Mom, you don't have a choice. I'm taking you."

Cliff looked at the cut on Lou's chin. "You're going, too," he said. "I think you might need stitches."

"And a tetanus shot if you haven't had a recent one," said Sam, coming back from his car with some blankets from the trunk for each of them. Anton and Karen huddled under theirs and went to get into the car.

Cliff pushed the blankets into Lou's arms, swept her up and carried her. Gandalf followed.

"I can walk. Put me down."

"I know you can, but you lost your shoes. Humor me. Here we are. Open the door." Gandalf scrambled in after and cuddled under their blankets with them.

Anton started the engine. Karen sat dazed, clutching the blanket, her hair stringy and dripping. Anton leaned over the console to hold her, their faces wet with rain and tears. The pounding of rain on the roof dwindled to a patter. Steamy heat filled the car; the windows fogged up faster than the defrosters could clear them. Eventually their hugs became less clenching. Their breathing quieted.

Karen roused from her blanket and said, "Let's go. We need to get dry and warm. Krista is going to be worried sick."

Pete came over to their car. Anton rolled down the window part way. "I'll come over in a few days if I may, Karen. It may be quite a while—a lot of wrap-up to be done. Vinnie's gone. Helene's in custody. Rest easy now. You're finally safe."

"Please come, Pete, and Sam, too, if he can."

"Sam will be on administrative leave, but I'll see."

CHAPTER FIFTY-SEVEN

As soon as their car reached a place with phone coverage, Anton called Krista and told her they were safe. He had decided that he would tell her about Vidar later. He asked Maria to get changes of clothing ready for himself and Karen to take with them and to add a couple of extra sweatshirts for Cliff and Lou. They would be there shortly and pick up Krista so she, too, could be with them when they took Karen and Lou to the hospital.

When Karen and Lou were safely in the hands of the hospital staff, Cliff told Lou he would pick her up in a little while. Anton drove to the vet's where Cliff left Gandalf to be checked out and stitched up. Krista petted Gandalf, kissed him, and said she'd see him soon. Then, they went to Cliff's house and the men finally had a chance for hot showers and warm, dry clothes. Krista found the hot chocolate packets in the kitchen and had hot drinks ready for them.

As Anton and Krista left for the hospital, he searched for the words to tell her what had happened. "Your grandmother will probably have to stay overnight, like I had to when I was shot. It was Vinnie you saw who hit her over the head and took her off in Vidar's truck. The doctors always worry about people who've been hit on the head, and they just want to make sure she will be okay. She probably will have a headache for a few days. We'll need to take special care of her."

Krista nodded solemnly. "Are we safe now, Daddy? Are all the bad guys really caught?"

"We don't have to worry any more now. There was a flash flood at the spot where they had taken Gramma and Vidar. Vinnie, the guy who stole Vidar's truck, got swept away in the flood. They're still looking for him, but it's pretty certain that he drowned. Pete will let us know when they find him."

"He couldn't just swim away and come back and hurt us?"

"I don't believe so. We saw him get hit by a tree and go under. I don't think he will be coming back."

"How did Gandalf get hurt?"

"Gandalf was very brave," continued Anton. "Vinnie had a knife and was going to hurt Lou, and Gandalf surprised him and grabbed him by the arm. That's when he got hurt. We owe that dog a lot, Krista."

"How about the other bad guy, Daddy?"

"The other one turned out to be a woman. A very bad woman. She's been arrested, and will go to jail for a long time. You knew that the two who kidnapped you were murdered?"

Krista nodded. "Pete told me. He said I didn't have to worry about them anymore, that they were gone, and that they could never steal any more little girls."

"I think the bad woman was the one who killed them." He pulled into a parking space at the hospital and turned off the engine. "This is very hard for me to say, Krista. That woman… she tried to shoot your grandmother. But Vidar jumped her and made her miss. They fought over the gun, and she shot again. That time she hit Vidar."

"Is he okay? Where is he? Is he in the hospital, too?"

"He died, Sweetie." Anton swallowed. "Vidar gave his life to save your gramma." Krista's wide blue eyes filled with tears. He brushed one away that rolled down her cheek. "He was very brave. Because of him, your gramma is still alive, and possibly he saved my life, and Lou's and Cliff's."

"I didn't want him to die." She cried against him, clutched in the circle of his arm.

"Neither did I. He was family." Krista held tightly to Anton, absorbing the enormity of Vidar's actions.

211

"Daddy," Krista said as she straightened up and looked into his eyes. "Does that mean that Vidar is in Heaven now with Mommy and Grandpa?"

Tears welled into Anton's eyes. "Oh, Sweetie, it surely does. They're together now." He squeezed her hand. They got out of the car and went hand in hand to visit Karen and give her some healing hugs before they went home to Maria and Diego.

◆ ❖ ◆

Cliff picked up Lou from the hospital and drove her home so she could finally get cleaned up. He said he'd pick her up in an hour, and they'd go eat.

As he drove away, he thought about where they might go and realized he wasn't in the mood to go to a restaurant and be around a lot of people in a public place. He just wanted to be with Lou. He felt a need just to hold her.

He stopped instead at his favorite grocery store and picked up some containers of hot soup, filled some boxes with all of the salad delicacies that he and Lou liked, and added a loaf of special walnut-blue cheese bread. When he went back to pick her up, she was ready.

"Mmm, something smells good," she said as she got in the car.

"I decided to get some take out. Is that okay?"

"Yes, better actually."

Shortly, they were settled in his kitchen, enjoying their feast. When they were finished, Lou stood up and put the dishes on the counter.

Cliff came up to her and took her hand in his. "I'm sorry," he said, lightly brushing the bruises on her wrist.

"You saved me. It's a good hurt."

"God, I was scared."

"Me, too. I'll never think of flash floods lightly again."

He pulled her into his arms. "I just need to hold you." Her heart beating against him, the warmth of her body nestled against his, the clean scent of her shampoo—he drew it all in. He could feel her hands idly stroking his back. He closed his eyes in sheer pleasure, savoring the moment. They'd come so close to losing each other. But this—this was good. She hadn't been snatched away. He'd found the power to hold on to her. Friends helped, it was true, but he held her. His Lou.

His eyes popped open…. His Lou? He set one of his hands against her cheek, tangling in her hair. He raised her chin and looked at her face. Her lids fluttered open, and he marveled at the luminous softness of her gray eyes. Wow, all this time. Why have I never noticed before? How beautiful she is! A little smile played on his lips, and he whispered, "Lou?"

His eyes shut again as he kissed her softly, tentatively, then as her lips opened under his, with joy and wonderment. He knew she could feel his physical reaction to her, but she wasn't pulling away. Her response just raised the heat. His hand slid through her hair as their kiss finally ended, to cradle the back of her head in his palm. This feels so right. My Lou, he thought, holding her snugly against him.

His phone rang, and he reluctantly let her go to answer it. It was the vet. Gandalf was ready to come home.

CHAPTER FIFTY-EIGHT

The next afternoon Cliff and Lou went for a walk. He finally mustered the courage to tell her what he'd been composing in his mind in the hours since he last saw her.

"I have realized something about myself, Lou. I think I know why I kept on choosing Ashleigh types. Deep down, I knew those relationships wouldn't go anywhere." They strolled, hand in hand, down the walk with Gandalf ahead on a loose lead, sniffing, reading all the doggie scents.

"It has to do with how I see myself—it goes back to Johnny's kidnapping. I felt guilty at not being able to stop it or to change anything. Even though I knew it was stupid—I was only four—but it didn't stop the terrible feeling of being powerless. Deep down I didn't feel worthwhile, I didn't feel loveable, and so I wasn't worthy of a mate whom I could really love. So I chose girls who didn't matter to me, without being aware that I was doing it or why. And I felt something else scary, too. If they can take a brother, they can take a parent, a wife, …my child. No one is safe."

They had reached his house. He unlocked the door and unhooked Gandalf's leash. They went to the kitchen and Lou filled some glasses of water for them. The late August afternoon was very hot for the 7000-foot altitude of Santa Fe.

As they sipped he continued. "I have always wanted to get married and have a family. It has been my dream to have little tykes of my own, to be a father. But what if I let them down? I hear their terror, hear them screaming, 'Daddy.' What if I couldn't protect them or keep them safe?"

"Oh, Cliff…life doesn't come with guarantees. Things happen. Accidents, evil people, mistakes, illnesses."

"I know. But now, since the attacks are over, I have learned I do have the power to make a difference. There are also good, caring people, strong people who act out of love, who would sacrifice even their lives to help. At the flash flood—that chain of folks was there with us, Lou. We worked together through this whole thing and we succeeded. Vidar's mother and Vinnie were out for themselves in the end. They wouldn't know sacrifice if it bit them in the butt." Cliff tugged her down to sit next to him on the couch.

Lou said, "You haven't given yourself enough credit. You are a strong person, Cliff. You have a lot to give, but I do hear you about the discovery. It is something new. It's exciting."

"I want to try again. I don't know why it took me so long to discover all this—I think Krista, Karen, and Anton have helped me more than I've helped them. They've been a gift in our lives. I do have the power. I could be a father worthy of those little tykes. I want them to have a mother who is also powerful, who is warm, who is loveable."

"And… is she a blonde?"

"No," he said, holding her gaze and catching a lock of her hair and teasing it with his fingers. "I think…I think her hair might be a lustrous, blue-black silk."

Startled, Lou sucked in a breath and pushed back a little, ducking her head. Why am I hesitating? she thought. Is he saying what I think he's saying? It frightens me—what I've wanted for such a long time might be so close. I've been on my own so long. I've changed. I don't want to stay in the shadow of a man. I should say something….

He drew her close and held her. "It's a new thought. Think on it. We don't need to rush it. This woman with the black hair—she will know that I get scared, that sometimes I still feel like that four-year old, but she helps me find strength to hold on and to make things right again. And that works both ways. My strength will help her, too."

Held against his chest she could feel the vibrating rumble of his voice, her thoughts continuing. This is wonderful, but it's also scary. I want a future with not only a mate, but a career. Can I have both? Will he support me in my dreams if I support him in his? An image came to her mind.

Then she spoke, softly and hesitantly. "Before we even think about the possibility of marriage and children, I want to talk about what you believe a relationship should be like. I went to a wedding not long ago where they had a unity candle as part of the ceremony. The bride and groom each had a lit candle symbolizing their lives. They lit one bigger candle with their individual candles, then blew out their own. That really upset me, and I've thought about it a lot. I think it's sad that symbolically their individual lives were extinguished. I know what the ceremony was trying to say, but it bothers me."

Cliff pulled back and looked at Lou's face. "This is important. Really important? I want to get it right," he said.

She nodded, and he continued. "I've seen that, too, and it didn't seem fair to the reality of two people who had already done a lot of living, and who are independent." He smoothed her hair back, so he could see her eyes. "What do you think—what if they had joined the two candles with a third of the same size and bound them together, all lit?" Cliff asked. "The third candle would be the new relationship—there would still be the old candles, but a newly-created one, too. Marriage must be bigger than the sum of one and one—he, she, and both. It is three."

Lou considered that. "Maybe. Each could give warmth and light, could nurture not only the other individual, but the relationship as well. Cliff, you might have made another discovery."

Cliff began to laugh.

"What? What is so funny?"

"The bell pull Krista gave me, maybe we have found a secret meaning for it that she never dreamed of. The Celtic knot—the triangle—seamless, never stopping, woven together—like the three candles—and it is intertwined with the heart—all bound together with love." He looked into her eyes, raising a questioning eyebrow.

She touched his face softly, tracing her fingers from his wild, curly hair, skipping over the bow of his glasses, down over his cheek, feeling the raspy drag of stubble, down to his lips. He caught her finger gently with his teeth and worried it with his lips and tongue. With her other hand she gently tugged him closer. "That's beautiful, Cliff. Do you think it could be like that?"

CHAPTER FIFTY-NINE

On Sunday morning Lou stepped into her parents' kitchen just as Pete and Akiko were finishing their breakfast and lingering over coffee. Their other children had eaten and gone their separate ways. Lou poured herself a cup of coffee, helped herself to a cinnamon roll, and sat down across from her dad.

"About Friday—a new rule from now on," Pete said. "I'm *never* going to let one of my children put themselves in danger in one of my cases again. Letting you be involved with the Bjornsons put your life at risk. You could have been killed."

Lou looked him square in the eye. "I'm sorry, Dad, but this was not a case of *letting* me do anything. These are my friends. I'm going to stand by them." She looked down briefly, then her chin came up as she looked again at her parents. "I *really* care about Cliff. I think I'm in love with him. You couldn't have kept me from his side. I belong there."

The kitchen was silent. Pete's face slowly got that stubborn German look Lou knew so well. Her eyes didn't waver, reflecting back her own newly-developed version of stubbornness that she'd learned from the master.

With a small pleased smile, Akiko looked at Lou, then at her husband. "Pete, do you remember back in Japan just before we got engaged, when those dealers had you cornered?"

Gray eyes startled wide, his gaze swung to her. "*Ach du Lieber*. I'll never forget." He put down his coffee cup.

"And who saved the day?" Akiko asked.

"You came charging around the corner into the fray. My Avenging Angel." He reached out to take her hand, kissed it, and brought it to hold against his heart.

"Your father just wants to keep you safe. And we're very happy about Cliff."

"Why didn't I become a librarian, or find another profession? Something non-violent.... Boring. Safe."

Lou looked at both of them, stunned by the glimpse into her parents' lives before she was born. "What's this? Before you were engaged? What happened? Tell me."

"Maybe I should retire and show dogs full time. No, on second thought, that's a cutthroat business." He shook his head sadly. "I could be an accountant, sit in an office, and crunch numbers all day."

Akiko's eyes still rested warmly on Pete's face. "Maybe someday we'll tell you, Lou, but not now. It's enough to know that he understands how you feel. He's your father, yes, but Cliff, perhaps, will be your husband. And, if so, he will come first."

"I'll open up a shop. Sell tea cozies, or I'll be a mechanic."

"You'd die of boredom in no time at all." Lou finished the last of her roll and sat back, laughing. "You know you thrive on your work. But thanks, Dad. I love you, too." She stood up and carried her dishes to the sink, throwing her mom a teasing glance. "Hmmm. Avenging Angel...."

CHAPTER SIXTY

Sunday afternoon the Circle Sleuths gathered for their last official meeting at the Bjornsons' home. Karen, looking relaxed, greeted everyone as they came. Diego, Maria, and Krista were welcomed into this Circle meeting. Pete brought Akiko with him. Sam followed them in with a cheery whistle. Gandalf—sporting a large, shaved patch on his side and a line of stitches—pranced in with Cliff and Lou. His usual fluid grace was hampered, but his enthusiasm and licky tongue were in top form.

"Gandalf, sit." said Krista. He immediately sat, accompanied by a chorus of approval. He didn't stay long, but it did show that Krista's lessons in dog training were paying off.

"You're looking wonderful," Lou said to Karen.

"The threat is gone. It's such a relief. I feel much better."

"It's a good thing that Norwegians have hard heads," Anton said.

A celebratory buffet lunch was spread on the counter between the family room and the kitchen. Maria, Karen, and Krista had fixed all of the foodstuffs. Krista pointed with pride to the lemon-caraway seed cookies. "I made those," she said. "They're Gramma's favorite."

Anton served wine and lemonade. Chatter and laughter set this meeting apart from all of the others.

Cliff and Lou stood next to each other. The others couldn't miss the looks that passed between them and the occasional touches, like Cliff's possessive hand on Lou's waist as they stood near the buffet. Pete's eyes became a little misty, and he blinked a few times. Sam, looking sideways at Pete, began whistling Purcell's "Trumpet Voluntary" softly, receiving a hard punch on the arm for his efforts, changing his whistling to laughter.

Krista, looking up from her play with Gandalf, caught Cliff and Lou holding hands. Her eyes went to her daddy's, and he winked at her, grinning widely. She knelt to whisper something in Gandalf's ear.

◆ ❖ ◆

Eventually the conversation turned to Vidar.

"His funeral will be on Wednesday," said Karen. "There's a police committee doing the planning. It's turning into a big event for a fallen officer."

"I've volunteered to play the pipes," said Cliff. "I want to do that for him. I've done it before for other officers, but I especially wanted to be a part of Vidar's."

"What are you going to play?" asked Sam. "Amazing Grace?"

"Yes, and I think "Flowers of the Forest" for the procession."

"I told them I wanted to say something, too," said Pete. "His sacrifice humbles me—the enormity of it is amazing. It hit me hard. I knew he was close to the edge, but I had no way of predicting this outcome. I catch myself wondering if I had seen what was going on earlier and intervened somehow, told the sheriff or something, that I might have been able to prevent his death. To put himself between that mad woman who was his mother and take a bullet for the woman he loved for mothering him was extraordinary."

"Don't beat yourself up over what you had no power to change," said Cliff. "That's some good advice I got—from you, I think. It is at Helene's and Vinnie's feet, and theirs alone, that the blame belongs. I'm just sorry I didn't get a chance to know Vidar better."

"Will it come out that it was Vidar's mother who did such terrible things?" asked Lou, having noticed that Krista was off with Gandalf out of earshot.

"I think we won't mention she was his mother," said Karen. "It may or may not come out in Helene's trial. That's up to her. Most people won't make the connection. They've no reason to. The name isn't even the same. None of her family live around here anymore. I think it would be better to paint Vidar as what he was, an officer who was killed while saving a life."

"She wasn't his mother in any way that counted," said Anton. "I agree with Mom."

"Pete, can you tell us what you found out about Vinnie?" asked Cliff.

"I can tell you something you'll appreciate," interrupted Sam. "Member Miss Bruton?"

"I can safely say I'll never forget her," responded Cliff.

"Well, I went to see her. Showed her a series of photos including Vinnie and some Vinnie look-alikes touched up with long, dark hair, and a bit of makeup. I didn't tell her they were men, just asked her if she had seen any of them before. She picked out Vinnie with no hesitation. 'It was her,' she said. 'I remember the cupid's bow mouth. Did you catch her?' She was thrilled to be asked, and was already planning how she would spread her story among her friends—that she helped solve the kidnapping and murders."

"Made her day," said Pete. "She'll get a lot of mileage out of that one. Now, about Vinnie. The autopsy said his cause of death was drowning. The press was told he drowned while attacking a hostage who had escaped his clutches because of a brave dog whom he injured in the process. The arroyo bank that he was standing on was undercut by the flood waters. He could have gotten out of there, but he chose to stay to do further harm. He sustained a non-life-threatening wound by an officer. His hostage and her rescuers barely escaped the flood. Another suspect was taken into custody. That's the story, and it's the truth."

"I'm still on administrative leave," said Sam. "Probably until midweek. Internal Affairs has to determine whether the shooting was justified. Standard procedure."

"Should only be a formality. Anyhow, when we searched Helene's home and Vinnie's properties, we found most of the ransom money. But what we found at Vidar's house and Vinnie's office was truly diabolical. Vinnie had used his skill in surveillance systems to set up video cameras at Vidar's. They had fixed it so they could not only spy on him, but had the ability to broadcast the 'voices from his father.' They had taken what Helene had already known about Walter's feelings of revenge and hate, and built from there. Vinnie had encouraged Vidar to talk about his father to him. He also had used material from the journal he told Vidar to write, which showed a man tortured beyond what he could bear by the lies and voices."

"Oh, my God," said Karen. "Several times Vidar tried to talk with me, but we were always interrupted. I wonder if that's what he wanted. He said it was okay; he'd see me later. I'd no idea what he was going through."

"None of us did," Pete said. "Those devils had skillfully woven all these ingredients into their plot to make Vidar think he was going crazy. They planned to lay all the blame on Vidar for wiping out the Bjornson family. Vidar had begun to suspect that Vinnie was spiking his drinks and he took some of the bottles in to be tested. Vidar's last journal entry, written before he went to work on that day, told of the results of the drinks' tests and his plan to confront Vinnie and ask him why."

"That's even more evil than I imagined," cried Lou.

"I can maybe understand the struggle over the gun," said Karen, "How that ended up with her killing her own son, but the cold-blooded plan to drive him mad, incriminate him to gain money, and kill him…. How can you do that to your own son? How can you not love him and celebrate that you brought such a wonderful being into the world? How can you not nurture him to reach his potential? It's monstrous."

"And what is Helene saying now?" asked Anton.

"She's been very busy trying to convince her interrogators that it was Vinnie who had been the leader in this plan. He was the one who hired Juan and Alfonso. She confessed that Vinnie wore Vidar's shoes while in Los Ojos. It was Vinnie who had hacked into Cliff's computer. The source of the porn was from a V Hawk client Vinnie had been blackmailing. She claimed it had been Vinnie who had done all the killings; she knew nothing of them and was not to blame. But then she would go off onto a spurt of hate that undercut her own testimony, and brag about her marksmanship and cleverness."

Diego said, "She's mental, that one."

"Quite possibly," said Pete. "She is still blaming everyone else, including all of you. It is, of course, all your fault that she is in trouble."

"Ah… Pete, Sam," said Diego, "I wanted to tell you I was sorry for being so noisy and obstructive the day you searched my house. My daughter was inside, and I didn't want you to know she was there. I shouted at you to warn her and give her time to hide."

"Where did she go?" asked Sam. "We sure didn't find her."

"When she heard me, she slipped out the back and into Maria's."

"No apology necessary," said Pete. "How is she doing in Minneapolis?"

"Says she likes it, and she's making new friends. It's a relief to have her away from that scum bag."

Gandalf and Krista came back into the circle. She brought with her a little plate of apple slices and settled down with Gandalf's complete attention.

"I've an idea," said Lou. "We should gather some of these papers about all the evil and pain and let them feed the flames at Zozobra."

"Is that Old Man Gloom?" asked Krista. "Where they burn up all the bad stuff inside that big puppet? We talked about it in school."

"That's it," said Anton. "I think that's a fine idea. It will be a way of putting everything behind us and starting fresh. I can get tickets for us."

"Uff da. I don't know if I'm up for that this soon. It would be this coming Friday," said Karen. "But it's a fine idea. I have some thoughts to put on paper that should be burned with all the gloom."

"Can I go too?" Krista asked.

Anton looked at her eager face. "I don't know. There will be big crowds, lots of strangers, and confusion. Wouldn't you find it scary?"

"Not if I'm with you and Lou and Cliff. I want to see the puppet burn. And I want to put some stuff in him, too."

"You'd have to stay very close to us," Anton said, looking at his daughter.

"I promise, Daddy. Can Gandalf come, too?"

"Sorry," said Cliff. "They don't allow pets. There will be a lot of noise and fireworks. Gandalf wouldn't like it. He would much rather spend the evening with his Airedale friends."

"He has Airedale friends?"

"Yes, Pete's dogs. He has three."

"You do?" Krista turned to Pete. "I didn't know that. Can I see them some time? Please? Do you have a lady dog that might have puppies?"

"Thanks, Cliff," said Pete, as laughter filled the air.

"I've been thinking. There's something I want to say to all of you." Pete looked around the group. "You know it's unusual for police to work the way we've done here. Allowing anything like the Circle Sleuths. I saw something very special among you. My gut told me we needed to work together."

"I, for one, am very glad you did bring us together," said Karen. "The villains are vanquished, but even more—I value the friendships we forged together."

"I've never told any of you," Pete paused. "But maybe it's time. I was a rookie when Cliff's brother was snatched. It was my very first case and it haunts me still."

"I never knew that," Cliff said. "I don't remember my folks ever mentioning it."

"I doubt they were aware of me—the young guy in the background doing the grunge work." He paused to take another sip of his wine. "When you started college and met Lou, I welcomed the opportunity to know you as an adult. I volunteered to be a resource for your books. I saw the tremendous need in you to be able to make a difference, to give strength to kids' lives. When you brought Krista back, I stretched a few rules to keep you involved. I wanted you to break that log jam of feeling helpless. And I needed you, too. You really do have an uncanny ability to come up with fresh insight. I hoped for success—we all needed it. Our working together may have solved this and saved lives. Each of you here has given strength to the Circle."

Anton stood with his wine glass in hand looking at each as he said their name. "To you: Pete, Sam, Lou, Cliff, and Gandalf...*skål*" He took a sip and looked at each again. "Thanks from all of us from the bottom of our hearts."

Chapter Sixty-One

Later that night Cliff stopped by his parents' house. He shared with them all the news from the last six weeks that they hadn't yet heard, and about Pete's being a part of the task force that had investigated Johnny's kidnapping. "If it's okay with you, I want to talk about that a little."

His mom and dad looked at each other and nodded. His dad reached over and took his wife's hand and held it tightly.

"We've never really talked about how we felt," said Cliff. "But it was always there, the elephant in the room, but we left it alone. I've always felt love and support from you both, and I know Erin has, too. We couldn't have better parents. But, I always hid my feelings—sometimes even from myself. In an odd way, this whole bit with the Bjornsons has given me the freedom to talk about it." He ran a hand through his hair and continued. "I always felt guilty because Johnny was taken. So powerless. I was surrounded by a loving family that he was stolen from. I was safe. He wasn't."

"I never knew you felt that way, Cliff," said his dad. "You hid it very well. God, that was almost twenty-five years ago. I think we *all* have tiptoed around and avoided talking about it, because it is so painful. Thanks for telling us how you felt. Maybe we can talk more now."

"In my books I've never wanted to write about anything related to a kidnapping. It was too personal, too scary. It was taboo. But I think I might be ready now—maybe in the next book, after I finish my current one. Like my other books, it might have the extra bit at the end with things to do that might make a difference. Anything I can do to give kids some power over what they can't change. I might even have Krista help me. For those left behind and for those taken, you do your best, you never give up, and you don't beat yourself up for what you have no control over or can't change."

"Sounds to me like that would be a blessing. A little bit of hope," said his mom.

As he settled down to sleep that night, Cliff felt strangely at peace about Johnny for the first time. Late into the night he and his parents had talked about Johnny at last. It was good sharing with his parents the feelings that had dogged him for all that time. He'd also begun to see his father and his mother in a new light. He'd never really looked at it from their point of view, nor appreciated the impact Johnny's kidnapping had had upon them. He thought their talking might have helped dissipate some of the burden they'd carried. It had been a good day.

CHAPTER SIXTY-TWO

The crowds were huge for the Zozobra, the burning of Old Man Gloom that kicked off the *Fiestas de Santa Fe* and Labor Day weekend. Zozobra stood fifty feet tall, a marionette that was stuffed with thousands of pieces of paper: shredded old police papers, paid-off mortgages, and notes each bearing someone's sad thought. All of the Circle Sleuths had contributed papers for the Gloom Boxes that had been emptied into the puppet. As Lou had imagined, it was kind of a new beginning, a purging of anxiety and anguish. It seemed to fit, as they looked over the last six weeks.

A red-haired man walking near them caught Cliff's attention. He looked a lot like what Cliff thought Johnny might look now. Like many times before, he couldn't resist the urge to start up a conversation with him, a subtle way of hoping against hope, that he might find Johnny again.

"Hi. Is this your first time at the Festival?" Cliff asked.

"Yes, I'm from out of state. I'm curious—does this event happen every year?"

"I think it's been going on for more than 70 years," Cliff told him, adding more about the long-standing tradition of Zozobra. "I hope you don't mind my asking, but you remind me of someone. Your name wouldn't, by any chance, be John McCreath, would it?"

"No, Ross Stewart."

"Oh, well. My real reason for asking is that when my brother was little, he was kidnapped. We never found out what happened to him. You look a lot like what I imagine he'd look like today. Sorry, I had to ask. I keep hoping that someday I'll find him. It'd take a miracle, I guess."

The young man's eyes widened. He rubbed his head and said, "I…I'm not surprised you stopped me. That's quite a story. Don't ever give up."

Then Cliff and Lou moved on to where they had planned to meet Anton and Krista.

The red-haired stranger watched them go, pain and confusion in his blue eyes. He took out a handkerchief and blew his nose, and turned to walk away. He tucked the handkerchief back in his pocket, and then his hand went to his car keys in another pocket. As his fingers caressed the little Koda figure on his key chain, he said softly, "John…. Johnny McCreath. I wonder."

About the Author

Betty Lucke holds a Bachelor's degree in elementary education from Macalester College, St. Paul, MN, and the Master of Religious Education and the Master of Divinity degrees from Princeton Theological Seminary, Princeton, NJ. She has fond memories of the summers worked at Ghost Ranch, NM. She lives in northern California with her husband and a Welsh terrier. She is a co-founder of the Town Square Writers, a weekly writing group associated with the library. She has also published *Festival Planning Guide: Creating Community Events with Big Hearts and Small Budgets.*